THE
EXAMINER

SETH CAGIN

*This book is dedicated to a community of great characters:
Telluride circa 2008, including many dear friends
along with my wife Marta and our son Carlos.*

Chapter 1

EYEBALLS

Tom was sitting in Erica Ortiz's office when he learned that Jay Cluff had been killed.

Erica was Tom's biggest advertiser in The San Miguel Examiner and his friend.

They were talking about the collapsing economy and what to do about it.

"We kept telling ourselves that the market would pick up," Erica said. "And it just kept getting worse. Now it's as bad as it can get. It's dead."

Erica had a television mounted high on the wall in a corner of her office, where she could keep an eye on it. It was perpetually tuned to a cable business channel. Tom glanced up at it. Crashing stock prices scrolled across the bottom of the screen while a reporter standing on the floor of the New York Stock Exchange talked.

Wall Street was only confirming what Erica and Tom already knew. The decade-long boom in Telluride real estate had started to tail off a year earlier. In March, real estate sales had come to a total halt. Six months later, Tom's biggest customers, including Erica, had fallen behind in paying for their ads. Tom was falling behind with his printing bills. The outlines of what would be called the Great Recession were in clear sight.

"Lehman is going down and nobody's gonna save it," Erica said. "Nobody can, except the federal government, and Bush is too chickenshit to try."

"Maybe Obama," Tom ventured.

"Fuck Obama. Nothing but a lot of pain will fix it. The slow economy was bad enough. We could have survived that. But now we're facing a total collapse of the financial system. You know that Lehman was the lender for the Mountain Village hotel project, right?"

"No."

But Tom should have known. The hotel was his biggest advertiser's biggest client, its luxury condos offered for sale at pre-construction prices in a full-page ad on the back page of every edition of The Examiner. Erica paid Tom $65,000 a year for that ad alone. It was beyond lucrative, it was essential, but it was also such a constant that Tom had come to take it for granted.

"I'm what's wrong with Lehman," Erica said. "I can't sell the condos, which a year ago would have sold overnight, which means Lehman can't recover what they've put into the project. And it also means I can't keep up with my own debt or pay you for my ads. I'm not the only realtor who's fallen behind with her advertising bills, am I? Properties are falling out of contract. Nothing's closing. Or haven't you noticed?"

"I assumed that you and all the other realtors were telling me the truth," Tom said. "That this year's slow sales were just a normal part of the real estate cycle, and they'd bounce back bigger than ever next year."

"I can't blame you for falling for our bullshit since we fell for it ourselves."

"Film Festival is coming up in three weeks. Got $40,000 in ads booked."

"We're all hoping some Hollywood fat cat will fall in love with Telluride, decide to buy a mountain retreat and save our ass. It won't happen. Even movie stars are paralyzed because they have no idea where their money's safe. There sure as hell won't be a truckload of them making an impulse purchase this week. Maybe one of us might get lucky. Or two."

"Ever the optimist."

"It might be me who makes the sale to Brad and Angelina."

"They're coming?"

"Who the fuck knows?"

Erica's sharp tone was startling. Tom had spent countless hours with her, conducting business in this very office and socializing over dinner with their spouses in one of Telluride's fine dining establishments or at one of their homes. He had witnessed her speak in public and interact with others in both professional and personal settings, engaging with colleagues, clients, and her two young daughters. He had never seen Erica lose her cool before, not even under pressure, not for a moment. Along with her good looks, Erica's polish offered reassurance and was the foundation of her personality and her business success. Now, cracks were showing, and Tom could observe her struggle, if only momentarily, to regain her composure.

"It doesn't take a psychic to see what's going to happen," Erica said, her tone reined back to a sympathetic register. "You'll publish a big fat paper full of all those ads we've booked. Then you'll owe a huge fucking printing bill, and you'll find yourself sitting on your hands waiting for the realtors who placed all those ads to pay their bills."

"What do we do?"

"Cut expenses to the bone and try to ride it out."

Erica had deep pockets. If she was scared, what was Tom feeling? Was it the first tremor of panic threatening to undo his equanimity?

That's when Tom's phone beeped.

He glanced at the screen. It was a text message from his senior reporter, Peter Barnard.

Tom read it out loud: "Jay Cluff found shot dead on his claim in Bear Creek."

Erica flinched and looked confused; the change of subject too quick to process.

"Cluff dead? Are you sure?"

"It's from Peter, so, yeah."

"Fuck."

"Well, the paper's not dead yet. Gotta go."

"The collapse of the economy will just have to wait, huh?"

Erica was reaching for the light irony she favored. But the subject was too big for that and there was a trace of something darker and more bitter in her voice.

* * *

Tom burst into the office to find Samantha, the paper's digital editor, covering the front desk.

"Where's Peter?"

Samantha nodded back in the direction of Tom's cubicle, the only place in the cluttered Examiner offices that afforded any privacy. Tom looked in the door to see that Peter was on the phone.

Peter looked up and mouthed the words, "Sheriff Owens."

Tom nodded and sat as Peter scribbled a few more notes, thanked the sheriff, and hung up.

"A hiker found him this morning on his claim up Bear Creek."

"I guess there are plenty of suspects."

"I'd say thousands of them."

Samantha had followed Tom into the office and was listening.

"This will go viral," she said.

"Let's get a breaking news teaser online a-sap," Peter said. "'Cluff Shot Dead in Bear Creek.' We'll fill it out as we go."

Tom snapped: "Is that really the most important consideration right this minute?"

They both looked at him like he'd lost his mind.

"Well, we are a newspaper trying to figure out how to stay relevant," Samantha said.

"Eyeballs," Tom muttered, the student slow to absorb the lesson the two of them had been working overtime to teach him. "Go ahead and post your damned teaser. What else have you got?"

"Cluff was doing his usual thing, standing guard outside his trailer with his rifle in hand," Peter said.

"So, he saw the killer coming up the trail and confronted him, thinking it was just another trespasser?" Tom asked.

"Nope. Sheriff said the killer had positioned himself behind a boulder just ten yards away from the trailer. Cluff's rifle had not been fired so there wasn't a shootout. Which suggests the killing was premeditated and the killer was a sniper."

Peter glanced at his notepad and continued: "Cluff was struck by a bullet from a small-caliber handgun, and the killer had good aim or was lucky and hit him with a single shot. And Cluff probably died quickly."

"Just probably?" Tom asked. "I wonder if he had time for any reflection before he died."

"Who would know that?" Peter asked, not as the snark Tom deserved but as if he were looking for guidance about whom to call for an answer to that question. Possibly the county coroner? Peter had none of Tom's existential—and irrelevant—curiosity: Did Cluff experience a flash of awareness that he'd made the ultimate sacrifice for his principles before he died? And if so, did it ease his passage?

"It was an idle question."

"Oh, right."

Peter resumed reading from his notes: "Nobody reported hearing a gunshot in Bear Creek yesterday. Cluff was dead about a day when his body was found by the hiker, who called 911 from a cell phone. The guy who found the body was a tourist and didn't know that the 'no trespassing' signs up there are for real."

"Do you know his name?"

"Sheriff seems intent on protecting his identity."

"Why?"

"The police procedural trick." Peter shrugged. "Withhold stuff only the killer would know so that if a suspect knows it, they incriminate themselves. Owens figures the guy who found Cluff would say too much if I got to him. But that's partly conjecture, partly off-the-record."

"Write up what you've got and let me see it—*before* you post it online, please."

Chapter 2

A JOURNALISTIC POINT

few years earlier, when he published the West End Forum newspaper in Naturita, near the Utah border with Colorado, Tom reported what was, for that small, isolated town, a big story: the disappearance of a local man. There was no risk that an auto mechanic's disappearance would go viral the way Jay Cluff's murder might, and the West End Forum didn't have a website in any case. Still, the citizens of the west end of Montrose County had already heard that Ray Walker had gone missing by the time the Forum could get the story out. That made the paper not the source of the news, but the record of it, validation to the readers and community that this event was important, at least for as long as the newspaper was on the racks and worthy of being memorialized for as long as there was a newspaper archive. It was almost a secondary function of the paper to sort out the facts from the rumors.

Now, in Telluride, word of Cluff's murder would spread much faster not only than a printing press could run, and faster not only than printed papers could be bundled and trucked and delivered, but even faster than a story could be posted on The Examiner's website. Even if Samantha didn't rush to post a teaser, people would send texts as quickly as the first rumor of Cluff's death reached them and someone would post the news on Facebook. But the newspaper still played the same role, of validation and supplanting rumors with facts.

Peter and Samantha waited impatiently while Tom read the story one last time. If they thought that he was taking his time to prove a journalistic point — accuracy before speed — they weren't wrong.

"We can change it two minutes after posting it," Samantha said. "If you find something wrong."

"We can do better than that headline," he replied, remembering the banner headline he had written in Naturita to report the Walker disappearance: MISSING, above Walker's headshot.

"Jay Cluff Murdered in Bear Creek," she read. "It's straight to the point."

"How about 'Cluff Clocked'?" Tom asked. "In an oversized font, all caps. And use that photograph of Cluff standing the near the trailer, the one we published in July when he posted the 'No Trespassing' signs."

The picture, which Tom had taken, placed Cluff standing possibly on the precise spot where he died, his broad back angled to the camera and his face in profile. Cluff had the physique of the West, he was all-sinew and a bit bowlegged, as if he had spent most of his life on horseback. He wore a cowboy hat and was holding a shotgun in the photo, guarding his claim, the notorious "no trespassing" sign off to one side.

"On it," Samantha said.

In a few moments she would tap a few keys on her keyboard and the story would be live at the speed of light.

CLUFF CLOCKED

Sheriff Asks Public Assistance in the Investigation

(Posted at 4:51 p.m., Tuesday, September 9, 2008)

By Peter Barnard
Staff Reporter

Controversial real estate developer Jay Cluff was shot and killed yesterday on his property in Bear Creek. No witnesses to the crime have stepped forward, and San Miguel County Sheriff William Owens said today that he has not identified any persons of interest.

Cluff's body was found this morning by a hiker in Bear Creek. The hiker, who was vacationing in Telluride and has not been identified, called 911 at 10:22 a.m. today to report his gruesome discovery. Cluff was found just outside the trailer he installed in June on one of his Bear Creek mining claims just off the Bear Creek road, his rifle by his side. The rifle had not been fired.

Cluff's fatal wound was caused by a small-caliber handgun, according to the sheriff.

"The bullet hit him square in the middle of the chest," Owens said. "The killer had good aim or was damned lucky, and Cluff probably died instantly.

"Right now, we're concentrating on collecting evidence from the scene and on conducting interviews," Owens added. "If anyone was in Bear Creek yesterday and heard or saw anything, we ask them to contact us. Someone must have heard the shot, which would help us establish the time of the incident. With all the people in town, and a bunch of them in Bear Creek every day, someone saw the killer on the trail or in the woods, and they might be able to describe him. Or her. It could be a woman. Even if they didn't know the person was a killer, someone saw him. Or her. We would, frankly, like to talk to every single person who was in Bear Creek yesterday."

Asked if he suspected a woman, the sheriff replied, "No, I'm just making my point. That it could be anyone. Also, that I'm not sexist. Even though most killers are men. Almost every damn one of 'em, in fact. Unless it's a love affair gone bad. But that's another story. Probably. Or maybe not. There are some peculiarities here."

Asked about the nature of the peculiarities, Owens said, "Well, I suppose every murder is peculiar, but not really. Most are cut-and-dried. Not this one."

The sheriff observed that Cluff was a controversial figure in Telluride. But until an investigation is completed, Owens said, "there is no reason to make any assumptions as to motive and every reason to keep an open mind."

"Heck, it could be political like a lot of people probably think it is, or it could be a love affair gone bad, it could be related to some other personal or business matter, or it could be totally random. The point is, we have no idea at this point. It could be somebody who knew Cluff or a stranger, somebody local or somebody from far off.

"But whoever it was," Owens vowed grimly, "we'll find him. Or her."

The political controversy alluded to by the sheriff concerned Cluff's announcement last summer that he had acquired mining claims at key locations in Bear Creek. He quickly posted "no trespassing" signs blocking unfettered public access to popular trails. This past May, Cluff announced an ambitious proposal to develop his Bear Creek property as the base for a new ski area.

If approved, the new resort would border the existing Telluride Ski Area, whose owners have expressed strong opposition to the concept. Cluff's application for the first of numerous required county approvals was scheduled for its initial consideration by the San Miguel County Planning Commission in just under six weeks, on October 20. He also filed paperwork required ahead of submitting an application for approvals from the U.S. Forest Service last month.

Political and legal observers have discounted Cluff's development threats as frivolous, citing the daunting government approvals that would be required for it to proceed and strong public opposition to any development in Bear Creek. Hikers and skiers have freely accessed Bear Creek for two generations or more. The county and the Telluride Mountain Club have both filed "adverse possession" claims, asserting that under Colorado law the trail and road that traverse Cluff's mining claims must remain accessible due to the long period of time that they have been used by the public.

Upper Bear Creek sits inside the Uncompahgre National Forest, although it is riddled with private mining claims, which, like Cluff's properties, may or may not be developable under existing county zoning and federal law. Whether the land is developable is precisely the question Cluff was pressing. He frequently asserted that if private property is not developable due to government regulations, then the land has been "taken" in violation of the Fifth Amendment to the United States Constitution.

Lower Bear Creek was acquired by the Town of Telluride in 1995 and placed in perpetuity in a nature reserve. It cannot be developed but it would be necessary to traverse it to access Cluff's proposed development, yet another formidable obstacle the developer would have to overcome. He predicted that public opinion would shift in his favor to resolve that problem.

"We could put in a new road outside the reserve," he told The Examiner last month. "Or we could use helicopters for access. Or maybe a gondola from the center of town. It just would make my development more exclusive."

The last murder in the Telluride region took place on August 6, 1990, when Ski Ranches resident Eva Shoen was killed by a late-night intruder whose motive was burglary and who later claimed his gun accidentally discharged when Shoen woke up to find him outside her bedroom. The killer, Frank Marquis of Albuquerque, was arrested in July 1993 and is currently serving a 24-year sentence at the Colorado State Penitentiary.

Stories about Jay Cluff's recent activities in Telluride can be found....

And there followed a list of a dozen hyperlinked headlines, starting with the first to alarm the community: "Developer Jay Cluff Acquires Bear Creek Claims," dated August 5, 2007.

Just a little more than a year after that, the Cluff drama had reached its violent conclusion, at least as far as Cluff himself was concerned.

Chapter 3

ONE MAN'S COMMA

The bit about the Shoen murder was Tom's contribution to the story. Feeling sidelined after Peter seized the initiative, he dug it up while Peter raced to break the story. Peter's urgency was purportedly driven by the new demands of digital publishing. But he reminded Tom of a big city cub reporter from an earlier era — more Jimmy Olsen than Clark Kent — hustling to get the scoop ahead of competing tabloids. Except that now, the competition was social media.

Let the cub have the glory, Tom thought, resolving to take the longer view that comes with maturity.

When was the last time someone had been murdered in Telluride? Was it in the modern period? That was a tidbit of information that would offer the paper's — and website's — readers some historical perspective. Crime was not unheard of in modern Telluride, as Tom knew from publishing the weekly police blotter, Police and Thieves, named after the classic reggae song and recently popularized by a Clash cover. But it was all petty stuff: there were plenty of DUIs and drunk-and-disorderlies after midnight, and the occasional brawl that would lead to an assault charge; there was frequent domestic abuse and shoplifting, but murder was all but unheard-of.

Tom put in a call to his predecessor as The Examiner's publisher and editor.

"Eva Shoen was murdered in 1990, or right around then," George Brooks said. "Story blew up national because she was the wife of an heir to the U-Haul fortune. At first there was a lot of speculation that it was related to a family feud over control of the business, but a few years later they arrested a guy from New Mexico, who had broken into her house to burglarize it. Before that, you'd have to go back to the late fifties. There was an affair gone bad, a jealous husband killed his wife, who was a schoolteacher, and her lover, who was a former student, over on Silver Pick Road. Then he shot himself. That was before the ski area, of course."

"Before the ski area" was Brooks's way of placing the Silver Pick Road incident safely in the past, a simpler age when a murder could be understood as a crime of passion and nothing like the chilling home invasion that randomly victimized Eva Shoen, never mind an all-too-modern act of eco-terrorism, if that's what Cluff's murder proved to be.

After he got off the phone, Tom pulled the bound volume of The Examiner from 1990 from the floor-to-ceiling shelves in his office to read up on the Shoen murder. It was just as George remembered it. Eva's young children found her body on the morning of August 6, 1990, at the top of the stairs in her Ski Ranches home. She had been shot in the forehead. Shoen had volunteered at the Telluride Elementary School and was active at Christ Church.

The story was featured on an episode of *Unsolved Mysteries* in December 1992, leading to the arrest of Frank Marquis. Marquis's brother-in-law saw the episode and called in to report that Marquis had bragged about having killed a lady in Telluride. Evidence was quickly unearthed to prove that Marquis was in Telluride at the time of the murder. He was arrested and confessed that he had been attracted by one of the town's famous summer festivals, imagining that there would be many wealthy people there to rob. He chose the Shoen house because it was dark and there were no nearby neighbors. Better yet, the door was unlocked. The gun he was holding discharged accidentally when Eva Shoen woke up to find him on the stairs leading to her bedroom. The weapon had been cocked and fired when he stumbled on a step.

Coincidentally, Eva's husband was out of town on business, which had contributed to the theory that someone who knew Sam Shoen's travel plans—possibly one of his own brothers—had planned or committed the crime. The potential for murder within the fractious Shoen family had been a real-life red herring, undoubtedly salacious but good only for distracting the investigation and fueling media interest and public fascination.

Reading The Examiner's coverage of the Shoen murder, Tom was struck by the whiplash the story induced. At first, because Eva so perfectly fit the profile of what Telluride was becoming—home to a growing number of wealthy young families seeking an idyllic childhood for their offspring—there was a rude shattering of the illusion that Telluride was a rarefied refuge, far from the ills of the world. The subsequent reporting about Sam Shoen's duplicitous family served as an antidote to the shock, offering reassurance that the Shoens likely brought the misery with them, even if they had tried to escape it by fleeing to Telluride. The discovery that the killer was a random intruder brought the story to an unsatisfying conclusion with no clear moral.

Now, 17 years later, Jay Cluff had been shot dead, its moral obvious at first glance: someone took out a villain who was asking for it. Even if the killing proved to be random, as unlikely as that seemed, Cluff deserved it by virtue of karma.

The Shoen incident cried out for editorial caution, similar to Sheriff Owens's refusal to draw quick conclusions. Yes, Cluff might have been shot by one of the thousands of residents deeply offended by his extortion of the community. Or by an eco-terrorist, an anonymous member of Edward Abbey's Monkey Wrench Gang, someone from virtually anywhere, motivated to remove an enemy of the environment and send a warning to others like him. The killing could have been in righteous defense of Mother Earth.

That would be an inevitable assumption for anyone who had been reading Peter Barnard's stories in The Examiner to make. Tom had not muzzled his young reporter in favor of journalistic "objectivity" because Peter's indignation was in perfect sync with the paper's readership. Cluff's crusade for private property rights, and his opposition to public ownership of land, fell on deaf ears in eco-liberal Telluride.

Cluff had made a business career out of acquiring environmentally sensitive land and then holding it for ransom by threatening to develop it in the most invasive manner he could envision. A local community, an environmental organization, or the National Park Service or the National Forest Service could purchase the property at an inflated price to preserve it, or it could refuse to be blackmailed and risk seeing the land and the acreage surrounding it spoiled. More than once, Cluff had started the bulldozers moving to demonstrate that his threats were not idle, and a few developments, including one on an inholding inside Black Canyon National Monument, had been completed. In the end, Cluff was equally happy to develop the land for profit or sell it to preservationists at the "market value" he established for it. He won either way.

"I do what all successful real estate developers do," he told Peter. "I look for properties that are distressed in some way. In my business model, it's because they are private inholdings surrounded by public lands and are therefore overlooked and undervalued. I acquire them and then I find a way to realize their market value. If it pisses off big-government liberals, that's just icing on the cake!"

Cluff's purchase of mining claims in Telluride's sacrosanct Bear Creek, just outside the boundaries of a nature preserve that had been expensively acquired by the town, was just the latest in his string of provocations, but it was his boldest move yet because it brought him to the heart of what he considered to be enemy territory, a community where private property rights were routinely and joyously violated. Telluride was a town of Earth Firsters and socialists, and Bear Creek was where they hiked in the summer and skied backcountry in the winter. Most of it was public land, so the deadbeats recreated on the public dime, which was bad enough. But even worse, inholdings of private property, old mining claims that dated back over a century, were routinely encroached upon by the public. After secretly buying up a few of those inholdings in key locations, Cluff first posted "no trespassing" signs and then announced he would develop a new ski area there, complete with a base area comprised of hotels, condos, vacation homes, restaurants, and bars. With the local resort economy booming, the threat was not entirely a bluff.

Happily playing the environmentalists' archvillain, Cluff carried a worn copy of the U.S. Constitution in a breast pocket. He would pull it out and to anyone who wanted to debate him he would point out the Fifth Amendment, and then recite the last clause, the takings clause, which reads, "nor shall private property be taken for public use[,] without just compensation."

Cluff had stopped by The Examiner office to introduce himself to Tom shortly after he announced his acquisition of the Bear Creek parcels, and he had tried the trick with him.

Cluff carefully enunciated each word, "nor... shall... private... property... be... taken..." as if this should have been all that was necessary to settle the question once and for all, with a sparring partner for whom it had to be spelled out only because he must be a damned communist not to know it in the first place.

"I'm sorry Jay, but I'm not a fundamentalist on property rights," Tom said, surprised to find himself more charmed by Cluff's earnestness than he was offended by his hardball tactics. "Governments exercise the right of eminent domain all the time, for highways, airports, schools, water systems and even for parks and open space."

"As long as they pay fair market value for it, I've got no argument," Cluff said. "But I will defend private property rights to my dying breath, because without property rights a man is nothing but a slave."

They went on to debate whether the takings clause in the original draft of the Constitution has the comma between the words "use" and "without," since some of the first copies of the Constitution, quickly reproduced by hand for each of the 13 colonies for their review and ratification, appear to have the comma and some don't. The comma or the absence of it could change the meaning, legal scholars say, the comma's presence granting more latitude to the government to take property for public use, with the comma subordinating the requirement for compensation to the government's overriding power to exercise eminent domain.

If the drafting of the original document was less-than-meticulous or if it was prone to error in being reproduced, or if the original contained a smudge that might be mistaken for a comma, Tom asked Cluff, then how could every word be taken as gospel? On this constitutional issue or on any other?

"If we can't agree to live by the words of the Constitution, as best we understand them, then how can we determine right from wrong?" Cluff countered.

"One man's comma is another man's smudge," Tom offered.

"I guess we can agree on that much," Cluff laughed, extending a hand.

They shook on it.

Now it appeared that Cluff had died as he claimed he was willing to do, in defense of private property rights.

Chapter 4

A SACRED TRUST

Tom had written another addendum to the Cluff story but had the editorial judgment to cut it before sending the story to Samantha for her to post it.

Cluff's murder also echoes an incident out of Telluride's historic period: the Nov. 20, 1902, murder of Arthur L. Collins, in the aftermath of Telluride's bitter labor war, which started with a strike in May 1901. Collins was the general manager of the region's largest mining enterprise, the Smuggler-Union Company. His killing provoked speculation that the assassin was a member of the local branch of the Western Federation of Miners acting on orders from union leaders.

Collins's killer was never identified or caught, but the incident nonetheless led to the declaration of martial law in Telluride and the destruction of the local union, a pivot in Telluride history away from a brief period of progress in the struggle for better working conditions for the town's legions of laborers, mostly immigrants.

Tom cut the Collins reference because it was one digression too many in the breaking story about the Cluff murder. Even more problematic, it hinted that the Cluff murder could have outsized political or social impacts, an irresponsible implication given the known facts. And while the Shoen incident was less than twenty years old and well within living memory, the century-old Collins killing was ancient history.

Tom had learned about the Collins incident shortly after starting work as publisher and editor of the San Miguel Examiner. He felt the weight of the paper's history the first time he sat at his new desk, a chestnut antique whose dings and ink stains only enhanced its beauty. Across from the desk in Tom's cramped new office were the bookshelves laden with bound volumes of old newspapers, not only editions of The Examiner, but also of The Examiner's rival, The Telluride Daily Journal, whose archives had likely been acquired when the Journal ceased publication in the 1920s. There was also a shelf devoted to a small collection of books that had been written about the town's history. Taken together, the newspaper archives, the histories, and the fact that The Examiner had been published nearly continuously for well over a century out of the same building — generations of editors sitting at the same desk in the same office where Tom sat now — impressed upon Tom that he had not only taken a job but had assumed a sacred trust.

Perusing the archives and books, Tom learned about the town's historic labor war, pitting a gifted young union leader, Vincent St. John, against powerful mining companies, whose union-busting campaign was led by Collins and the famous labor antagonist, Pinkerton detective James P. McParland, whom Collins and the Telluride Mine Owners Association had retained. Most intriguing, The Examiner's founding publisher and editor, Charles Sumner, was drawn deeply into the conflict, which put him on the opposite side from the editor of the Daily Journal, Francis Curry.

By the time Collins was murdered and the town's anti-union forces were heeding McParland's advice by loudly declaring that St. John had ordered the hit, Sumner—whose reporting struck Tom as convincing—was fully in the St. John camp. In contrast, since history is written by the victors, the books on Tom's office shelf broadly characterized the union as a cabal of foreign agitators and violent anarchists, rightfully run out of town by patriotic Americans. The story of the five young men, one of them shot by a sniper, had the makings of a terrific book, Tom thought—editor versus editor, union leader versus mine manager, the four of them manipulated by a nefarious detective—one he would write when he found the time.

Tom's book might exonerate St. John, honoring his predecessor's work by revising the prevalent anti-labor characterization of the town's history, and right a profound historic wrong.

Lost in his stray thoughts, Tom was interrupted just five minutes after the Cluff story was posted by what viral sounds like.

Most of his staff, about a dozen people, was huddled around Samantha's computer, watching the screen.

He heard loud whoops and then, "That's fucking awesome!" It was the voice of the paper's gregarious sports editor, Gus Jarvis.

Tom walked to his office door.

"What's fucking awesome?" he growled.

"We're watching web traffic, boss," Peter offered.

"It's spiking," Samantha said. "Already."

Tom leaned in and could see a graph showing real-time website visitation.

"How many are there now?"

"Just over seventy," Samantha said. "Up from about 40 before the story posted. Traffic was already spiking because of the teaser. The most we ever had at one time before was 23, when we posted Gus's story about the co-ed broomball championship game."

"That one was a classic!" Gus interjected.

Tom shook his head. He couldn't say what he was thinking: that this spike would do nothing more for The Examiner's finances than the broomball story had. The paper had not implemented a paywall because Samantha had convinced him they needed to build traffic first. Real estate ads were the paper's bread-and-butter, and there was no way to draw a line from web readership attracted by a juicy murder story—never mind broomball—to a speedy recovery of the real estate market.

"It's at 102," Peter muttered, awestruck.

Back at his desk, ignoring the celebratory noise emanating from the office bullpen, Tom studied the paper's financials, working to ground himself. His accounts receivable number was growing as invoices were increasingly past due. His payables were also growing as he was falling behind with his own bills. Ignoring cash flow and overdue invoices, the paper was still profitable. Tom fiddled with the scale of x and y axes, so that the worrisome graphs on his computer showed crashes, a reverse mirror of the graph that engrossed his staff.

The encouraging spikes on Samantha's computer did nothing to offset the distressing crashes on his.

Chapter 5

EVERYTHING IS REAL ESTATE

The office slowly grew quiet as Tom's employees left for the day. A knock on his door.

"This story is breaking huge," Peter announced. "Over a thousand hits already. In less than an hour! And they're not bouncing. Samantha says the website visitors are spending an average of almost *four minutes* on the page and they're linking to it. We're starting to get hits from far away, and I don't mean Naturita. From Denver and L.A. There's even one from London!"

Tom recognized the jittery energy of the young reporter on a mission: to seize this golden opportunity that would make his career. As always, Peter reminded Tom of a younger version of himself. He was likely imagining that in the very near future—a day or two—he'd be invited on CNN.

Tom could easily picture it, or Peter's fantasy of it, anyway.

"Well, Wolf," Peter would explain, "Jay Cluff pissed off pretty much every citizen of San Miguel County, and a bunch of other counties where he conducted his brand of legal extortion for the last twenty years. Let's face it. The guy was a class A dick."

Time to rein the kid in, Tom thought, as Peter took a seat. In the two years Peter worked for him, they had developed a close working relationship. But it was more complicated than Peter could guess. There was an element of self-interest in Tom's mentorship, as if he might redeem himself by shepherding Peter to a successful career. Tom had sabotaged his own career in big-city journalism ten years earlier, fired from the Boston Mail for having fabricated quotes. No, it was worse than that, so painful that he shaved the truth even in his recollection. In his rush to build his reputation, careless because early success had gone to his head and he'd been partying too much and was cultivating a runaway cocaine and alcohol problem, he had fabricated an entire story. More than one, in fact. Because it was easier on a Monday morning, blasted after a long weekend in the clubs, to make shit up than to report something true. He was good enough at fabrication to get away with it. Until he didn't. It was his flight from the humiliation of the scandal, reported on the front page of the Mail, that propelled Tom to the remote twin towns of Naturita and Nucla, Colorado, in the West End of Montrose County, 90 miles west of Telluride. To hide out there. Peter didn't know Tom's shameful secret. Nobody did, except for Sarah, who did him the favor of burying it even more deeply than he had.

Peter was the age now, 28, that Tom was then. Peter could have been his kid brother or, if Tom was a decade older and had married young, his son. It was more than Peter's youthful ambition. It was his agreeable nature, bordering on disingenuous, that reminded Tom of his younger self, something he had long since abandoned for crustiness, as if having once been too likeable was his fatal flaw. Like Tom, Peter had a countenance that made him approachable: good looking but not intimidating, clean-cut, an everyman demeanor. Sources and interview subjects quickly confided in him, often telling him more than they'd intended to, a natural advantage for a reporter and likely one Peter was unaware he possessed.

Peter assumed that Tom would fully support his jumping deeply into investigating the Cluff story. But Tom pulled back.

"It's a big story," Tom allowed.

"They don't get any bigger," Peter countered.

"The collapse of the economy isn't bigger?"

"You think it's related?

"Everything is real estate."

Peter leaned back, hesitating, and then responded to Tom literally. Though Cluff's political provocations made him countless bitter enemies, his murder could as easily be tied to business.

"Cluff had shady real estate deals all over the West, and I've barely scratched the surface," he said.

"Which means there are plenty of suspects. Hidden relationships that could have soured."

"I've had this idea that the ski company secretly wants to expand into Bear Creek and they were using Cluff as a stalking horse."

"That's a reach. Unless you've got reporting to back it up."

"Cluff was never the wildcatter he pretended to be. Rugged individualist, acting on his own to defend capitalism. Who does that shit? There's got to be money involved. Too much for the killer to have been some anonymous eco-terrorist."

"This is fun," Tom said with a sigh. "But we need something you can actually report. What about the public implications? That's what makes it news."

"There are lots of murders with no public implications and newspapers report the crap out of them just because readers love a good whodunnit. Like that Eva Shoen murder you stuck at the end of my story."

He's getting feisty, Tom thought.

Leaning back in his chair and measuring his words to avoid sounding defensive, Tom explained himself.

"The treacherous family in that case made great copy," he said coolly.

But had it really been necessary for him to put his thumbprint on Peter's story?

He continued: "There was a backstory insiders wanted to talk about. In this case, everyone will assume Cluff was shot by some hairy and unwashed eco-dude camping out in the woods, and that guy's not talking."

"Wasn't there someone like that?" Peter asked, breaking the tension.

"The Unabomber. Loner lived in a shack in the woods in Montana and mailed bombs to political targets. He was a math genius, a political theorist, and a serial killer."

"So, what do we do?" Peter said, resigned to Tom's determination to play the downer. "No follow-up story would be totally lame."

"What happens to Cluff's Bear Creek plans now?" Tom asked. "Does somebody else pick it up and try to carry it forward? Or does it die? Check with county officials and the Forest Service. Call Cluff's office and see if they have any comment. See if you can find any of Cluff's partners in the Bear Creek deal who are willing to comment. Get a reaction from the ski company."

"Boring."

"Who told you reporting is all fun and games?"

Peter's arms were crossed.

"You've got to start somewhere," Tom said. "If you poke around, you could find something interesting."

Peter stood and put up a good show of obedience.

"Yes sir," he said, with a salute.

Then he turned and walked out of Tom's office.

Walking toward home, on Main Street, Tom saw more viral activity.

"Whoa, dude, check this out," a young man said, handing his phone to a friend.

"Holy shit! Cluff clocked!"

I'm still good for something, Tom thought. His sensational "tabloid" headline was helping the virus spread. He pictured it happening everywhere, his words jumping from device to device. It was not as easy to observe as readers on a main street bench, holding a fresh edition of a printed edition of the newspaper in their hands, as they had only a few years earlier when the paper hit the racks. But this was faster and possibly more effective.

Still, he took some comfort in knowing that Sarah would not have already heard that Jay Cluff had been murdered in Bear Creek because she was rarely online—using her cell phone strictly to make calls—and worked by herself at home. Her reaction could not be predicted, but the news would almost certainly elicit an emotional response. Their marriage had been forged in the aftermath of a murder, the disappearance of Sarah's husband, the very auto mechanic who had gone missing in Naturita and was later presumed dead. They'd become close when Tom interviewed her, digging into her biography as he reported the story. If the echoes were faint, they would nonetheless be audible as the new murder would trigger memories of the older one. Sarah would instantly sense that their reality had shifted because there was now this new momentous event that they would remember for the rest of their lives, which would be a chapter in the town's history. Whether that chapter would be important or incidental, long or short, simple or complex, was yet to be determined, to some extent by Tom himself in his role as publisher and editor of the local paper.

This is how the events in a person's life form a narrative, Tom thought as he walked up Pine Street to the decrepit miner's cabin where he and Sarah and their adopted child, Tyler, and Sarah's son Ray Jr., lived. There was no connection between Ray Walker and Tom Cluff other than the fact that a specific newspaperman, Tom himself, wrote bold headlines to announce their deaths. The unrelated stories he reports become threads in the fabric of the journalist's life; their meanings — or lack of meanings — must inevitably inform each other, at least in the journalist's mind. And in his reporting, as well.

Chapter 6

A WONDERFUL SURPRISE

When he stepped through his front door, Tom couldn't tell Sarah the news of Jay Cluff's murder because the past was not just echoing. It was booming, sitting in the flesh on the sofa: Sarah's daughter, Angie, had come home.

"Wow," Tom said. "How long has it been?"

Tyler sat uncomfortably in Angie's lap, his very existence the answer to Tom's question.

Tom shifted his attention to the boy, who was reaching for him. Angie was the boy's natural mother but had left in the messy emotional aftermath of her father's disappearance, when Tyler was an infant; Sarah and Tom had adopted him and were the only parents he knew.

"How old are you, Tyler?" Tom asked. He had only just learned to answer the question, a sign of his development that Tom and Sarah had welcomed, even if it came to him a bit older, it seemed to them, than most of the children he played with.

"Four," Tyler said.

"Angie is back," Sarah said, with a mother's happiness and no trace in her voice of the dismay Tom was feeling.

"When did you get here, Angie?" Tom asked.

"About an hour ago. I thought I'd surprise you."

"It's a wonderful surprise," Sarah said.

Sarah was instantly ready to forgive anything and everything her daughter had done, all the things she knew about and anything she didn't know about for good measure: a blanket amnesty that certainly covered future transgressions as well. Just as instantly, Tom assumed that Angie had turned up after four years of absence only because she had run out of string and had nowhere else to turn. It would be a sad story that he would hear soon enough.

"Aren't you happy to see me, Tom?"

"Of course. How is California?"

The last they had heard from her was a post card from Los Angeles, a week after she'd left home, leaving Tyler and a note promising she would be in touch once she got settled and assuring them that she hadn't mysteriously disappeared like her father had, but just couldn't stay. In the circumstances, Tom told Sarah, a new life for Angie was likely a necessary move. She deserved a new beginning and didn't know how to get one without a clean break from her past. But Sarah never accepted Angie's abrupt departure. She told Tom she had faith Sarah would come back someday. As, in fact, she just had.

"California is great," Angie said. "And Mom tells me you got married. I mean, wow! And congrats!"

"Almost three years ago," Tom said. "Thanks."

"We have so much to catch up on," Sarah said.

Tyler squirmed free from Angie's arms and ran to Tom, who picked him up.

"How are you doing big boy?" Tom asked.

"Good."

"Where's Ray Jr.?" Angie asked, as if she'd only just remembered she had a little brother.

"He's at the University of Colorado," Sarah said proudly. "He got a full scholarship."

"College?" Angie said. "That's *crazy*."

Over dinner, Angie described her previous four years in California as she might to a stranger seated at the next barstool. Her life was a series of close girlfriends and good jobs in hair salons, loyal clients who "wouldn't let anyone else touch a hair on her head," and lazy Sundays at the beach.

"Maybe you'd let me do your hair," Angie said, reaching over to apply her hairdresser's touch to her mother's head.

"Ooh, I'd love that," Sarah said.

Watching them interact as if he wasn't there, with Tyler squirming in his lap, it seemed to Tom that their long separation had somehow brought Angie and Sarah closer, not least in appearance. They looked more like sisters than a mother and daughter. The previous few years had softened Sarah, who was in her mid-thirties and looked younger, but had hardened Angie, who was in her early twenties and looked older. Angie now wore a diamond stud in a pierced nostril, like Sarah's. Both were so thin they might be anorexic. Either might be mistaken for an urban sophisticate with artistic leanings, belying their origins in one of the most remote corners of the Mormon West.

When their plates were empty but not yet cleared, Sarah reached over, cupped Angie's hands in hers and said, "Well, honey, you seem so good. It sounds like California has been great for you."

"I belong near the sea."

"I am so happy you learned that about yourself. I only wish we hadn't lost the last four years."

Angie bit her lower lip and suddenly looked like the child she still was at 21-years-old, and not the grownup she'd been pretending to be. "Mommy, I didn't come back so you could blame me…."

Tom quickly interrupted: "If you can handle Tyler, I'd like to go out for a walk and let the two of you really catch up. I didn't want to spoil your reunion by telling you, there's a big story I've got to follow. Jay Cluff was murdered."

"Oh, wow," Sarah said. "When?"

"Yesterday. They found his body today."

Angie looked up at Tom dully.

"It's work-related," Tom said. "You know. Local news."

"Yeah," Angie said. "Sure."

"Do they know anything?" Sarah asked.

"Not that they're saying."

"I guess you can tell me all about it when you get back."

"I will, and you can catch me up with all of Angie's news. Don't worry about the dishes. I'll clean up when I get back."

Tom's excuse for abandoning her had been accepted and Sarah was far too distracted by Angie to give Jay Cluff's murder another moment's thought.

Chapter 7

MAN OF THE HOUR

The midsummer night was clear and crisp, the sky lit up with stars, the Milky Way stretching north to south from horizon to horizon. Tom had been in Telluride for three years and had lived for another few years before that some eighty miles to the west in Naturita, in the West End of Montrose County, at a much lower elevation, but still isolated in the American outback where the sky was pitch black and the night air was cool even in August. Telluride, with its fancy restaurants and mansions that were their owners' second or third homes seemed a world away from Naturita, and both Telluride and Naturita were a world away from the America of freeways and suburbs and a perpetual glow in the sky from city lights that washed out all but the brightest stars and dimmed even a full moon.

But Telluride was hardly remote from the America where everyone was out to make a buck and those who pulled it off on a grand scale lived like 17th-century European royalty while those who scraped by worked as servants, with fewer and fewer people in the middle. Telluride and Naturita epitomized that America of haves and have-nots, with many of the residents of Naturita, commuting the 160 miles round-trip from their decaying old uranium mining town to Telluride for the closest work they could find, cleaning hotel rooms and vacation homes, staffing restaurants and shops, shoveling snow in the winter and taking care of extensive landscaping in summer, working construction or for the ski resort. The uranium mining in the West End had long since shut down, as had the cleanup of the radioactive pollution the mines had left behind. Ranching employed only a few dozen people over a thousand square miles and paid barely enough to cover a family's supply of rice and beans. Economic despair was the obvious if not-entirely-sufficient explanation for the meth epidemic that had ensnared Angie five years earlier.

And now Angie, by her unanticipated return, had plunged Tom into a flurry of conflicting emotions. He was pulled in one direction by Jay Cluff's murder and his own role in reporting it. Though there was an act of violence at its core, the Cluff incident aroused in him oddly pleasant feelings — the curiosity elicited by a real-life whodunit, seasoned with the satisfaction of professional relevance related to his role as a minor character, the newspaper publisher, in the mystery. The chaos represented by Angie was anything but pleasant. She was the baggage that came along with his marriage to Sarah. Whereas the mystery of the Cluff murder could potentially be resolved, Angie's return home promised only discord and destabilization.

It was psychological physics — repulsed by the unpleasant, drawn to the intriguing — that drove Tom to seek an escape from Angie by fleeing to the office, where he imagined he might work with Peter on the Cluff story. But Peter was not there. He was likely out tracking down a lead. Or maybe he'd done enough damage for one day and was out on the town with Hailey, his girlfriend, accepting accolades for the reporting he had already done and fielding theories from friends about who had clocked Cluff. Tom wondered idly if anyone offered a compliment for the headline, "Cluff Clocked," and if so, whether Peter would just nod and take the credit for it. Probably, he would.

Why not?

Someone else might ask, "Why was that Eva Shoen bit stuck on at the end of the story?" And Peter would say, exasperated: "I have no idea. My editor stuck it on there."

Again, why not?

Tom sat at his desk. He felt restless. He rarely went back to work at night. Since marrying Sarah and adopting Tyler he had been happy spending every evening at home, luxuriating in domesticity, something he had not experienced since adolescence, and so, it seemed, was something he needed in high dosages now, in middle-age. He and Sarah were devoted to helping Ray Jr. come of age and giving Tyler a chance in life, if only by not fucking him up too badly. Tom knew that if Tyler was their anchor, that was in itself a good way to fuck him up. But he would at least be fucked up in a better way than if he was raised by Angie because the world is divided between kids who are well cared for and take advantage of it and kids who start out with all of the disadvantages of being born to teenage meth-head parents, and then lack the spunk or luck to come from so far behind that they can't even envision a realistic safe harbor.

It could happen but was not common for a kid to defy his origins and cross over to the other tribe, for a born winner to tank or a born loser to beat the long odds. Tyler was born to teenage meth-addled parents but then had the good fortune of having his father killed in a meth lab that blew up and his mother abandon him long before he reached the age of awareness. And so, he was left with Tom and Sarah, who were themselves far from perfect, but had somehow become fundamentally responsible human beings by their mid-thirties. Tom took enormous satisfaction from knowing that Tyler had a chance, despite being born with meth in his system, and as one of Tyler's two legal parents, Tom had vowed that he would never let Angie interfere with his upbringing. He had been confident that Sarah, Tyler's other legal parent and natural grandmother, agreed. Or did she? The sight of Sarah and Angie engaged in intimate conversation had introduced unwelcome doubt.

Meanwhile, Ray Jr. had demonstrated encouraging resilience after his father's disappearance, helped by the move to the new surroundings of Telluride. For him to be accepted at the University of Colorado, much less win a scholarship, would have seemed a highly unlikely destiny just a few years before. No graduate from Naturita High School since the 1970s, at least, went on to higher education, whereas Telluride High had an excellent record of college placements. Maybe, Tom liked to think, he had something to do with Ray's success, too — something more than helping him with his college essay.

From where Tom sat at his desk, his thoughts free-associating, the newspaper archives on the opposite wall gazed down at him reproachfully, reminding him of his responsibility to be worthy of them. The Collins murder was not entirely irrelevant to the Cluff murder. History doesn't repeat, Mark Twain was reputed to have remarked, but it often rhymes. It was rhyming now like Kanye West on speed dial. Telluride in 2008 as in the mining era was dominated by organized business leaders, the Telluride Mine Owners Association then, the Telluride Association of Realtors now. Now as then, underpaid legions of workers worked long hours to grease the wheels of commerce. Cluff, like Collins, made news as a prominent member of the business class, and one whose notoriety might have motivated an assassin to take him out.

There was someone Tom needed to talk to. He wouldn't exactly be reporting the Cluff murder by talking to Chuck Small, but the self-anointed local historian shared Tom's interest in the Collins murder and had filled him in on many of its details, always insistent that the past loomed over the present. And Tom knew exactly where he would find Small pontificating to anyone willing to listen.

But Small was not at his usual perch at the Elks Club bar, where the two of them occasionally met over lunch to talk history.

"He's over at the Sheridan," the Elks' bartender said, tacitly acknowledging that on a night of big news ripping through the community, that's where the action would be.

Tom had avoided the heavy drinking scene in the ten years since he was a bartender at a tourist trap in the Florida Keys. There he had finally crashed after a decade of booze and drugs and had become sober overnight, had gone cold turkey without twelve steps or counseling. As he crossed the New Sheridan's threshold out of necessity, looking for Chuck Small, Tom observed that he trusted himself back around alcohol; it came as a blast of self-awareness that felt almost precisely how it used to feel when he tossed back the first shot of whiskey at the start of a night out.

The place was hopping, and Tom was acquainted with many of the patrons. They were his advertising clients, real estate agents mostly; and his sources of news, local elected officials and town and county employees; and his readers. Life in Telluride flowed easily from business and small-town government to the street and the saloon.

"Man of the hour! Cluff Clocked!"

It was a young realtor whose name Tom couldn't quite recall until after he moved past. Making his way to the bar, Tom was greeted, slapped on the back, and shook more than a few hands. He took a seat and ordered a club soda with lime, heeding the unspoken rule that if you're the sober guy in a bar you should at least order a drink that looks like it might contain booze. No serious drinker wants the buzzkill of a stiff hanging out with him.

"Anybody could have done it," someone opined.

"The fucker got what was coming to him."

"Can I join you?"

Chapter 8

HISTORY RHYMES

Chuck Small slid on the stool next to Tom before he could answer, sparing Tom from having to admit he'd come looking for him.

The bartender stepped up.

"Double Jack Black, and I'll buy Tom another one of whatever he's having."

Small eyed Tom's highball. It obviously looked suspicious to him, girly, whatever it contained, though he probably couldn't have guessed it was alcohol-free. That would be incomprehensible.

"Shee-it," Small said. "You've got yourself an un-fucking-believable story to report now. Maybe not. It's more like in-fucking-evitable. Course, it'll never be solved."

"Just because the Collins murder wasn't?"

"No. But for the same reasons. Too many suspects. And because it doesn't matter who did it. Everyone will be sure it was an eco-terrorist type killed him. Capitalist pig Cluff knocked off because of his beliefs. That's what people will say, even if there's never any evidence to prove it, even if a jealous girlfriend is arrested and convicted for killing him. They'll just say she was in on the plot."

Small's paternal grandparents were early Telluride settlers, miners. Even though Small himself was born and grew up in Grand Junction, where his ancestors relocated in the early 1900s, he had moved to Telluride as a young adult so he could assume his rightful place as a Telluride old-timer. The third-generation identity was so important to him that he embraced it fully, his hair long and unkempt, his beard untrimmed, dressed in buckskin and heavy woolen clothing from the turn of the last century. In defiance of his surname, he was a large man with a big gut, and well over six feet tall, which suited the illusion that he was so set on creating, that he was a character out of an earlier time.

"The night Collins was shot, one hundred and six years ago, this bar was packed with people talking about it, trying to figure out who did it and what it meant," Small said. "Killer could have been right here, in the New Sheridan, soaking it all up, enjoying the drama he'd created. Just like they're talking about Cluff now. The place even looks the same as it did then."

Small was right. Not only was the bar they were sitting at original, dating to 1895 — built after the Sheridan Hotel burned to the ground and was replaced by the New Sheridan — so were the mahogany wall panels, leaded glass dividers, and filigree light fixtures, all carefully restored. Listening for it, Tom hadn't been able to pick out a single conversation occurring in the bar that was not about Jay Cluff. The killer could easily be among them.

Tom saw the lead for his next Up Bear Creek column, which consisted of his random musings about life in Telluride.

"The New Sheridan was buzzing like a swarm of mosquitoes at the Beaver Pond at dusk in July. 'Who Clocked Cluff?' the bar patrons asked. Everyone had a theory and everyone is a suspect, but all agreed that the victim was probably whacked by an eco-terrorist."

From there, the column could delve into the way Telluride history was repeating itself, up to and including the buzz in the very same bar. The Up Bear Creek column was where the Cluff-Collins correlation belonged, and Tom had been right to pull it from Peter's hard news story about the discovery of Cluff's body. Which was … where, exactly? Coincidentally, it was up Bear Creek. As long as everything was rhyming so beautifully, Tom might even give Small credit for the insight.

"It was my idea back in the seventies to get the town designated a national historic district," Small boasted, characteristically seizing more credit than he was due and uninhibited by the fact that he had told Tom about his instrumental role in preserving local history several times over.

Tom expected Small to play the blowhard and didn't interrupt him.

"Got the town's preservation ordinances passed. Helped write the regs. Property owners fought it because they thought it would devalue their buildings. We beat them but look what happened. Their property values went through the roof. I helped make the greedheads richer!"

Tom's rejoinder was equally well rehearsed: "You fucked up."

"Ha!"

Small tossed back what remained of the Jack in his shot glass and grimaced.

"At least the tourists like it."

"But Collins ran the biggest mine in the district," Tom said. "Cluff was just a grandstander."

"Maybe so. They sure as shee-it were hated just as bad. But you're right. Collins lowered miners' wages and cut back on safety measures. Forced the miners' union to strike. It was a bloody mess. Before Collins came to town, Telluride was called the 'town without a bellyache.'

But Collins put an end to that, pretty much single-handedly. It wasn't all his fault. It was also geology."

This was a new wrinkle Tom hadn't heard before.

"How so?"

"Most of the ore here was low quality. That meant they had to process a lot of it to extract a small amount of silver, which made it difficult to make a profit. That's why they brought Collins in. From England. He was an expert assayer, chemist, mine engineer, you name it. He was only thirty or so but had experience in mines all over the world. The mining company brought him in to solve a difficult mining problem and a difficult business problem. It was either that or shut it all down and they'd spent a lot to buy the mine and they didn't really want to walk away. That's why Collins cut labor costs. To satisfy his Jew partners back east."

"Jew partners?"

"The Rothschilds were big investors in the mines around here," Small shrugged. "It's not antisemitic to say it if it's true, is it?"

"I didn't say you were antisemitic."

"Ah, why don't you just go fuck yourself?" Small muttered.

Small had always been quick to take offense, so Tom let it pass. Small nodded to the bartender, who set a full shot glass down in front of him. Tom's club soda was in no need of replenishment.

"Collins and Cluff. A couple of greedheads, a century apart," Small said, resuming his discourse. "It's the nature of the place. It attracts 'em, then it destroys 'em. The low-grade ore is what led to the labor troubles. Just like the fact that the best mines were at high altitude forced my grandparents' generation to commercialize alternating current electric power. They were using mule trains to bring the ore down from the mines, but that was extremely inefficient, especially in winter.

Shee-it, they lost tons of ore, not to mention mules — oh, and a bunch of men, too, though they weren't as valuable as the mules — swept away by snowslides. People want to get rich off the mountains. But the mountains always get the last word. You know these mountains are the most avalanche-prone in the world, don't you?"

Tom frowned and shook his head.

"Because the mountains are not too steep to collect snow, but steep enough for it to slide easily. Then our weather systems deliver snow in big dumps followed by bright sunshine. The sun melts the surface of the new snow during the day, which freezes at night, forming a layer of 'Wedding Cake' crust. Then another dump comes in. Sun comes out again after the storm passes. The ice layer underneath the new snow is like a sheet of ball bearings. It gets lubricated by snowmelt trickling down to it from the new layer, and whoosh! Snowslide. That made this a dangerous place for mining a hundred years back. And for skiing now. Big dumps of fresh snow on slopes just steep enough to hold it, followed by sunshine? It's beautiful skiing if it doesn't kill you."

A skier died in an avalanche the first winter Tom ran The Examiner. He'd run into the longtime county coroner, Chet Ramsey, shortly after the news broke, "Backcountry Skier Dies in Ophir Slide."

"Helluva thing," Tom had said, making small talk with someone he saw as a colleague, because, after all, they'd both responded professionally to the incident. While Ramsey had been around for decades and had collected numerous bodies, Tom was the newbie, making it incumbent on Tom, not Ramsey, to chew the fat.

"Yeah," Ramsey had said. "He's right here in my car."

Ramsey gestured to where Tom could see a body bag through the rear window, the victim's skis and poles and knapsack lying next to it.

Though Tom hadn't recognized the deceased by his name, Rob Shultz, his photograph, emailed to the paper for publication by a friend, looked familiar. Then again, there were many dozens of young men his age and demeanor in Telluride, strapping athletes who skied in winter and played town league softball in the summer and worked in restaurants or construction or both. In the photo Shultz was wearing his softball uniform, advertising the team's sponsorship by the Roma bar and pizzeria, swilling a beer after a game. He could be someone Tom had passed on the street a day or a week before.

Why should it have seemed surprising, Tom wondered as he and Ramsey parted ways, that the corpse was resting, at that moment, in the back of an SUV? Who else but the coroner would transport the body to the mortuary in Montrose? And how else except in his vehicle, in a body bag, along with the deceased's personal effects? And when, if not just a few hours after the body was recovered? Was it surprising because an unexpected death is always a surprise, even to a coroner? Ramsey himself had remarked that the corpse was at hand, right there in his car, expressing not jadedness, but the opposite.

"Just think about how much of our lives is shaped by fate," Small was saying. "Where we're born. Where we choose to live. Geography. History. Where was I…?"

"Electricity."

"Right. The mining companies needed electricity to power their mills and ore buckets. And it wasn't feasible to haul coal or wood by mule to fuel power plants in the high basins. They went against Edison's idea that electricity would be delivered by direct current. You can't transmit direct current efficiently over long distances and the distance from the best locations for hydro and the mines was long. So, they were forced to innovate with Westinghouse's idea of alternating current and that's the real history that was made here. The world's first AC power plant at Ames was financed by L.L. Nunn, who was a local banker and had an interest in the Gold King Mine, and was a homo, by the way. He didn't make much of a secret of the fact that he brought in the young engineering students from Cornell University to develop the power system — and for his sexual pleasure."

"How would anyone know that?"

"My grandparents knew," Small shrugged. "They called him 'L.L. AC-DC' and if they knew, everyone knew."

"You think that's the source of the expression AC-DC?"

"You never know," Small laughed. "It sure as shee-it makes sense that it could have been. People back then were talking about AC and DC all the time, it was on their minds, and L.L. with his perverted sex drive was right at the heart of it. If they're the ones who started calling queers AC-DC it would just be another of Telluride's unsung contributions to history."

He gave Tom a long look, as if he was newly appraising him.

"I hate to admit it, but I like how you think," he said. "History is geography, economics, and politics, but also greed and lust. Whether old L.L. developed A.C. to satisfy his D.C. or it was his lust for profit or because he was a true visionary, or all three, A.C. soon powered the whole world, and it was first commercialized right here in Telluride. That's the real history that was made here. Shee-it, there were a helluva lot more cable tramways around this valley back in the late 1800s than there are lifts at the ski area now."

"Hard to imagine."

"There was a shit-ton more people and a lot more businesses then than there are now. It looks a little different, but nothing's really changed. We're still using aerial cable systems with electric motors powered by AC electricity to access the high basins. A hundred years ago it was to bring ore down and now it's to haul skiers up. It's Telluride's geography. The goods, the rich ore and the deep snow, are in the upper basins. Industrialists like L.L. Nunn, Arthur Collins and Jay Cluff want to get at the goods by putting in lifts. They piss people off and get shot. History repeats itself."

"Or at least it often rhymes."

"That's good! You just come up with that?"

"I'm not that good. Mark Twain said it."

"Old Samuel Clemens knew a thing or two," Small said with a chuckle. "You know there's a lot of Jews in Telluride now, don't you? Jew investors, in hotels and whatnot. More than you'd think. They pretty much run the town. Or am I not allowed to say that either?"

"Say what you want, Chuck," Tom said with a sigh. "This isn't an interview. If it was, I'd ask if you want to say something like that on the record."

"So that's how you work, huh?" Small said, pouncing as if Tom had committed a gaffe. "You tell people what they can say and what they can't say *on the record*? Is that what they mean by 'the power of the press?' Thanks anyway, but I'll say what I want to say, and I'll stand by it, too."

There was no point in arguing with Small, so Tom deployed an old reporter's trick by changing the subject to something safer: "You don't think it could have been an eco-terrorist who killed Cluff?"

"Maybe," he shrugged. "They never did figure out who killed Collins. The mine owners were sure it was the union. But they'd say anything to get St. John. The miners called him 'Saint,' so you know he was a real thorn in their side. Shee-it, Collins himself said it was the union before he passed.

"The miners tried to say it was the husband of a woman Collins was banging who shot him, or someone he'd ripped off, but the mine owners didn't want it investigated unless they could prove it was a miner because it's all the excuse they needed to crack down on the union. Hell, it worked out so good for them, they could've had Collins shot themselves! They sure as shee-it destroyed the union, got the governor to declare martial law, ran the anarchists out of town. The spirit of the place was broken."

"What's a town without anarchists?"

"You got that right! But we came back in the seventies. I'm glad I got to experience it. The town without a bellyache, act two. It was paradise for a few years there."

"That's nostalgia talking."

"It's not. It's the karma of the place. Along with the greedheads Telluride attracts idealists and anarchists. The stars align and for the briefest of moments it seems like anything is possible. Some kind of … harmony. But then, what you said."

"What did I say?"

"History rhymes," Small proclaimed. "And someone gets shot."

"Come to think of it, you better hope the damn history doesn't rhyme too much," he added. "You know what happened to Charley Sumner, don't you? The founder of your paper? After they declared martial law?

Tom shook his head.

"They put his ass on a train and ordered him never to come back."

* * *

Maybe Chuck Small shot Jay Cluff.

He was cast in the mold of the Unabomber. Political theorist.

Hatred of greedheads. Self-described anarchist. Eccentric loner with an ax to grind. He even lived, like the Unabomber did, in an old miner's shack.

Small might have decided that recounting history and preserving historic buildings was not enough, not with Bear Creek threatened. He might have resolved to make some history of his own. With the Collins murder unsolved a century later, Small had good reason to think he could get away with a copycat crime by melting into the crowd at the bar. He might even have enough confidence to boast about his deed to the town's hapless newspaper publisher—who like his predecessor was on the wrong side of history and about to be exiled to oblivion.

What could Tom do to hurt him? What facts could Tom uncover? None if Small had slipped away unnoticed after committing the crime.

The history Small knew so well could have served as a roadmap to a perfect murder. Maybe he was the culprit and had judged correctly that he could easily hide in plain sight.

Chapter 9

BLOWING SMOKE

I t's workmanlike," Tom said.

He had just finished reading Peter's copy about the status of Jay Cluff's proposed development in Bear Creek, the story Tom had assigned him to follow up the news of Cluff's demise.

"Oh, that's great," Peter scowled. "That's just great."

"It's a compliment."

"No, it's not. You're just blowing smoke. It's a news story that says there's no news. Nobody in Cluff's orbit will talk and the officials with development applications on their desk have no idea what's going to happen. I want you to kill it."

"I'm not killing it. It's stuff we needed to report."

"Then take my name off it."

"Come on, Peter. Even if you're the guy who is going to break this story wide open, it might take you more than a couple of days to do it."

Peter had turned his head to the side, pointedly looking away from Tom. They'd never before reached such an impasse. Mentoring can mean occasionally being a dick, Tom thought. He could play the downer again, handcuffing Peter, but that risked pushing Peter further away. Tom's impulse was to do the opposite, to support an ambitious kid he cared about and help him succeed. Plus, he didn't want to "blow smoke."

"Have you got any leads you want to follow?"

"Maybe."

"So, tell me."

"I'd like to go to Cortez for a day or two, poke around, see if I can get people who knew Cluff to talk to me."

"When?"

"If I leave early, I can get a full day in tomorrow."

"What are the leads?"

"They're not exactly leads, OK? They're more like hunches. If I tell you, you'll shoot them down and then I'll have nothing."

Tom frowned. The odds were better than even that Peter's mission would be fruitless and produce no copy. But tracking down hunches, even when most of them will inevitably fail to pan out, is what makes a good reporter.

"What would you be missing here?"

Peter brightened, like a puppy let off-leash.

"Someone would have to cover the meeting tomorrow morning of the town parks and recreation commission," he said. "There's an application for that proposed Trance Music Festival next summer in the park. I doubt they'll approve it, but they might and then it would go to council."

"So, if I cover it for you, that means I can't stand up and speak in opposition to the damn thing?"

"That's right, boss. You'd have to pretend to be impartial in the interest of letting me report the biggest story in this paper's history. And if I'm gone two days, the county commissioners might make some news at the regular meeting on Friday morning. The agenda's pretty thin, though."

"I'll cover parks and rec for you. See what you can dig up. I'll book a room for you for tomorrow night. But I want you back here first thing Friday morning to cover that commissioners' meeting. I'll need more than hunches if you want to stay another day.

"And your byline stays on this story."

Tom had covered so many governmental meetings that he could compose the story on his laptop as it played out, even devoting just a portion of his attention to the proceedings of the Telluride Parks and Recreation Commission.

The proposed midsummer Trance Music Festival was a major event that would attract visitors who would spend money in town hotels, restaurants, and shops, (some of which would flow down to the newspaper for ads). Sure, the town was already busy in peak season, but that was valuable to offset the long, quiet off-seasons. Or the festival would be a loud disruption to town residents and would displace recreational users of the park for yet another major event in a town that already hosted more than enough of them.

Tom's mind slipped easily from the argument unfolding in front of him to the much bigger picture that preoccupied him, the imminent collapse of the global economy, which threatened to drag him, his newspaper, and the Telluride economy down with it. If that was the real story of the day, it was irrelevant because there was no way to report it in a story about a festival application. He recalled his own advice to Peter just two days before.

"We need something for you to report," he had said, when they were discussing how Peter might pursue the big Cluff story. That direction had produced something "workmanlike," a news story reporting that there was no news.

"You're just blowing smoke," Peter retorted when Tom justified the assignment, an accusation that stung and had its intended effect: Peter was in Cortez pursuing hunches while Tom was doing workmanlike for him.

"We can't afford to say no to this event," Graham Hall was telling the parks and rec commission. He owned a Persian rug store on main street. "We need every last tourist we can bring to this town."

Graham was scrambling financially, like every merchant and realtor in town and like Tom himself. Tom knew this because Graham was thousands of dollars behind in paying for his newspaper ads, which was why he had just opened a kitschy fondue restaurant downstairs from the rug store, in the basement, hoping to dig himself out. Graham had invited Tom to dine at Elsa's Melting Pot so it could be written up and generate business. Tom declined, but assigned Samantha to do it, willing to provide the publicity in the hope it might pay off for Graham so that he, Tom, might get paid at least some of what Graham owed him. Tom's dealings with Graham were a perfect example of the mutual backscratching required of a small-town newspaper publisher and his advertisers, which had reached a frenzy as the economy worsened. Even if Graham was not likely to keep up his end of the bargain, at least Tom was able to throw the perk of a free meal to his digital editor, hoping that she might somehow find new revenue to sustain the paper.

"There comes a point when more commerce and activity is just too much," said Jerry Green, a town resident since the early seventies, and owner of a local bakery. "We're past the tipping point. We always wanted to grow this community big enough to be sustainable, but without selling out."

This argument could also be discounted as a form of self-interest, because like Chuck Small, with whom Green was sitting, Green wrapped himself in nostalgia for the golden age of his youth. Plus, he had purchased real estate decades back when it was dirt cheap. This meant, as far as Green and Small were concerned, town residents who had arrived after they did were less entitled to the boom-town spoils.

Surely Small would agree that the entire argument — permit another summer festival? or reject it? — was trivial compared to early twentieth-century arguments about the rights of miners to safety on the job and a living wage. But the history did rhyme. A hundred years later, the human drive to build wealth still came at a cost, albeit one — a little more crowding — that could be defended as reasonable. Just as the opposite view, that the cost in unwelcome noise was too high, could be reasonably asserted.

Perhaps there had been a century's progress: Today's civic debate wouldn't lead to anyone's murder.

Or would it?

Tom entertained the stray thought that the Cluff murder could be tied to the proposed Trance Music Festival. What if Cluff was the festival's secret investor and was knocked off by a homeowner in east Telluride, across the street from the Town Park stage and violently opposed to another high-decibel event that would disrupt his serenity by rattling the dishes in his cupboards? While that notion might be absurd, Cluff's death could easily be connected to high stakes real estate development, which shared the same growth imperative as the festival industry.

Tom was the last person to rule out the possibility of hidden alliances—mutual backscratching—influencing business and political outcomes, far removed from public awareness. Exhibit B might be the story he assigned Samantha about the cozy new fondue restaurant in town that appeared in the previous week's Examiner. The prime exhibit, Exhibit A, was more scandalous than that and more obscure: the fact that Erica Ortiz was more than Tom's biggest advertiser.

She was also his silent partner.

Chapter 10

EVERYTHING IS EVERYTHING

Erica had called Tom in the early winter of 2005 at the West End Forum to ask for a meeting. They met in Tom's office in Naturita. It had taken her just a few minutes of small talk to get to the point.

"I'm going to make you a business proposition, Erica said. "But I have to ask first for your complete discretion."

"We're off the record," Tom said with a nod. "As far as I know, you're not a news source."

"I appreciate that. You may know George Brooks. He's been publishing The Examiner up in Telluride for almost forty years and he's ready to retire. He's burnt out. He would like for you to buy it from him. He's been impressed by what you've been able to do down here with The Forum."

"What I've done in this backwater? Compared to Telluride? I'm surprised George has ever seen an issue of the Forum."

"It's not just George. It was my idea, too. Actually, it's a group of us who want to help George retire. He's been a fine editor but he's not much of a businessman. In the last twenty years Telluride got too big for him, too sophisticated. On top of that he's pushing 80, and he's not as sharp as he once was.

"George could just sell The Examiner to a newspaper chain, cash out and walk away. The paper is prospering along with real estate. But that's not his preference. And he's not the only person who thinks that the town would be better served if the paper stays independent. Your name came up as the right man for the job."

"The Examiner is profitable?"

"I spend over $150,000 a year in ads with George. The other brokers in my firm also advertise weekly. And we are just one of the six big brokerages in town. Plus, there are a bunch of small offices and independent realtors. And there are other advertisers, too, though they don't amount to much compared to real estate."

A hundred and fifty grand was twice the annual ad revenue that Tom took in with The Forum.

"I appreciate the offer, but I can't afford it."

"The paper is profitable enough to support the financing that we can arrange for you. This works because there's a seller who is looking for the right buyer. And he has friends like me who want to help him and who care about the community."

Tom leaned back and studied Erica. She was in her mid-fifties, conspicuously fit, and radiated self-assurance. Her voice had a sexy huskiness to it.

"We need to discuss the catch."

"No catch. I'm a broker with a business to sell, representing a seller who would prefer to find a buyer who shares his values."

"I'd like to look at the financials and give it serious consideration."

"That's all I can ask," Erica said, standing and extending a hand. "I hope we can make it happen."

The financials were promptly delivered. Though the bookkeeping was full of holes, it was clear that the paper was prosperous, judging from revenues alone. When Tom called Erica back to pursue the deal, she surprised him by offering to personally loan Tom the money for the acquisition, with the caveat that Tom would keep his financial participation strictly confidential, and so would she.

"It would hurt the paper with the other realtors in town if they knew they were supporting a competitor by advertising with you," Erica explained. "They'd assume I was self-dealing, giving myself all the prime placements, which is ridiculous since I already have the back cover and inside front cover under contract with George. But appearances are important."

"Sounds reasonable."

"It doesn't even have to be a loan. I'll put in cash for 51 percent of the equity. You'll put in sweat for the other 49 percent. Since I want to do right by George, he'll be paid plenty, which means the paper's valuation will be high and your stake will be valuable from day one, if I ever decide to sell. All you have to do is keep the paper profitable so you're not coming back to me looking for more capital. That means pay yourself as much as the paper can afford and still turn a reasonable profit, almost half of which is yours, after all, so you have plenty of incentive to keep your damned costs under control—and provide me with quarterly accounting and my share of the profits. We can work out the details in an operating agreement, keep it as arms-length as possible between us. How does that sound?"

"Too good to be true."

"I believe in the Telluride community. As long as you run a good, honest, and profitable paper, I'll be getting what I want out of the deal."

"Can I keep The Forum and hire someone to run it?"

"I don't care."

"If I don't keep The Forum alive, the West End won't have a paper."

"That's why George and I approached you. You've got integrity."

. . .

Tom had long since given up the hope that he'd ever catch another professional break. Not after spectacularly blowing up his career in Boston; not living and working in the obscurity of the West End, where he'd fled. He liked publishing a very small paper in the middle of nowhere, processing the weekly school lunch menu for publication and affixing address labels by hand to copies of the newspaper to be mailed to subscribers, most of whom resided in nursing homes. He had adapted to scratching out a modest living and to the glacial pace of life in the outback. His relationship with Sarah had deepened after it became clear that her husband, Ray Walker, would never be found because he was almost certainly dead following his disappearance, and they had begun to talk about getting married.

But Erica's timing was propitious. Enough time had passed, and Tom's secret history was buried deeply enough, that he was receptive to the possibility of rejoining the bigger world where there might be a better chance at redemption. Or would it just be a second opportunity to fuck up, since failure always lies on the flip side of aspiration?

Why risk it?

There was Sarah to consider. She had her own reasons for wanting a fresh start in a new setting, away from the trauma of Ray's disappearance. And there was Ray Jr., who was flailing at Naturita High. Tom resolved to step up to the opportunity. He was ready to recover his professional pride. He was not the same person he'd been in his twenties. Hadn't Erica observed that he had integrity? Even if Tom knew that wasn't true, nobody else did. Plus, he was sober now and maybe that was enough.

There was a catch, of course, that was never articulated because there was no need to speak of it. Tom, the new publisher of the venerable San Miguel Examiner, found himself paying deference to Erica. He told himself that Erica's ownership stake was not the reason, because he would have shown the same consideration to his biggest advertiser without it. Even if that were true, would it be any less salient? Because if Erica suggested Tom look into a story that she, Erica, was personally interested in, usually something to do with zoning or a land use policy that could affect property values, Tom dutifully did it. Moreover, Tom ensured that Erica was included prominently as a source in any story about the state of the real estate market, burnishing his silent partner's reputation as the region's leading broker. And though Tom could barely acknowledge his own self-interest, even to himself, he never paid much attention to the views of the no-growthers like Jerry Green and Chuck Small, who always struck him as crackpots.

That's how self-interest works. It feels reasonable to the self-interested party: natural, ordinary, obvious. It can even feel a lot like friendship.

Everything is everything, Tom thought—the urban street expression Springsteen employed as a lyric, a frequent earworm, precisely because it applies to everything, always, somehow—even the pending parks and rec board vote on the question: Trance Music Festival or no Trance Music Festival? At this moment, everything was a singular thing whether it was called self-interest or commerce; wealth accumulation or job creation: it consisted of real estate development and music festivals; Persian rugs and Swiss fondue and full-page newspaper ads. It was human endeavor, or just call it greed, and it was all about to bust, even if few people had come to grips with this fact ... yet. The purported idealists like Green and Small were no less self-interested. But they also had a point.

Now Graham was making a final argument: "The town needs its merchants to prosper. We pay sales tax and provide jobs. Visitor surveys rank the shopping experience among the five things visitors love most about Telluride, not far below the skiing and the scenery. We merchants need this festival so we can do our part to support the community."

Green couldn't restrain himself from blurting out: "The town has no obligation to bend over for a merchant!"

The board chair banged down his gavel once, twice, three times, the loud cracks an official expression of irritation.

"Now we'll have none of that. Please speak only when you are called upon or you will be asked to leave the meeting."

"I'm sorry," Green muttered.

But Green wasn't really sorry. This bit of drama was routine in Telluride and Tom's mind had wandered back to an extraordinarily awkward dinner at Graham's house six months earlier, an invitation to socialize with Graham and his much younger wife, the Elsa of Elsa's Melting Pot, which he accepted because he couldn't think of a graceful way to decline.

The evening started out with a quick tour of the couple's Beaver Pond condo, including a pass through the bedroom where the bed was perfectly made and there was a bottle of champagne chilling in an ice bucket, and not two, but four glasses on a nearby tray. Tom glanced at Sarah, who nodded back.

Cocktails were served, followed by a well-cooked meal of grilled salmon and asparagus with hollandaise. Graham, a polished British transplant by way of an earlier career on Wall Street, seized the opportunity to impress Tom with his Telluride cred, since he'd been in town much longer and had plenty of opinions about governmental dysfunction that made it difficult to survive in a retail business. The two of them were engaged in the same battle for economic survival, admittedly ancillary to the town's main business of real estate, but essential to its success, Graham providing fine Persian rugs to lay on the floors of the homes that Tom helped sell with ads in his newspaper.

Sarah and Elsa operated out of opposite schools of style, Sarah displaying the unlikely flair of a fashionable streak in her hair despite her artisanal leanings and Elsa looking like she'd just walked out of a Parisian boutique wearing the latest cashmere sweater, leather miniskirt, and high-heeled boots. Tom overheard them describe their respective backgrounds. Sarah the daughter of Mormon fundamentalists on the remote border of Colorado and Utah and Elsa the daughter of a famous chef in Zermatt couldn't have had less in common.

"A daughter and two sons," Tom heard Sarah say, offering a family inventory and no personal details, not even her children's ages, much less their complicated provenance: the wayward adult daughter, the first son fathered by a dead husband, the second her adopted grandson.

"My period is late, and we are hoping," Elsa replied, her voice pregnant even if she was not.

Elsa stood and then began to clear the dinner dishes. "I have made a lemon tart with strawberry coulis," she said. "Let's have it in the living room."

Elsa served the dessert and then, while Graham poured cognac, she flicked on the television.

Graham and Elsa turned their attention to the screen, so Tom and Sarah followed suit. A couple walked into a hotel room holding hands.

They started kissing, fell onto the bed, pawed each other, ripped each other's clothes off, and began having sex.

Graham was kissing Elsa.

Sarah knew exactly what to do.

"I have had a very long day," she said. "Topped off by this lovely evening. But I have got to get home soon and or I'll fall asleep right here on this couch."

"Oh," Elsa said, pulling away from Graham. "But you are welcome to stay."

"That is so gracious, and dinner was wonderful, but I prefer my own bed."

They kept their cool until they were safely outside, but then burst out laughing.

"Did that really just happen?" Tom asked.

"They could have just asked us if we swing," Sarah said.

"They pretty much did ask. But I guarantee it's not me they're interested in."

"Don't be so sure."

The board was voting, and Tom reined in his daydreaming to add the final vote tally and otherwise update the lead of his story—the rest of which was complete—on his laptop.

"The Telluride Parks and Recreation Commission narrowly rejected on Thursday a request by a festival promoter for a major new event next July in the Telluride Town Park. By a vote of three-to-two, the commission concluded at the end of a two-hour discussion that Town Park is already fully booked with numerous recreational activities next July and will not be available to host the proposed Telluride Trance Music Festival at that time. While the commission indicated that it would be more receptive to dates in September or May, festival promoter Craig Gamble said that only a mid-summer date would work for his audience."

Then Tom felt a sharp chill. It was terror, the ice that freezes the blood of even a Hollywood star.

The global economy was crashing.

What if this was the very last story that The Examiner would publish?

Chapter 11

GOOD ECONOMIC THEORY

As he walked out of Town Hall, Tom got a call from Peter.

"How did that parks and rec meeting go?"

"They killed the trance festival."

"That's cool. Listen, I'm onto something big."

"Yeah?"

"No time to talk now. I'm heading into an interview."

Peter interrupted his conversation with Tom to greet someone, "Hey, I'll be right with you…." And then he spoke again to Tom: "I'll need another day. At least. County meeting tomorrow is all yours. And don't worry, boss. I assure you it will be worth it."

Tom was about to protest, to tell Peter he should pack it in, there was no point in continuing because…. but the kid had already hung up.

Tom felt a rush of anger and called Peter back, ready to blurt out that Peter was out of a job, fired! But the call went straight to voice mail. In the time it took to wait out Peter's recorded greeting, prolonged by a few catchy bars of reggae, Tom wondered if cell phones were diabolically designed to foster mistrust. Does a call go to voice mail because the person you are calling actively declines to answer? Or because he turned off the phone or silenced the ringer? Maybe he misplaced the phone? Or the battery suddenly died? The caller might have been blocked. Possibly, the person you are calling has moved out of cell range. Or it could be a random technological glitch. Weren't there more than enough ways to miscommunicate before cell phones?

By the time Tom heard the beep to begin recording his message he had calmed down enough to keep his options open.

"I said I need more than hunches," he said gruffly. "Something big doesn't cut it. Call me."

Across the street from where he stood, Tom could see Graham and a couple of other main street merchants continuing the rarefied argument about the town's identity with Jerry Green and Chuck Small — as if there were no global financial crisis about to crash down on them all, rendering the question moot. Perhaps it was fortunate that Peter hadn't answered when Tom tried calling back. Nothing would be served by pulling the plug on The Examiner one moment sooner than necessary. If there was time for Graham and Jerry and Chuck to debate how much commerce is too much commerce, and time for Peter to chase hunches about the Cluff murder, then there was also time for Tom to regain his equanimity and think through his next moves.

* * *

Tom needed a break, so instead of returning to work, he went home. It was Sarah he really needed to talk to.

He found her in the living room, huddled with Tyler over a coloring book.

"Where's Angie?" Tom asked, looking around as if she might be hiding in a closet. Even home wasn't entirely a safe place.

"I told her that if she is planning on staying with us for more than a few weeks she had to get a job. So, she's out looking for work at the hair salons."

Tom nodded and sat on the sofa. He had already assumed that Angie wouldn't be leaving anytime soon because she wouldn't have come back if she'd had anywhere else to go.

"Good work," he said to Tyler, pointing to the outline of a giraffe in a coloring book that was covered in crayon scribbles. Tyler chose a new color and scribbled some more, oblivious to the lines.

"It will be all right," Sarah said. "She's matured, except she expects a lot, that he'll love her like a mother, just automatically. Her presumption that he belongs to her scares him. And you can't blame him because she's a stranger to him."

The boy was scribbling furiously, as if to shut out the adults' conversation. Tom handed him a crayon of another color.

"I've had a rough day, too. Cash flow has dried up as the economy tanks."

Tom couldn't tell whether Sarah was slow to comprehend the implication of what he was telling her or just didn't know what to say in response. So he spelled it out.

"I'll probably have to fold the paper."

Now she gasped.

"I thought it was the real estate cycle."

"I did too. But it's a lot worse than that."

"Why?"

Sarah really didn't know. She was practical and knew that Tom had been worried about his business. But she didn't follow national news in the slightest, had never voted and rarely glanced at a newspaper, even after she married a newspaper publisher. She was born and raised outside Nucla, to a Mormon family that lived in isolation precisely so they could practice polygamy without state interference and had never been further from home than Grand Junction until she married Tom and they drove to a beach in Baja California for their honeymoon. Her life had not lacked for challenges, but they were contingencies, like her daughter's meth addiction. She had found equilibrium and earned a living by making artisanal soap, and packaging and selling it at local farmers markets and gift shops. It was her groundedness that made her such a good match for Tom, who so frequently lost himself in abstraction.

"The market is crashing. Not just here, but everywhere. It's all over the news. I really don't know what to do."

"You always know what to do."

"I fake it."

"You do not."

"I've been saving for a down payment. So, we're good for a while, and after that, I don't know."

"My sales are growing. Maybe because the realtors are buying soap for their wives because it's a small luxury they can still afford."

"It's as good an economic theory as any. Plus, there's the website."

Tom had asked Samantha to moonlight, building and managing a site for Sarah's Handmade Soap, and it had already begun to pay off in online sales. There was an opportunity for Sarah to grow the business faster, but she was reluctant to hire the help she would need to produce more soap.

Why was Sarah's website bringing in more money than the newspaper's, even though the newspaper had far more traffic?

"It's an e-commerce site," Samantha had explained. "The newspaper website isn't selling anything. Just ads. And there are lots of places people can advertise online."

Now, Tom thought, the potential to sell a tangible product online—Sarah's soap –could turn out to be his family's salvation. They could build the brand. Expand the product line. Who knew what might work in a brave new world without newspapers?

"I can learn to make soap."

"You'd never have the patience for it. But you could spend more time with Tyler and let me work more hours. Like now, before you go back to the office. Let me get another batch of soap started early. It could be worth an extra $200 in sales this week."

"Sure," Tom said.

Just that easily they had begun to imagine a future in which Tom didn't publish a newspaper.

After Sarah left, Tom opened the coloring book to a page yet untouched by crayon.

"It's a zebra," he said to Tyler. "What does a zebra have?"

"Stripes!"

"Let's color in the stripes."

"OK."

Tom carefully colored in a stripe and handed the crayon to Tyler, who promptly scribbled across it.

"Not like that!" Tom exclaimed. "Let me show you."

Tyler watched impatiently as Tom colored in another zebra stripe, staying within the lines. Then Tyler took the crayon and scribbled some more.

"Oh, my God," Tom said. "You're right!"

He took the crayon and scribbled the way Tyler had done, to the boy's peals of laughter.

And that's how Tom spent the last of the fading afternoon, helping his son fill the coloring book cover-to-cover with unruly scribbles.

Chapter 12

WORRIED ABOUT WHAT?

That's the problem with Peter, Tom thought: He is too old to be scribbling outside the lines.

Tom tried calling his off-leash reporter later that night, and the next morning when he got to work, but both times there was no answer.

"Let me know what's going on," he said, leaving a message. "Call me as soon as you can."

He tried to sound casual, calling not out of worry — because what was there to worry about? — but rather from an editor's duty to his reporter in the field. He sent the same message as a text. He called the motel where Peter was staying and asked them to transfer the call to Peter's room. But there was no answer there either.

Tom could imagine Peter getting so involved in his reporting that he didn't have time to call back. He could understand that it might not occur to Peter that Tom would be concerned since they had spoken just the previous day. Assuming there was nothing seriously wrong, Peter might not have any reason to think Tom was worried.

But Tom didn't think Peter would flat-out ignore his calls and texts. At the very least, he would text back to tell Tom that he would be in touch soon, that his story was coming along, or to say he was on his way back to Telluride.

Maybe he was on his way home and out of cell range, or his phone battery was dead. Maybe he'd lost his phone. These were weak arguments against the overriding fact that for Peter to be incommunicado was deeply out-of-character. He could have called from his motel room. Or have stopped in at the Cortez newspaper offices to introduce himself and borrow a phone.

Though Peter might be a younger Tom, he was a better version, similarly dogged in pursuit of a story but more responsible. Peter had Hailey, who worked at the Telluride Gallery of Fine Art and was as career focused as he was. Peter didn't seem susceptible to the allure of drugs or alcohol. He had a goofy streak—"aye, aye," and a salute when Tom gave him direction—but Tom was usually more charmed than annoyed by it. Not this time. Tom was seriously irritated by the tease of Peter telling him he was onto "something big" without offering the slightest hint of what it was and ending the call before Tom could ask.

Tom almost called Hailey to ask if she'd heard from Peter, but he didn't want to worry her. He decided to let her call him if she was worried. He imagined the two of them, himself and Hailey, separately starting to worry, leaving messages on Peter's phone, fearing the worst. But that was probably not the case because Peter had not been out of touch for all that long, not even 24 hours, and he hadn't necessarily told Hailey he was onto "something big." He probably told her he'd be gone a day or two. Or he had been in touch with her because he knew she would worry, not imagining that Tom would.

But the weight of Tom's worry was heavy twice over. He loved the kid like a kid brother, and he was also Peter's boss.

At noon, sitting at a picnic table in the park outside his office, finishing a sandwich, Tom called and left Peter another voice mail, letting his irritation show: "Fucking call me. Now. What the fuck is going on?"

Tom's phone beeped, signaling a new text message.

But it wasn't from Peter. It was from Erica.

"Cancel all of my advertising effective immediately."

*   *   *

He should have anticipated it, but still it landed like a sucker punch.

How could it come now, with Tom consumed by a far more immediate crisis? And like this. By text. From Erica.

Tom thought they were friends. How many times had they been invited to a dinner party hosted by Erica's husband, Ramon, who assembled guest lists to introduce Erica's wealthy real estate clients—who were contemplating a move to Telluride, at least part time—to interesting locals like Tom, the local newspaper publisher, and his wife Sarah, a talented local artisan? Ramon, who was a professional host as owner and front-of-the-house man at The Depot, the town's most elegant dinner reservation, effortlessly made business into something social and a dinner party into an intimate gathering that could grease a real estate transaction. Now, Tom saw with sudden clarity, he and Sarah had been nothing but handy props.

There was panic welling up inside, threatening to break him open and display his guts, right there in public, so he sat perfectly still working to keep his expression placid. There were strangers passing by on the nearby sidewalk; and there were familiar faces, acquaintances and friends who made eye contact and nodded. It came as a relief that they could not see that he was a ruined man. Or perhaps they could see it clearly and looked away in embarrassment. Maybe they were ruined too, each in their own way. Or they were about to be ruined and just didn't know it yet, the way Tom himself had imagined only moments earlier that his crash was a dozen miles down the highway and might yet be avoided.

"Hey."

Samantha sat next to him.

"I can't reach Peter."

Was this a form of mercy, displacing a meltdown with a mere crisis?

"When's the last time you talked to him?"

"Yesterday afternoon."

"Me, too. It sounded like he was onto something."

"I think so."

"What?"

"He didn't tell me."

Tom slammed a fist on the table: "Why the fuck is he playing games with us!"

She frowned. "I don't feel it's games, exactly."

"Have you spoken to Hailey?"

"She hasn't been able to reach him either, not since yesterday afternoon. She said he sounded normal; told her he had found some 'amazing stuff,' so he was going to stay one more night."

"'Amazing stuff?' And you have no idea what it was?"

She shook her head.

"I shouldn't have let him go."

"It's not unusual for a reporter to look into the background of a murder victim. Is it?"

"Not at all."

In fact, as Tom had recently learned, The Examiner's coverage of the Eva Shoen murder 18-years earlier included deep speculative dives into the family's business entanglements, no matter that they later proved irrelevant.

He picked up his phone and placed a call, putting it on speaker so Samantha could hear everything.

"Anasazi Motor Inn. This is Maria. How can I help?"

"This is Tom Austin. I prepaid for a room for my employee Peter Barnard for last night and I need to extend the stay through tonight."

"I was about to call you," Maria said. "Mr. Barnard missed the check-out time for today. He left his belongings so we assumed he would be back for tonight. Fortunately, we have availability. This is still our busy season."

"I'm sorry for the inconvenience. Peter's been detained and I'll be arriving in Cortez this evening to join him. We'll be sharing the room, so I'll need a key from you in case he's not back by the time I arrive."

"OK, I'd better check with my manager," she said, and put Tom on hold for a moment.

"She says OK," Maria reported back. "Usually, we'd need a photo ID that has the same name as the name who has already checked in on the reservation, but since you paid for the room, we'll just need to see the credit card that you used. When do you expect to arrive?"

"I should be there by five."

"Oh, good. I'm on duty until six."

"One last question," Tom said. "When is check-out time?"

"It's noon, but it can be extended to one or two if you ask. Do you want me to extend it for tomorrow?"

"I'll let you know. I was just wondering how long Mr. Barnard has been away."

"I can't say. I'm here from nine to six and I haven't seen him today. I don't know if anyone else saw him and there's a back door where a guest can leave or come back using their key card without walking past the reception desk. He could have left early this morning. "

She lowered her voice to just above a whisper.

"Or, well, I probably shouldn't say…"

She stopped talking.

"But?"

"The housekeeper said that the bed wasn't slept in."

Chapter 13

'I KNOW THAT DUDE'

C all the cops," Samantha said, when Tom hung up.

"They won't take it seriously. He hasn't been gone long enough."

"He was investigating a murder, and we can't reach him. That's more than enough."

"It doesn't matter. I have to go down there. Which means that you need to cover for me here, handle anything that comes up. And we need to stay in close contact. I'll text you every move I make. And if you don't hear from me, you can call me, and if I don't get back to you within half an hour, then…."

"Then what? I drive down looking for you and we can make it three missing reporters in Montezuma County?"

"Then you call the cops. They couldn't ignore a report of two reporters missing in their county within a day of each other."

"Are you insane?"

"What's the alternative?"

"Call the cops now."

Tom stood and they started to walk back to the office.

"Give me time to get into his room and see what I can learn," he said. "If something bad has happened, getting the police involved now won't change it. If he's all right and we call them now, we'll have to justify ourselves to them. Which could be a huge headache. Law enforcement doesn't like reporters looking into a criminal investigation."

Tom glanced at his watch. Time was short. He had to reach the motel before the clerk who promised that she'd let him check-in to Peter's room was off duty.

He decided on his way home to grab an overnight bag and the car to tell Sarah that he landed a last-minute interview with Jay Cluff's daughter in Cortez. There was no need to alarm her and no time to persuade her that his mission was urgent and that there was no alternative to his looking for Peter himself. She had her hands full with her daughter and would hardly notice his brief absence.

Because there was surely a logical explanation for Peter's silence, and he would prove to be perfectly all right.

Wouldn't he?

* * *

Tom texted Samantha from the parking lot of the Anasazi Motor Inn: "Just arrived motel. Will call when get to room."

He was welcomed at the front desk by Maria herself.

"I appreciate your help with my unusual situation," Tom said, as he showed her his credit card.

She was in her late twenties and appeared to have some Native American or Mexican ancestry. She leaned toward Tom to draw him in closer and tilted her head slightly. Her meaning was clear. Her manager, sitting at a desk in the office nearby, might not appreciate her butting into a hotel guest's personal affairs. Tom could see what Maria couldn't: that the manager was, indeed, paying attention, glancing up from her work and looking right at him. Tom smiled past Maria at the manager, hoping Maria would understand they were being closely observed, if not easily overheard. But her curiosity would not be denied.

"It is unusual, I would say," she muttered, beneath her breath.

"Did you see something?" Tom spoke in an equally low voice, establishing a quick bond of mutual confidence.

"Yesterday, at about this same time, just before I got off work," she whispered. "Mr. Barnard was walking around while he was talking on his phone."

"He was talking to me right around then."

Maria's words tumbled out.

"I just checked him in a little before, so that's how I know it was him. Then this dude shows up. And Mr. Barnard gets off the phone and they say 'hi,' like they're just meeting for the first time, shake hands, and they go off together."

Tom wanted to hear more, but not now.

"Can we talk later?" he said, lowering his voice another notch and shooting a more pointed look toward the manager's office. He used the pen he had just used to sign his credit card voucher to scribble his cell number on a nearby note pad.

"Yes, sir," Maria said in a stronger voice, for the manager's benefit, as she handed him his key card and pocketed the note. "Breakfast is from six to nine right over there in our breakfast nook. I hope you have a very pleasant stay with us. If you need anything, just let us know."

Peter's overnight bag on the table next to the television was unopened. Tom unzipped it and looked inside: fresh socks and underwear, a clean shirt, a toiletry kit. The knapsack he used to carry his computer was gone. Other than that, there was no sign that Peter had been there. Housekeeping might have straightened everything out, almost as if to purposefully remove any clues. The meager evidence that Peter had been there only made the room seem more sterile.

Tom could deduce that Peter had not gone straight to the motel when he arrived in Cortez on Thursday morning. Maybe he was hungry and went for lunch. Or maybe he had something scheduled. Peter hadn't revealed his "hunches" so Tom had to imagine what he would have done if he were doing Peter's job. Head downtown to visit Cluff's real estate office and try to strike up a conversation with someone there. Have lunch at the closest restaurant, chat up the waitress or some of the regulars, and bring up the subject of the murder in Telluride. Maybe meet with a reporter from the local newspaper. Possibly swing by Cluff's home to try to talk to someone there.

Sometime around four Peter had checked in to the motel, had briefly gone up to his room, and then had returned to the lobby and to meet the man Maria had described. He called Tom while he was waiting. But for whom? Someone with whom he made initial contact earlier with plans to meet later at his motel, if Maria's observations were to be believed, and she certainly seemed to have an eye for detail.

His phone rang.

"The bitch just fired me," Maria said.

"She was watching us pretty closely," Tom said. "Probably overheard too much."

"I don't even care. I'd about had it with her riding me all the time anyway."

"How long did you work here?"

"About six months. It's OK. I can find another ten-dollar an hour job in a day or two. There's lots of good jobs like that around here. Heck, maybe I can get ten-fifty."

"Where are you?"

"Behind the motel."

"I'll be right down."

He found her in a weedy vacant lot, sitting behind the wheel of a beat-up Hyundai. He climbed in the passenger seat.

She greeted him with a theatrical snarl.

"What the hell, man! You're the dude who just got my ass fired! What more can you do for me?"

"Hey, I saw what happened. You got yourself fired. You didn't give a damn what she heard."

"Can't deny it," she shrugged. "Story of my life. It's always my bad attitude gets me in trouble. I just kind of thought if I guilt-tripped you a little, maybe you'd feel like you owe me dinner or something."

"I'm good for that much. Let's go big. What's the best joint in town?"

"Maria's," Maria said. "No relation, but a great name, don't you think?"

"I wouldn't take Maria anywhere else."

Maria started the car and put it in drive. They lurched forward.

"I don't think we'll make it very far," Tom said, pointing to the fuel gauge on her dashboard. "You're riding on empty."

Maria frowned.

"You got five bucks you could front me? I'm out of cash until payday."

"Don't sweat the five bucks. I'll fill your tank."

"So you do feel bad you got me axed!"

"Nah. OK, maybe a little. What reason did she give for firing you?"

"I told you that she said it was OK to give you the key to Mr. Barnard's room, but I didn't really ask her. I put you on hold a sec to figure out if I could help you find your friend, because I already knew that's what you were trying to do. I was getting nervous I'd be off work before you got here and then it would have blown up anyways when you told her that I said you could check in without the right ID. She got suspicious when she watched me check you in. She wanted to know what room I put you in and got pissed when she saw it was Mr. Barnard's room, because that cost her money, not making you get your own room. So, I guess I was ready to leave this fricking job anyway. Heck, I didn't get fired! I quit! But it looks like I'll get a free tank of gas out of it. So that's like half a day's salary right there."

"Yep. And dinner, too," Tom said.

"Like a real date?"

"Except that I'm a happily married man."

"Story of my life" she said. "All the good men are taken."

"I thought it was your bad attitude getting you into trouble."

"Yeah, that too. Now you know my whole life story, both chapters."

She pulled into a gas station. Tom climbed out of the car to run his credit card and she started to fill the tank.

Tom could read the headline in a paper on a nearby rack: "Local Businessman Killed in Telluride." He walked over to it, fished into his pocket for quarters, and grabbed a copy of the paper.

"Prominent Cortez businessman Jay Cluff was shot and killed on Monday, apparently while he was guarding property he owned in Telluride," the story read. "A lifelong Cortez resident, Cluff, 58, owned Cluff Properties, with offices on Main Street in Cortez. In addition to brokering real estate, Cluff was a developer and owned properties here and in the region. He purchased the property in Telluride's Bear Creek last year and was pursuing plans to develop a ski resort there."

The editor in Tom immediately wanted to ask the writer who or what Cluff was "guarding" the property from. But perhaps to the Cortez readership, the need to guard one's property was obvious, just as it was obvious to Tom's Telluride readership that people had the right to use a long-established hiking trail that traversed private property.

"Look over there," Maria said in her low voice, indicating a late-model matte black Tacoma pickup tanking up a couple of lanes over. "That's the dude who met your friend yesterday afternoon."

He appeared to be in his late twenties and wore blue jeans and cowboy boots. His hair was military short. An American flag tattoo on a skinny left upper arm peeked out below the sleeve of his t-shirt.

"Is he following us?"

"You got any reason to think someone might be tailing you?"

"With Peter missing, I can't rule it out."

She had finished filling the tank and was back in the driver's seat. Tom had climbed back into the passenger's seat next to her.

"Well, just in case, let's blow this popsicle stand."

She had inched to the edge of the gas station lot, where she abruptly peeled out onto the highway. She took a sharp right and expertly found a gap in the oncoming traffic. Tom looked back to see whether the truck owner was paying attention. He looked up as they left, but indifferently and only prompted by the screech of Maria's wheels.

"I know that dude," Maria said. "And that's how I knew there was something not right about your friend not sleeping in his bed and not checking out on time and then you calling about him. The whole thing.

"Like, I'm asking myself, what was a normie like Mr. Barnard doing with a skank like Lionel Fucking Cluff?

Chapter 14

'THIS IS A MURDER INVESTIGATION'

Who was Maria?

Could it be a coincidence that the clerk at the motel where Peter was staying knew the man Peter met just prior to disappearing? And that they then spotted him at a gas station? And he just happened to have the last name of Cluff?

Why not, in a small town?

The fact that the questions occurred to him might be evidence that Tom was becoming paranoid. He had good reason to feel vulnerable, even if there was no reason for anyone in Cortez to know who he was—other than Maria. And yet coincidence can be the trick that enables conspiracy to hide in plain sight. Or it might be serendipity that brings the twists of a complicated plot into relief where it can be apprehended. There was no sure way for a witness like Tom to know the difference.

"How do you know Lionel Cluff?" he asked, as Maria pulled up to a Mexican restaurant on the far end of the town's main street.

"Lionel and me were in Law Enforcement Academy together," she said. "Couple of years back, for 18 weeks. He was a smart-ass. Should have flunked out. But he still got hired the day he graduated. I saw him around after that in his shiny uniform, driving a Cortez Police Department patrol car. But he got fired."

"You don't like him."

"He's a total douche. Didn't recognize me when he came to the motel to meet Peter. I was just the clerk behind the counter. Of course, I was invisible to him back when we were in the class together, too."

They had made their way into the restaurant and were being seated.

"Why do you say that?"

"I'm Native. Half Ute."

She explained once they were seated: "A lot of Pinks look right through us Natives, like we're not even there. Especially Native women. Unless they feel like raping someone. Then we can come in handy."

"Pinks?"

"You don't really look all that *white* to us," she said. "And what the fuck is *Anglo*, anyway? It's not a color, is it? I mean, you can't exactly paint your bedroom wall *Anglo*, right?"

"Word," Tom said.

The waitress approached.

"What should we eat?" he asked Maria.

"Chicken enchiladas, green chili, rice and beans."

"Two orders," Tom told the waitress.

"So, I'm Pink?" he asked when the waitress had left.

"Yeah, but don't worry about it none. I'm half Pink myself. In case you're wondering."

"Why would I be wondering?"

"People do," she shrugged. "So, I'm clearing it up for you just in case. My mom is from Towaoc. My dad is from Cortez.

"Cool."

"There ain't really nothing 'cool' about it," Maria said. "The Natives are OK with it. But not the Pinks. I've got a Mexican-sounding last name, Sanchez, because my dad is Chicano. Which makes it worse, even though he's not Latino."

"What's the difference?"

"Chicanos have been in the U.S. of A. way longer than Pinks, but not half as long as the Natives. Latinos are new. Wetbacks. Go back two, three generations at most. Us Chicanos go back to the conquistadors. Lots of Chicanos have Indian blood. Of course, the Latinos who come from across the border have lots of Native blood, too, but Mexican Native blood, like Olmec or Maya blood, not Ute or Navajo or Apache blood. But the cowboys and roughnecks from around here still think this country belongs to them, even if they got here, like, yesterday, so they give me shit because I don't look like them or have a last name like them. I just tell them I'm a mutt."

"Is that why you're not a cop?"

"Good guess. I got the best grades in the class. But fuck me, all I could land was a crummy desk job at the county sheriff's office.

"'You talk too much for an Indian,' my supervisor says to me. I told him my dad is white. Worked for County Road and Bridge for forty years. I got the gab from his mom, my grandma. He didn't care.

"'You want to get ahead here?' he says. 'Then you've got to stay in your lane for a few years and prove yourself.' I didn't go to the Cop Academy to sit at a desk, so I applied at the city police department, and they called my supervisor for a background check, and he fired me the next day because he said I wasn't happy there. And then the police department didn't want nothing to do with me because the sheriff's office fired me. So, I'm not a cop. I'm a front desk clerk at a shitty motel. And I'm not even that anymore. But, hey, I'm on a date with you at the best joint in town, so what've I got to whine about?"

"It sucks to be told you're too smart for your own good."

"You got that right. Like, what does it even mean? It means you're too female? Skin too dark? Too broke? But don't mind me. I'm not bitter or nothing."

"I'd hire you in a heartbeat if I had a job to offer."

"You sure you don't have one?"

There was no reason for a digression into the painful subject of why he would be laying off his entire newspaper staff, and would be out of work himself, within the week.

Tom opened the copy of the Cortez Journal he had bought at the gas station and put it in front of her.

"You know that guy?" he asked, pointing the photograph of Jay Cluff, the same head shot that appeared on the Cluff Properties website.

"Whoa," she said, her eyes widening. "Lionel's granddad. This is a murder investigation."

"Peter is a newspaper reporter who works for me up in Telluride, and he was here to dig up anything he could about the murder. And now you're telling me that Lionel Cluff is a douche, but does that make him dangerous?"

"Hell yes, he's dangerous. Killed his granddad. Probably killed your man Peter, too."

"Why would he kill his grandfather?"

"Jay Cluff was one of the richest men in the county and Lionel's a loser. What more do you need? He might have stood to inherit something. Or they could have had other issues. Except...."

"Except what?"

"Except the killer is never the first one you suspect. And if it is, there is always more to it. Some twist."

"Like what?"

"Like," and she paused to let the theory develop a bit before she continued, thinking aloud. "Maybe Peter was working for Lionel as a hired hitman, he took the job with you to go undercover to do the hit on Cluff. And then he met with Lionel yesterday to get his pay-off, and then disappeared because his work is done."

"Peter a hitman?" He laughed. "Peter doesn't have a violent bone in his body."

"Are you *sure* about that? Remember, it's always the very last thing you'd guess. The bad guys look good because they're cons. And the good guys look bad because everyone's got something to hide."

"What kind of hired killer would take a job as a reporter to go undercover? I think maybe you've watched too much *Law and Order*."

"Most TV stories are based on true crimes, and you can learn a lot from watching them. I'm just saying you've got to consider Peter could have a secret, too."

"If there's one person who doesn't, it would be Peter."

"Then I've got a real bad feeling about it. One way or the other, he got caught up in something that was too big for him. You'd best prepare yourself for the worst."

Tom felt the small hairs on the back of his neck stand up, an involuntary response to her validation of his fears.

"I bet he wasn't packing."

"Are you packing?"

"Always," she said, patting the knapsack sitting next to her. "Are you?"

"No."

"He was getting close to Cluff's killer, even if it wasn't Lionel. Killer had to shut him up."

"If someone killed him to shut him up, then that'd be another murder that the cops would start looking into and that would make it more likely they'd get caught."

"If it's Lionel, he'd figure the cops would look the other way, and he'd be right if it's local cops. Or the killer could have just disappeared Peter. Who'd go looking for him except for you and maybe his parents?"

"He's got friends. And a girlfriend."

"Good luck with that. They wouldn't get the time of day from the Montezuma County sheriff or the Cortez police. The missing person isn't a local resident, so it's not their problem. And he hasn't been missing all that long, so they'd say, 'give it a few days and he'll show up.' I heard them say that all the time at the sheriff's office and usually that was right. They'd show up. But plenty of people go missing around here all the time and they never show up. Especially Natives. The body gets dumped in some wash way out in the desert, the vultures and coyotes scatter the bones, and that's it. Or someone just drives away from this shithole without looking back, and nobody goes looking for them. There's a list of missing persons long as your arm over at the sheriff's office."

"What do you think I should do?"

Tom felt that she was studying him, weighing her response.

"Hire me," she said, slapping a private investigator license issued by the state of Colorado on the table in front of him.

"I'm only Level 1," she said. "That means I passed the jurisprudence test, but don't have 4,000 hours of experience to be Level 2. You'd be my first paying client. Which means I'd be cheap. Only a hundred dollars a day. Plus expenses and a testimonial if I do good."

"OK," Tom said.

"I got the job?"

"Only I want to pay you a hundred and fifty."

"Plus out-of-pocket?"

"Sure."

She put her hand up in the air and Tom met it with a slap.

"Woo-hoo!" she said, and then caught herself.

"It's not right for me to be happy for myself," she said soberly. "Because especially if he got on the wrong side of Sheriff Bruce, your reporter is in a lot of trouble."

Chapter 15

WESTERN MYTHOLOGY

Back in Peter's room at the Anasazi Motor Inn, Tom eyed Peter's overnight bag, resting near the television where he had left it. The everyday object seemed obstinate, as if it willfully refused to offer up even a tiny clue to its owner's whereabouts, though it could if it only chose to speak.

Tom called Sarah.

"How are things with Angie?" he asked.

"Hold on a sec…." He could hear some commotion in the background. "Sorry. Tyler was just trying to climb up the back of a kitchen chair."

"Oh."

"Hey Angie," Sarah shouted. "Can you come help me with Tyler?"

And then Angie's sluggish voice: "Yeah, awright."

"Sounds like you have your hands full," Tom said. "I'll let you go."

"It's nothing," she said. "When will you be home?"

"I'll let you know," he said. "It depends. A day or two. I'm following a couple of leads."

"OK," she said. "Love you."

To which he replied, "Love you."

The routine expression of devotion as they ended the conversation only underscored the extraordinary circumstance that Tom found himself in.

Why, he wondered, did he tell Sarah so little?

It was not only because she was preoccupied with problems of her own. It was also because, despite the rapidly mounting evidence of foul play, Tom clung to the hope that there would be nothing of consequence to tell, no catastrophe he would be obliged to reveal, not only to Sarah but to the world. Peter might enter the room at any moment with a wild story of having been held hostage by a deranged Lionel Cluff and having just narrowly escaped. Or there would be a benign explanation for his absence. He had gotten lost on a backcountry road where he had run out of gas, and it had taken him hours to hike out. Better yet, he was home in Telluride with Hailey and the two of them were so happily ensconced in bed together that it hadn't occurred to either one of them to get in touch with anyone else.

But then Peter's bag caught his eye again, and he realized that it did speak, and with absolute authority: "He would not have left me here," the bag said.

It felt like an emotional betrayal of Sarah that Tom called Samantha to update her on his investigation into Peter's whereabouts.

He had earlier texted that he was having dinner with a source and said he would call when he got back to the motel. Now he told her the source was the motel clerk, Maria, who had identified the person Peter had met the previous afternoon as Lionel Cluff.

"That's no surprise."

"She knows him. Says he's a lowlife. Ex-cop. Fully capable of murder."

"Call the cops."

"Maria worked at the sheriff's office. Says the cops can't be trusted. Hell, Lionel was a cop!"

"Do you trust her?"

"At this point I'm not sure I trust anyone. Not even you."

She answered with silence.

"That was a joke. About my own sorry state of mind."

"Not funny."

"I'm sorry."

"If we can't trust each other…."

"I know," Tom said, cutting her off. "I hired Maria to help me. She's got a private investigator's license. She's going to try to get to Lionel Cluff tomorrow morning, see if she can learn anything talking to him, or talk to people who know him, learn where he's been hanging, what he's been doing, while I make a visit to Cluff Realty."

"I'll see what I can dig up about Lionel Cluff online."

"All right," he said. "I've got to try to get some sleep."

* * *

Tom dreamed he was a newspaper editor in an earlier era. In the dream, a voice cried out: "Arthur Collins has been shot!"

Tom was reporting the murder. Telluride circa 1902 was smoky, noisy, crowded, and cold. He jostled with rough miners for space on the street in the town's busy "gaming" district. He visited a fortune teller who occupied a "crib" in an alley. Her name was Madame LaFarge, and she was really a prostitute and an opium addict whose fake French accent was a gimmick. She knew who shot Arthur Collins—Collins was a client—and Tom was willing to pay her rate for her to tell him who did it. But she drugged him with opium and seduced him instead, distracting him from his purpose.

Why, he wondered when he woke up, is there so often a sexual element in a dream? Is it to distract from the dream's deeper meanings, as if the subconscious mind was determined to keep its secrets? Madame LaFarge was real. Peter had written a story about her for the summer visitors guide, a magazine that the paper published the previous May. Decades after she was run out of town — disappearing who knows where, "lost to history," as Peter had written — she was still good for local color, served up as an example of the sort of rootless grifter who settled the lawless frontier, reinventing herself to survive.

How far had the West advanced in a century? Who in Telluride or anywhere else in the rural West wasn't staking a claim to some bit of Western mythology?

Chapter 16

INTRODUCING HAY CAMP MESA RANCH

Tom pulled up to the Cluff Properties office on west Main Street just before 9 a.m. and parked. A sign on the locked door indicated that office hours on Saturday were 10 to 5, so he took a moment to study the properties advertised in the window.

The most expensive home was a brand new, three-bedroom, three-bath on 35 wooded acres for $595,000. Most homes were in the $75,000 to $150,000 range. There were vacant lots for as little as $5,000. The prices were several decimal points removed from the real estate ads that Tom published in The Examiner, where you couldn't find a broken-down miner's shack or barely buildable vacant lot for less than $750,000, a modest home was well over $1 million, and there were plenty of listings for "estates" and "retreats" at upwards of $5 million.

Tom looked for a more discreet vantage point where he could wait for the office to open, finding a parking space around the next corner with a clear view of Cluff Properties' back entrance. One of two reserved parking spaces was occupied by the antique Ford pickup Jay Cluff had driven around Telluride. As a property owner in Bear Creek,

Cluff had a key to the gate and was permitted to drive up the Bear Creek road, and the red pickup was often parked conspicuously on his land. If it was there when Cluff was killed, it had been returned to the family in very short order, no more than a week after the murder, a reflection of either Sheriff Owens's efficiency or the Cluff family's diligence in looking after their property.

His phone rang. Samantha.

"Where are you?"

"Waiting for Cluff Realty to open."

"Don't go in there."

"Why?"

"I followed Lionel down an internet rabbit hole into a Reddit forum, a subreddit."

"A what?"

"It's a website, like a digital bulletin board, where people with common interests can post content and interact with each other. Like Facebook but not as public, because you need an invitation to join a subreddit.

"I created an alias. They let me right in. They don't seem worried about being busted or exposed. There's something like 850 members. I think they assume that because they are on Reddit, they're below the radar. Maybe they are. Maybe the FBI isn't onto them yet.

"The topic of the subreddit is the preservation of the White race in Southwestern Colorado. They're a chapter of a secretive national organization called the Aryan Patriots and they've got this plan to take over Montezuma County. You can't believe how twisted it is. Timothy McVeigh, the Oklahoma City bomber, is their big hero, and David Koresh, the Waco guy. Remember that? When federal agents raided a polygamous Seventh Day Adventist sect and something like

80 of the followers died? But what has them really fired up now is Obama. They're freaked out that an… '*N word*' … could be the next president. They're convinced that if Obama wins, the first thing he's going to do is confiscate all their guns, so they are busy practicing marksmanship and creating secret armories.

"They believe that only ordinary armed citizens can defend freedom, they say they're like the 'three percent' who fought the American revolution. And *when*, not *if*, the feds come after them, they won't be outgunned this time, like what happened at Ruby Ridge and Waco. And ElCee—Lionel Cluff—is all over it. It's partly a real estate play. He's pushing real estate for these whackos to buy where they can hide out with their ammo."

All of this was frightening, Tom thought, but not terribly surprising. There might be a similar conspiracy group online for half of the rural counties in the country, each egging the others on. Like his grandfather, ElCee was a perfect candidate to have joined one of them.

"OK," Tom said.

"There's more. Open your computer and check your email," she continued. "I sent you a link."

While he dug into his knapsack to retrieve and power up the computer, Samantha continued.

"I was researching the Cluff family before Peter left. Cluff and his two adult children were big donors to this guy, Dan Bruce, who was elected Montezuma County sheriff last year."

"And?"

"This guy Bruce ran on an extreme far right-wing platform. He promised he'd be a 'constitutional sheriff.' It turns out there's this movement of people who believe that county sheriffs have more legal authority in their county than any federal or state official because counties are sovereign jurisdictions, and the 'high' sheriff derives from English common law that the Constitution was based on. It's a complicated conspiracy theory and it's not easy to make sense of it."

"Which confirms that Cluff was a far-right nut job," Tom said calmly, as if to counter the alarm that rose in her voice the longer she talked. "No news there."

"Which is exactly what Peter and I thought! We set it aside. But did you get the email?"

Tom had already clicked on the link and was reading.

"Yeah," he muttered.

He knew what he was looking at instantly: a page from the Cluff Properties website, littered with cheesy animations of American flags flapping in the wind. He had visited the site several times to glean what it might reveal about Cluff, which was not much: there were property listings and photographs of Cluff, the managing broker, and his adult daughter, Connie Cluff Barnes, described as an associate broker.

The headline proclaimed: "Introducing Hay Camp Mesa Ranch." The subheading beneath it read: "A highly secure location that will be offered exclusively by Cluff Properties to White Christian American Patriots, in a county governed by sovereign Sheriff Dan Bruce."

"Holy shit."

"Yeah," Samantha said. "You were so right not to call the cops."

"How did we miss seeing this?"

"It's a hidden page on the Cluff website. I got the link from one of the nut jobs on the subreddit."

"This has got to be the big thing that Peter didn't have time to tell me about yesterday on the phone," Tom said. "Maybe he found it following the same path you did, on the subrrrr…"

"Subreddit."

"Or he could have learned that Cluff was developing this secret white supremacist compound some other way."

"It has to be connected with Cluff's murder," Samantha said. "I wonder if Sheriff Owens knows about it."

"I'm sure he knows that the Montezuma sheriff is a wingnut. But not necessarily Cluff's involvement with him. Hell, he probably knows that, too."

"Maybe it's not relevant."

"Oh, it's relevant," Tom said. "Start with the fact that this Haystack Mesa Ranch is a federal fucking crime all by itself. No colored need apply? It's so unbelievably ... brazen."

"They talk on the subreddit like they'd welcome a fight with the feds. So they could take them out with AK-47s blazing. Start a civil war."

"Sounds like bravado."

"You could write it off that way if it wasn't for the website page, which is like a billboard designed to draw the attention of the FBI."

"Right," Tom agreed. "Which just means they're delusional. On top of that, the Nazi subdivision opens up all sorts of possible motives and suspects for anyone investigating the Cluff murder, drawing attention, like it did from Peter, even if it's totally unrelated."

"And what are the odds of that?"

"Low. Which is why cops don't like reporters who dig shit up that can make them look bad or tip off a suspect."

They sat silent for a moment, the phone line open, listening to each other breathe.

"Peter was underselling it when he said he was onto something big," Tom said in awe. "This is like a two-scoop."

"Is that a newspaper thing? Or an ice cream cone?"

"Just ice cream. It popped out of my mouth."

That drew an involuntary laugh.

"Don't think for a minute I'm laughing," Samantha warned. "I'm not. I'm hysterical, is what I am! Where the fuck is Peter?"

"He's probably a prisoner of war in a work camp on Hay Camp Mesa. Or under interrogation in Sheriff Bruce's Montezuma County jail."

"They could keep him forever and how would anyone know?" Samantha said, closing in on full-panic mode. "If that's what happened to Peter, they could make you their second POW. You've got to turn around and get out of that county fast!"

"And just forget about Peter?"

That was obviously not an option, pausing both of them.

"I don't think Connie Cluff or anyone else in that office will pull out a gun and shoot me if I do exactly what I was planning to do, and just walk in there to talk to them," Tom said.

"They've got to be all-in on the Hay Camp Mesa stuff, right? And Connie is probably as whacko as the other Cluffs."

"I'm sure she is."

"And you're still going in there?"

She sounded incredulous, Tom thought, not so much because she disagreed with his decision or was in awe of his fortitude, but at finding herself at the crux of so much danger unfolding in real time, and with no way out.

"Yep," Tom said. "If you don't hear from me in a couple of hours" — he glanced at his watch — "say noon, then sound the alarm."

"What does that even mean? Sound the alarm?"

"Start with Sheriff Owens," Tom said.

"How do we know he's not a neo-Nazi?"

"I don't think he's the type."

As they ended the call, Tom experienced an immediate loss of confidence. He thought he knew Owens pretty well. But he could easily be a member of the Aryan Patriots subreddit forum, even a proud property owner in Hay Camp Mesa Ranch, busy stocking his own secret arsenal.

If he was, Maria's warning would sufficiently explain it.

The bad guys look good because they're cons. And the good guys look bad because everyone's got something to hide.

Chapter 17

MUTUAL UNDERSTANDING

A few minutes before 10, a late model Chevy Tahoe pulled into the vacant parking space behind Cluff Properties. Connie Cluff got out of the vehicle unlocked the back door to the office and disappeared inside.

Tom recognized her from having seen her photo on the Cluff Properties website. He also knew from the Cortez newspaper story, which included a paragraph about the deceased's survivors, that Connie was the older of Jay Cluff's two children. Lionel Cluff was the youngest of five grandchildren, and the son of Cluff's son, Will Cluff, who owned a construction company. Connie was Lionel's aunt.

Tom also knew that Connie was likely a white supremacist, as fully involved with the Aryan Patriots as her father and nephew were. That might be to his advantage: that he knew more about her than she likely could guess, and he could either hint at what he knew or play dumb, depending on how the conversation played out. On the other hand, she might not give a damn who knew about her political beliefs and affiliations. As to his personal safety, Tom reminded himself that no matter how dangerous Connie Cluff might be, she was unlikely to pull out a gun and shoot him on the spot in her Main Street office. Any menace now would be the threat of future risk.

Tom gave it a few minutes, and then walked back to main street, finding the Cluff Properties' office now open for business and Connie settling in at her desk.

"Good morning," she said, rising to greet him. "How are you today?"

"I'm fine thank you," Tom said, handing her a business card. "I'm Tom Austin. I run a newspaper up in Telluride."

Connie's warmth instantly evaporated.

"I don't have one word to say to you," she said, as if Tom likely had a hand in her father's violent death.

"I'm very sorry about what happened to Mr. Cluff. We knew each other. He came to my office several times to explain his project in Telluride. I respected his strong commitment to his beliefs."

The hard lines in her face did not soften.

"My father was very passionate about his principles."

"He was. Are you sure I can't have just a moment of your time?"

She sighed and indicated a chair next to her desk.

"I'm Connie Cluff."

"I admired your father's fighting spirit," Tom said, as he sat down. "He struck me as a happy warrior."

"And what was your opinion of his proposal for Bear Creek?"

"I guess that depends on what he was trying to achieve. His objectives struck me as political as much as anything. He enjoyed being provocative."

"He did. But he also sought justice for the property owners."

"He made that clear. He said he valued my role in bringing his perspective to the public."

"It was his hobby, sticking it to the left, that's all. I told him he was wasting his time. But it shouldn't have cost him his life."

"Well, we don't know who shot him."

"I think we know. Maybe not the individual far-left radical who pulled the trigger. But we know the kind of person it was."

"You believe it was politically motivated, then?"

"What else?" She shrugged.

"I'm actually here because I'm concerned about a young reporter I sent down here the day before yesterday," Tom said. "I haven't been able to reach him since Tuesday afternoon."

Tom was studying Connie's face while he talked and thought he could see her wince very slightly.

"His name is Peter Barnard. Did he contact you?"

"He did," she said slowly, as if deciding whether to cop to it. "Tuesday around noon. He asked about Jay. I spoke to him very briefly, against my better judgment."

"Why against your better judgment?"

"Because I have nothing at all to gain by encouraging you or anyone else to put another damned thing about my father in a newspaper. He liked publicity. I don't."

"Understood. I'm not here to report on your father. We're off the record. I just want to find Peter."

"I can't help you with that. If he's missing and you're concerned about it, you should probably talk to the police."

"Do you think I might have reason for concern?"

"I can't say."

"Why is that?"

"Because you don't know and I don't know who shot my father. But I would think that whoever did it would not welcome a reporter's nosing around. Which your cub reporter was clearly doing. By harassing me, for example."

"Do you think Peter could have gotten crosswise with the kind of radical who would kill your father? Here in Cortez? I get the idea you think the killer would have been more of a left-wing radical of the sort you would expect to find in Telluride than a far-right radical you'd be likelier to find here."

"I wouldn't know. I've lived here my entire life and have never met a far-right radical. I don't even know what that is."

"Your father's ideas weren't exactly middle-of-the-road."

"They were around here. Ask anyone who knew him and they'll tell you he was an American patriot. I'm sure he considered you to be an extreme leftist."

"I'm sure he did. Do you think I had a hand in killing him?"

"Honestly, you don't strike me as the type," she said with a note of condescension, as if to suggest that Tom likely lacked the balls to carry out a good murder, even in self-defense or for the most righteous patriotic cause. "But when reporters from *Telluride* start asking *me* questions about my murdered father and *our* business, I just have to wonder if maybe you think *I* had a hand in it."

"That's not exactly how reporters think about it."

And then he understood that maybe that is precisely how reporters think about it, how he and Peter thought about it: that by asking questions they might shed light on the crime, and it might well have been a family member who killed Jay Cluff. And they might break the story.

She was studying his reaction.

"I guess we assume that someone with nothing to hide won't mind talking to us," Tom offered, thinking aloud. "And that someone who won't talk must have something to hide."

"Well, then," she said, her lips pursed. "Maybe we do understand each other. Seeing as how you set yourself up as investigator, prosecutor, judge, and jury."

"I'm sorry if Peter was too aggressive. Do you mind my asking what he asked you about?"

"The same questions he asked when he called a few days earlier. I told him I had no comment then, which he reported accurately in his story in your paper, keeping my name out of it, which I appreciate. I don't really know why he persisted, asking me who controls the partnership that owns my father's Telluride property. I told him, off the record, that it's in probate and probably will be for a while."

"I understood your father was the majority owner."

"He was the managing partner. There's a difference. With his death, there are lots of issues to resolve surrounding ownership interests and what happens to them now. But I really don't want to talk about those details, even off the record, because it's a private matter."

"Wouldn't it be public record?"

"Look it up then." She shrugged.

"Was that your father's office?" Tom asked, indicating a glassed-in cubicle near the rear of the storefront.

She looked back. "Yes, it was," she said. "I'm not quite ready to move in there yet."

"It looks very organized, as I would expect from what little I knew of your father. He seemed to have a very organized mind."

"I really don't see how that line of inquiry will help you find your missing reporter, Mr. Austin."

"You are right. I'm sorry. I understand that you don't have time for small talk.

"I'm sorry I couldn't be of more help," she said, standing to bring the interview to a close.

They'd reached a stalemate.

"Thank you for your time," Tom said as he also stood. "Again, I'm so sorry for your loss."

Chapter 18

THE DEVIL'S HIGHWAY

Tom placed a call to Samantha as he walked around the block to his car. She answered on the first ring.

"You're OK!"

"I told you she wouldn't shoot me in there." An ironic chuckle. "She'll find a better time and place for that."

"How can you joke about this?"

"Who's joking? But let's focus here. Peter met Connie Cluff on Thursday. She wouldn't say much. Just that they met. But that tells us a lot."

"Like what?"

"Why do you think she agreed to talk to me?"

"No idea."

"I thought it was fifty-fifty when I walked in that she'd kick me right out the door the second I identified myself. But she wanted to size me up. Which suggests that she's up to her eyeballs in it, whatever it is."

He was climbing behind the wheel of his car where he would be safely hidden, he hoped, by his tinted windshield.

"She's cold-blooded enough to be a suspect in her father's death.

She could have had a financial or personal motive to be rid of her old man, and might have killed him, or had him killed, confident that 'radical' environmentalists would be blamed for it. That's what she said. It was radicals, and that includes you and me, by the way, and Peter, because we live in Telluride and work at a newspaper."

"So, she suspects that we killed her father, and we suspect that she killed him?"

"Except that we know that we didn't do it."

Connie Cluff was exiting the real estate office from the same back door she had entered half an hour earlier.

"She's leaving. In a hurry. My meeting with her provoked something."

"Where are you right now?"

"In my car, watching her."

"Does she know?"

"She's looking around."

As Connie's gaze swept past him, he felt himself flinch.

"What are you going to do?"

"She just got in her car. I'm going to follow her."

"No, you're not!"

"I'll keep a safe distance behind."

"This is nuts!" Samantha said, raising her voice. "It's too dangerous. I'm going to call Sheriff Owens."

"Not yet."

"Why not?"

"Because there's nothing he can do to help. He's too far away and this isn't his county."

"He could call Sheriff Bruce and let him know that he knows you are down there, and that Peter is missing. That might put Bruce on notice not to do anything stupid."

"Bruce is fucking in on the conspiracy. Stay cool. Back me up here. I'm going to follow her from a safe distance."

"Where are you?"

"Heading out of Cortez, north toward Dove Creek."

"Fuck!"

Connie was traversing an intersection where the traffic light was already yellow, so Tom pressed the gas pedal to avoid being trapped behind the light when it turned red. His pulse quickened as the car sped up.

"Peter posed as a white supremacist who wanted to look at property," Samantha said. "His tour of Hay Camp Mesa Ranch would have made for great copy. He'd even have pictures for the big story he was planning to break, revealing that Cluff and the sheriff were in business together. Connie set up an appointment for Lionel to show it to him. But it was a trap, because she knew who he was."

"How do you know all that?"

"It just hit me. Like, 'duh,' of course. Isn't it something you would have done?"

"If I was going for the scoop," Tom said, feeling Samantha's insight in the pit of his stomach. "But then I'd think about how dangerous it was and … I guess I'd go ahead and do it anyway. Or at least I would have when I was younger and dumber."

Tom couldn't see it until Samantha said it because it was too painful. Peter had flat-out lied when Tom asked what leads he wanted to pursue in Cortez.

"They're not exactly leads. They're more like hunches. If I tell you, you'll shoot them down and then I'll have nothing."

But Peter had more. He probably knew about Jay Cluff's White Supremacist real estate development. What broke their relationship of trust? Was he competitive with Tom and trying to preserve the scoop for himself? Or just afraid that Tom wouldn't let him go if he knew what Peter was planning? Because it was too dangerous.

"Connie would recognize his voice if he said he was looking for property where a White Christian patriot could hide out," Tom objected. "They had recently talked on the phone."

"Just a few words," Samantha said. "And he could put on a great Southern drawl."

"Plus, she might have seen his picture on our website."

"So maybe he came right out and identified himself, admitted that he knew about Hay Creek Mesa Ranch, and asked for a tour of it. And she arranged for Lionel to take him there, and he walked right into the trap that way."

Tom could picture Peter doing just that, overconfident that they couldn't risk harming him. As if the power of the press bestowed upon reporters an invisible coat of armor.

"Maybe she's leading me to him."

It was a frail hope, tossed out as a sop to her and to steady himself, a way to stay the course, to keep following Connie Cluff because no alternative presented itself.

"I am begging you, right now, to stop and turn around," Samantha said. "Let's just take some time to think this through."

But Tom's mind was racing, and he barely heard her.

Peter walked into a trap, meeting with the treacherous Connie Cluff thinking he could outsmart her. But she saw through him, knew he presented a threat, and she and her nephew put an end to it, most likely by "disappearing" him, just as Maria had suggested they easily could have, because such things were routine in Montezuma County. Vultures and coyotes were likely already doing their part by dispatching Peter's corpse.

And Tom, now, was at extreme risk of meeting precisely the same fate. Because at the very least Connie had to be concerned that she could be implicated in Peter's disappearance, unless Peter turned up unharmed, which was highly unlikely at this point. If she was involved in whatever happened to Peter, then she might conclude she had no better alternative than to disappear Tom, too, as risky as it was. She couldn't know that there was a nosey motel desk clerk involved or that Tom was sharing everything with Samantha, either one of whom could connect the dots, which meant she wasn't constrained by that possibility. In any case, she enjoyed the protection of the sovereign Montezuma County Sheriff and his right-wing militia.

Discounting all this speculation, there was no doubt whatsoever that Connie was assessing the risk Tom presented to her with at least as much diligence as Tom was assessing the risk that she presented to him.

There was an important difference, though, which came courtesy of Maria's instruction into survival strategies in the rural West: Connie was likely armed.

"What the fuck am I doing?" Tom muttered.

"What the fuck *are* you doing?"

"Driving into a trap, according to you."

"Where are you now?"

"Highway 491. Five, maybe ten miles north of Cortez. Did you know it used to be named U.S. Highway 666? People called it the devil's highway. Which is why the number was changed."

"I don't get it."

"It's in the Bible or something. 666 is the number of the antichrist."

"I'm not superstitious."

"I might be. Still not sure. Maybe about to find out."

"Looks desolate, judging from the map."

"Wheat fields. Farmhouses. White supremacist compounds protected by concertina wire and guarded by German shepherds."

"What?!"

"Well. I assume they're out there somewhere. I mean, where the fuck is Hay Camp Mesa?"

"It's north and east of Cortez. You're heading north and west."

"That's reassuring, I guess."

"Could she be aware that you're following her?"

"I'm pretty far behind her."

He kept as far back as he could because she might assume he was on her tail, literally tailing her, and not just as an abstract threat. Or would she assume he lacked the fortitude? When your best hope is that your adversary thinks you're a pussy, you are in some seriously deep shit. On the other hand, she did read him as more than a pussy, or she wouldn't be on the move now.

"If I lose you, it's just because I'm driving out of cell range," Tom said, lying because he wanted to end the call and knew she'd argue. Samantha's presence on the line was becoming a distraction and she couldn't help him anyway.

"Turn around!" she shouted, and then Tom hung up on her just as Connie signaled an intention to turn off the highway.

Tom followed Connie's Tahoe into an aging subdivision of single-story tract homes and doublewides on large, weedy lots. She pulled up to one of the homes where Tom saw a familiar vehicle: Maria's battered Hyundai.

He was flooded with relief and terror at precisely the same instant. This might be Maria's home, and she and Connie Cluff could be working together against Tom. But this required more coincidence than even Tom's rampaging imagination allowed: that the motel clerk where Tom booked a reservation for Peter just happened to be in a conspiracy with Peter's killer, assuming Peter was dead, even before the killing was planned. Peter's disappearance was the circumstance that brought Tom and Maria into contact with each other in the first place.

The other possibility had to be correct. This was home of Lionel Cluff, and Maria was following up on her self-assigned task of trying to learn more from him. As he inched his car to a better position to remain out of Connie Cluff's line of sight, he saw another familiar vehicle: Lionel Cluff's black Tacoma, parked behind the home. The truck was buffed and belied the ramshackle condition of the house. Was it because its owner had recently come into some money? Or because he loved his vehicle far more than his home? Regardless, Maria had worked her way inside his house and was in a position to hear whatever was being said in a conversation between Connie and Lionel. But not for long. She was ejected just moments after Connie entered. Tom watched her get into her car and drive away. He started to follow her, and quickly called her cell number.

"I'm right behind you," Tom said.

"You followed Connie," she said. "She was way pissed at him. How did you fire her up like that?"

"I just asked about Peter."

"They killed him."

"Probably."

"I had to scram, fast. Before I could get anything out of him."

"How did you get in there in the first place?"

"He sells weed. My brother knows him. You owe me fifty bucks I had to spend on bud. I had to smoke a little. You know, to maintain my cover. So, I'm a little buzzed. But I'm not paranoid or nothing. This shit's real."

Chapter 19

SUPER UTE WOMAN

They parked both of their cars by a house that looked unoccupied, partly hidden by some scrub, but with a good angle from fifty yards away on Connie's Tahoe and Lionel's Tacoma. Tom joined Maria in her Hyundai.

"He still didn't remember me," she said. "Which just proves again that being invisible can come in handy."

"It's your superpower. Native female crimefighter can't be seen by bad guys."

"That makes you a bit player in my comic. You good with that?"

"Uh huh. I'm a Clark Kent, mild-mannered newspaperman, but one who doesn't turn into Superman. He's just tight with Super Ute Woman."

"Connie can't know that you saw Peter with Lionel Tuesday afternoon," he theorized. "She doesn't know you. Doesn't know you're working with me. So, for her to rush over here right after I asked her about Peter is pretty much a signed confession. She's in on it. Am I right?"

"Yep. She knows something happened to Peter and that Lionel did it. Except why was she ragging on him just now? What did he do wrong?"

"Maybe he wasn't supposed to hurt Peter," Tom suggested. "He was just supposed to threaten him, warn him off. So, it was news to her that he's missing."

"Got any evidence of that?"

"I think maybe I saw it. She might have flinched when I told her I was looking for Peter."

"I'll buy it. Gotta trust your instincts. Maybe Lionel took it a step too far. Showed initiative when he was supposed to follow orders. And because he disappeared Peter, now Connie's got you breathing down her neck. And she's pissed off about it."

"So, she's probably yelling at him right now, 'Where's that snot-nosed reporter? How come he's not back where he came from?'"

"I'm Lionel," Maria said. "And I go… 'I dunno.' Cause playing dumb comes real natural to Lionel."

"I'm Connie and I say: 'Don't lie to me. What happened?'"

"'Nothing happened, Aunt Connie!'" Maria said in her whiney Lionel voice. "'I did what you said. Told him he was in over his head. Should stop asking so many questions or he might get hurt.'"

"I'm Connie and I smack him."

"'I swear Aunt Connie.'"

"That's why she didn't just call him. She knew she'd have to work him over. That's why she jumped in her truck and drove over here." He reverted to his Connie voice: "'I know you have a hot temper, Lionel. Did that boy say something to piss you off?'"

"'He didn't take me serious. I had to rough him up, just a little.'"

"Look," Tom said. "Something's happening."

Connie had burst out of Lionel's house and was climbing into her car.

They slunk down in their seats to be out of sight when Connie drove past.

"Our theory is wrong," Tom said. "She just told Lionel to take care of me. Like he took care of Peter."

"You got a target on your back, for sure."

"Should we follow her?"

"I'm more interested in what Lionel does."

"You're right," Tom said. "Because … for every action there's an equal and opposite reaction. My meeting with Connie sent her out the door and now she's gonna send Lionel out the door. And he's gotta go out hunting for me. Because what else is there?"

"For sure."

Lionel walked out the door of the house, glanced around like a man with good reason to fear surveillance, and got into his truck. He pulled out and Maria followed him. At the highway, he turned south, back toward Cortez, and then turned east on a county road.

"He's not looking for you out here," Maria said. "It's something else. He's kicking up a lot of dust. Which means we can stay back and not lose him. Good thing you filled my tank."

"If he's not looking for me, it's got to be Peter."

"That'd be my guess."

Driving back past the desolate farmhouses and barns, Tom scanned the landscape looking for ….

"I forgot something," he blurted out. "What direction are we going?

"East."

"Toward Hay Camp Mesa?"

"Kinda. It's east, then north, I think."

"There's this subdivision," Tom started, and he told her about the hidden page on the Cluff Realty website.

When he finished, Maria turned to him, furious: "And you forgot to tell me this, until now, when we're headed right there?"

"I just found out about it this morning and there was a lot going on," he said, sounding like a schoolkid who forgot to do his homework because he was so caught up in Grand Theft Auto IV.

She shook her head at his incompetence.

"You're lucky you got me, is all I can say. But I'm not surprised. If the rednecks are gonna start shooting anywhere, why not here, where they run a whole Sheriff's department?"

"We're coming up on a highway," she said, tapping the brake.

Sure enough, the county road ended at the state highway that ran north to Telluride and south to Cortez.

Lionel turned north.

"So that's where he's headed," Tom said.

"If he takes the next right."

Ahead, Lionel's right turn signal blinked.

Maria stepped on the gas, signaling to Tom that the late intelligence he had provided would not change their plans, but only made their mission all the more urgent.

"Hope nobody's home," Tom muttered.

Ahead, Lionel was signaling a left turn.

As Maria slowed the car to stay back, they passed a brown Forest Service sign indicating that the turn ahead provided public access to Hay Camp Mesa.

Lionel turned and Maria continued straight ahead, pulling off on the right hand shoulder. She looked back to her left and Tom looked the same way to see that Lionel's tires were kicking up more dust.

Maria wheeled the car around to follow Lionel up the Forest Service access road. The dust hanging in the air just above the gravel road surface provided excellent directions, leading them to a gated side road marked by a NO TRESPASSING sign. A second sign read: "WARNING! We Shoot First. Ask Questions Later."

Dust in the air on the other side of the gate indicated that Lionel had passed through the gate, which was now closed to them. Maria displayed no hesitancy, but accelerated into the gate, knocking it open.

The road climbed up a couple of miles into woods. Around a curve, they saw Peter's Wrangler parked by the side of the road, Lionel's Tacoma pulled up behind it. Maria put the car into reverse and backed down to where she could park out of Lionel's line of sight.

"We've got to move fast," Maria said. "In case Peter is still alive." Tom was happy to see she was clenching her gun in her right hand.

They climbed out of the car and made their way quickly, keeping off the road and under the protection of the sheltering aspen, toward the two vehicles.

As they drew close, they could see that Lionel was struggling to move Peter's inert body from behind the wheel of his car.

"Maybe he's just tied up," Tom whispered to Maria.

They crept closer, to within thirty or forty feet of Lionel, whereupon Maria nodded, indicating she was ready to make a move.

"Stay behind me so all he sees is the gun," she whispered.

She stepped forward, coming within twenty feet of Lionel before she said: "What up, Lionel?"

Lionel jumped, and spun around shouting, "What the fuck?"

"I sure hope that boy is alive and you're just trying to help him," Maria said.

Lionel's lip curled and then he abruptly lurched toward his own truck, presumably where he had a weapon stashed, so Maria fired a shot at Lionel's feet, stopping him in his tracks.

Her gun was aimed right at him.

"I know you," Lionel sneered. "You just bought weed from me. What the fuck are you doing here?"

"Your racist eyes can't even see me, can they?" she said. "Didn't recognize me."

"Huh?"

"From the Law Enforcement Academy."

"Oh, yeah," he said dimly, as if he was finally able to place a face that had looked vaguely familiar. "Are you a cop now?"

"Did you kill that boy?" Maria asked. "Maybe you're having second thoughts about leaving him here? Now you want to give him a proper burial? Or just hide him real good? Cause your aunt found out what you did?"

"What's it to you, bitch?"

"Besides the fact that I don't like murderers?" She nodded toward Tom: "Check his truck for a weapon."

"You're not cops," Lionel said, squinting at Tom. "He ain't even armed."

Lionel's calculation—that he could easily take this pair of posers—was conveyed by a smirk. He darted his eyes and bolted for the truck.

But he had miscalculated.

Maria fired and Lionel fell to the ground, twitched, and was dead.

"Holy shit!"

"He finally remembered me, but he forgot that I was the best shot in the class."

"It happened so fast."

"It's what they teach. You'll be dead before you can think twice, so you have to react instinctively."

"He's dead," Tom said, referring not to Lionel but to Peter, the awful truth washing over him in a wave of nausea. "He must have been surprised by how quick it was."

"He probably didn't feel nothing."

Was she thinking of Peter or Lionel?

Tom heard a sound and realized it was coming from him, and he was keening, an involuntary reaction. Maria put a hand on his shoulder, and he glanced up to see that tears glistened in her eyes. Maria was not grieving for Peter, whom she hadn't known, but from the sheer release of emotion, from having killed a man, and from fulfilling her life's ambition of solving a crime in the worst possible way.

The two of them stood there paralyzed by emotion because the violence was no longer an abstraction; they were awash in it, the rank smell of Peter's decaying corpse, a faint gurgling as blood pulsed from Lionel's body into the dirt.

Now time slowed as Tom's understanding of what had happened came into focus.

Peter had died as collateral damage in a twisted family drama, the Cluff family drama, and its toxic business of politicized real estate ventures, which is to say, he died for no reason at all. Jay Cluff had likely died of the same cause, but while Cluff had died of a pathology of his own making, Peter had lived his short, sweet life utterly without guile.

Chapter 20

QUAKIES

It seemed to Tom that he and Maria would never be able to make a move. That they would be frozen in this moment of horror forever. But it was only a few minutes before Tom thought to check his phone to see if he was within range of a cell tower. He saw that there were missed calls from Samantha and Sarah.

"We have to call 911 or we'll incriminate ourselves," he said.

"Wait," Maria said, her law enforcement training once again brought to bear. "When you tell them you're at a crime scene the 911 dispatcher won't let you hang up. They'll ask a lot of questions, and it will all be on tape."

"Right."

"Are you ready for that?"

"I don't know."

"You can't lie. Not when you're talking to 911 and not later when they take us in for questioning. Not even a small lie. After they get here, they'll separate us so that we can't hear what the other one is saying or see how the other one is acting. So, we both have to say only the truth. Because we have nothing to hide. We didn't do nothing wrong."

Tom nodded.

"I shot Lionel in self-defense." Maria said. "He was lunging for a gun, right there in the truck."

"Is there a gun?"

They looked to confirm that there was one, a menacing looking Glock, right on the passenger seat.

"Even if there wasn't a gun, I would have been justified," Maria said.

"Yes, but it would have been harder to prove," Tom said. "I'll grab a picture of it."

Luckily, Peter and Samantha had urged him to spring for the upgraded iPhone 6 with it's novel camera feature to help him "go digital."

He moved closer to Peter's car, and was sickened again by the sight and smell of Peter's bloating corpse. Burying his nose in the crook of his elbow, he forced himself to snap the photo.

"Peter's knapsack's in there," he said, backing away. "His computer's there. If they take it, I might not get it back."

Maria reached through the door Lionel had left open, snatching the knapsack and handing it to him.

"Where are you going to put it?" she asked. "If you try to hide it in the woods, they'll find it. You wouldn't be able to come back and get it. Crime scene. And even though they're not supposed to, they'll search my car, so if we leave it there, they'll get it."

"I'll carry it like it's mine," Tom said. He had left his own knapsack in his car, back at Lionel's trailer.

"I don't like it, but I can't think of a better idea."

Tom slung the knapsack over one shoulder, as if to get comfortable with it.

"They'll ask why we were following Lionel."

"We were looking for my missing reporter."

"They'll ask why we looked ourselves and didn't call them."

"Because he wasn't missing that long."

"I was helping you because you hired me," Maria said. "I didn't even know Peter."

"That's right. I met you at the motel, we got to talking, you lost your job because of me, we had dinner, and I learned you have a private investigator's license. I thought you could help me find Peter."

"All true. They know me, and they know I'm nosey. I'm trouble. We've got nothing to hide, except that we took the damn knapsack."

"Here's something I picked up from watching *Law and Order*," Tom said. "Don't volunteer anything. Just answer the questions they ask as simply as possible."

"You watch *Law and Order*, too?"

"Who doesn't?"

"I guess we're good with calling them. It wouldn't be good to wait too long."

Tom started to dial, but Maria stopped him: "Wait!"

"What?"

"I'm thinking we might feel a lot safer if somebody else knew what was happening to us right now."

"You're right," Tom said, as he dialed Sarah. "Maybe there's somebody you can call," he added while the phone rang and before Sarah answered.

But Maria shook her head.

"Hi," Sarah said, glad to hear from him.

"There's something awful. Peter is dead. He was shot …"

Sarah gasped.

"I just called so you know where I am. In case."

"In case what? Are you in danger?"

"I don't think so. Not right now. But they'll question me, and I might not be free to call you right away, and …." The magnitude of the potential risk became manifest as he completed the sentence: "… the Montezuma County Sheriff could be involved in the killing."

"How involved?"

"Way involved."

"Should I come down? Or call someone?"

"Call Rod Irons. It would be foolish to go in for questioning with a corrupt sheriff in a murder case without a lawyer at least knowing where I am. Tell him to call the sheriff to let him know I've got legal representation. I don't want it to seem like I need a lawyer because I'm guilty of something. But there's another man dead, too."

"Who?"

"Jay Cluff's grandson. There isn't time to explain it all now. I'll tell you later. But you've got to call Rod, now."

"OK."

"Tell him that Peter came down on Thursday to poke around the Cluff story and must have gotten into some kind of trouble. I couldn't reach him. Which is why I came looking for him. I didn't say anything to you because I didn't want you to worry. And now I found him, dead. And call Samantha and tell her. She's been working with me, and she'll be worried when she can't reach me. I left her hanging."

"OK."

"Gotta go. Make the calls fast."

"OK."

He hung up.

"I read that dope phone can text a photo," Maria said.

"Good idea," Tom nodded, tapping his phone. "Done."

"Now call 911. Put it on speaker. Remember, only the truth."

* * *

"911. What's your emergency?"

"I'm calling to report a murder. I'm at the scene."

"Where are you sir?"

"I'm at Hay Camp Mesa Ranch, north off of Hwy. 184."

"Yes sir. I'm sending officers. And I need you to stay on the line until they arrive."

"O.K."

Tom felt sick again, and sank to his haunches, crouched over Peter's knapsack. Gazing at it, he saw that there was some blood splattered on it. He looked up at Maria, caught her eye, and pointed it out to her.

Several minutes ticked by.

"Are you still with me, sir?"

"Yes, ma'am. I'm just getting a drink of water."

He unzipped Peter's knapsack, knowing there was likely a water bottle inside.

Finding it, Tom handed the water bottle to Maria, who took the knapsack a few steps away off the side of the road to rinse it clean.

"Are you in any danger right now, sir?"

"No."

"Are you alone?"

"I'm with a private investigator I hired to help me find Peter."

"Is that the name of the deceased?"

"Yes. He was my employee, my friend. Peter Barnard. He was missing and I went looking for him and found his body in his car."

"What is your name?"

"Tom Austin."

In the distance, he could hear a siren.

"I want to hang up now."

"Hang on with me for a moment longer, sir. Help is almost there."

"I hear them."

He listened to the siren draw closer.

Maria handed Tom the knapsack. Then the first sheriff's car careened to a halt nearby and the 911 operator said, "You can hang up now."

Tom found himself retching as a deputy emerged cautiously from his car, gun drawn.

"You're OK," Maria shouted, as the deputy approached Lionel's corpse, where it lay on the road. "It's Lionel Cluff. He's dead."

"Is that Maria?" the deputy said. "Maria Sanchez?"

"Yeah, Dale, it's me."

Tom was still on the ground when a second sheriff's car arrived, followed by an ambulance. A deputy stood over him, and was asking, "Are you injured?"

"No," Tom said, rising to his feet. "Just in shock, I think."

"Are you armed?"

"No."

"Can I pat you down?"

"Sure."

He looked over to see that Maria was explaining something to the first deputy, Dale, who was peering into Peter's car.

"Can I look in your knapsack?" the deputy who had finished patting him down asked.

"Sure."

Tom was confident Peter didn't pack a weapon. He hadn't seen one when he had opened the pack to look for the water bottle. But he held his breath anyway as the deputy unzipped Peter's knapsack and rummaged inside. Nothing. The deputy zipped the knapsack closed and handed it back to him.

Then he was sitting in the back seat of a sheriff's car by himself, having been separated from Maria, just as she predicted. He watched as Maria was escorted to another sheriff's vehicle, which had just arrived.

He opened Peter's pack to make sure it wouldn't contain any surprises if it was searched again, more carefully. There was the laptop, charger, headphones, pens, notebooks, the water bottle, a packet of tissue, wet wipes, a small toiletries kit, a clean pair of socks and underwear, a couple of protein bars, a pocketknife, a book. It was everything a young reporter might need if he found himself stranded for a couple of hours in an airport, or on assignment in a war zone: a survival kit.

Tom opened the book Peter was reading, *In Defense of Food*, and read the first line. "Eat food. Not too much. Mostly plants."

Great lede, he thought.

"Keep it simple" was Tom's standard advice to young reporters struggling with a story. "Get to the nugget of the story and spit it out. That's your lede. The rest will flow from there."

He put the book back and examined the outside of the pack to see that Maria had gotten it clean. There was a spot that might be a speck of Peter's remnant blood, so he used one of Peter's wipes to rub at it — and the surrounding area, for good measure — then shoved the used wipe deep into his pant pocket.

I just wiped Peter's blood off Peter's pack with Peter's wipe, Tom thought. But this was both less and more than a tongue twister.

Tom studied a deputy who was standing a short distance away. He was out of central casting: skinhead, too-tight shirt on a sculpted torso, dark sunglasses, military bearing, holding an AK-47. He was standing at a vantage point where he could survey the entire crime scene. He was possibly a lookout. There might be danger lurking in the woods. It seemed like a reasonable precaution.

Tom craned his neck to see what the lookout was studying, but from his low position on the wrong side of the car he could see only the tops of tall aspens, swaying in the breeze as if they were the Earth's lungs, peacefully breathing, exhale, inhale, exhale, life ongoing, even after a person or two have died.

Quakies, Tom thought. What old-timers called aspen.

"I'm going to take you to the sheriff's office for questioning," a deputy said after opening the driver's door and climbing behind the wheel.

Chapter 21

THE CONSTITUTIONAL SHERIFF

Less than an hour later, Tom was in a barren interrogation room, recounting everything he did the few days leading up the gruesome discovery of Peter's body.

"Did you learn what Peter meant when he said he was onto something big?" the investigating officer, whose name was Ross Weston, asked.

"Just the obvious theory that he was getting close to Jay Cluff's killer," he said, wondering if Weston already knew that it was his boss's participation with Cluff in marketing Hay Camp Mesa Ranch. Weston could be a property owner there himself. If so, the question had a double edge.

"What about Peter's family?" Tom asked. "I need to tell them what happened."

"We're on it. A police officer near their home could already be on his way to their house. Probably with a social worker. That's protocol with a homicide."

Of course, Tom was reminded. That's how people learn that the worst has happened, that time has stopped, that nothing will ever be the same: the cop at the door, hat in hand, who says, "I am here to inform you that your son has been murdered."

"Are we finished?" Tom asked, feeling suddenly exhausted. "Can I go?"

Weston leaned back in his chair and frowned. He was a good-looking young man, about thirty, sandy hair, blue eyes—very *Aryan*, Tom thought—but with an open expression.

"I feel like maybe you haven't fully grasped the full nature of your situation," Weston said.

"How's that?"

"You may not realize how things are in this county. How things work. You're not from here. You're from Telluride."

"Not originally. I'm from Boston."

Weston nodded, as if Tom had just confirmed that he was out of his depth.

"People in the rural West don't exactly appreciate having a stranger poking into their affairs. It's what draws them here in the first place. They want to be left alone."

"I lived in Naturita for four years. I didn't come down here to cause any trouble. I just came to find my missing reporter."

"You sent him here to begin with."

"A tragic, unforgiveable mistake," Tom said, choking up.

"Don't make it worse. It's dangerous to poke a stick at a coiled rattler. That snake can strike faster than you can react."

"Who's the snake?"

"Well, now, that's just the problem. There's one hiding under almost every rock."

"Huh," Tom said, as if he'd just been apprised of a curious fact of life on the range, akin to, "We eat deep-fried bull testicles and call them Rocky Mountain Oysters."

"What am I supposed to do with that bit of wisdom?" he asked.

"I didn't mean to insult you. Just be careful, that's all. I don't believe you are engaged in illegal activity or have bad intentions."

Weston might be sincere but was more likely playing the good cop, working to gain Tom's confidence and elicit more information from him on the reasonable assumption that Tom hadn't told him everything. His attempt to offer friendly advice sounded disingenuous. There was no reason to think he wasn't also a rattler, poised to strike.

"I appreciate your concern. Am I free to go?"

"Sheriff would like a word with you first. With you and the other party involved in this incident."

"Can I make a quick call first? My wife will be worried."

"Sure. I'll leave you alone."

As Weston opened the door to leave, Tom glimpsed the impassive deputy who'd been on lookout duty at the crime scene, standing in the corridor.

Tom's phone displayed a half dozen unanswered calls and voice messages from Sarah.

A series of text messages from Samantha were a terse chronicle of rising panic as she couldn't reach him — "please call me," "I'm getting worried," What should I do?" "I'm going to give it half an hour and then I'm calling Sheriff Owens," — culminating with, "Sarah called," texted at 2:21 p.m.

Sarah answered on the first ring.

"Thank God," she said.

"I'm OK."

"I can take Angie's car if I need to come down."

"It's not necessary. I'll be leaving soon and will drive right home."

"Are you sure?"

"I'm sure."

"The sheriff told Rod he wasn't holding you. That they were just taking your statement."

"Yeah, that's right. That's almost finished. I've just got a short break, so I wanted you to know I'm fine. And Samantha…."

"She's right here with me."

"That's good."

"I'll put you on speaker."

Sarah knew everything that Samantha knew, and Tom could cut to the chase.

"Maria and I followed Lionel Cluff to Hay Camp Mesa Ranch and interrupted him as he was trying to dispose of Peter's body. We were hoping Peter was alive, but he wasn't. Lionel lunged for a gun and Maria shot and killed him."

Telegraphed, it was not a complicated story.

* * *

A few minutes later, Weston was back.

"We're going next door," he said, and led Tom past the impassive lookout, who had not budged, to a slightly larger room where Maria was sitting at a table. The plainclothes woman detective who apparently had interviewed her was standing in a corner.

"Hey," Maria said with a slight nod, in a tone meant to convey some degree of solidarity, perhaps.

Weston indicated that Tom should take a seat and stepped into another corner of the room.

The Montezuma County Sheriff walked in, followed by the lookout, who closed the door behind them and then stood with his back to it.

"I'm Sheriff Dan Bruce," he drawled.

Bruce was short, with slicked back gray hair that didn't cover a bald spot and a generous paunch. He eyed them with a look of curiosity, as if they were unfamiliar specimens.

"Y'all have had quite a day, haven't you?" he said.

"I'm in a state of shock," Tom said.

Bruce turned to Maria.

"I'm fine," she said, meeting the sheriff's gaze.

"We don't have a lot of homicides in our county," Bruce said. "You know that I'm a fairly new sheriff, and this … I should say *these* … are my first two violent deaths. So, me and my deputies are having quite a day as well.

"Is there anything a-tall you want to add to what you've already told us?

Tom shook his head.

"Deputy Weston was very thorough," he said.

"My investigator was too," Maria said, nodding toward the woman whose nametag read "Yost."

"From what I know now, I don't see a high likelihood that you will be charged," Bruce said. "It appears that you, *Señorita* Sanchez, shot Lionel Cluff in self-defense. And it happens that I believe in a person's God-given right to self-defense. It is fortunate that you were armed and able to defend yourself and Mr. Austin, or the two of you surely would have been shot dead. It seems clear that you interrupted a killer while he was in the process of disposing of a body."

"The question is why," Tom said. "Why did Lionel Cluff kill Peter?"

"With both of them deceased, we may never know," Bruce said. "It could have been something between them. Like a drug deal gone bad. Mr. Cluff had a record of arrests related to illegal drugs."

"But Peter wasn't here to do a drug deal. Peter was here to do a story about the murder of Lionel Cluff's grandfather."

"We all know about this *alibi*," Bruce said. "I've talked to Sheriff Owens up in San Miguel about these connections and we discussed your involvement in all of this, too. I told Sheriff Owens that I would advise you in the strongest possible way to leave the investigation from this point forward to law enforcement. We've got good investigators here in Montezuma County and they've got 'em up in San Miguel, too, and we'll all be working together on this, what with these related homicides in our two counties, a San Miguel resident killed here, and a Montezuma resident killed there. If you think of anything you forgot to tell us, or if you learn anything new, don't do nothing stupid. Just call us.

"As for you, *Señorita* Sanchez," Bruce continued. "You were fired from your position in this office for cause. As a result, you are no longer in law enforcement. And although I admire your courage in defending yourself and Mr. Austin out there on the mesa this afternoon, I do not want to see you interfere with law enforcement again. Or there will be consequences."

He paused.

"You are free to go," he said, and then seemed to think better of it. But this was pure theater.

"Oh, there is *one* more thing before I let *you* go, Mr. Austin," Bruce said. "I heard from a Mr. Rod Irons, who asked after you. Can you tell me why you felt you might need a law-yer to represent you in this matter?"

Tom might have answered, "Because you have secretive political and business ties to the Cluff family, including an interest in Hay Camp Mesa Ranch, where my reporter was killed, so you could be complicit in Peter's murder. And besides that, you're a white supremacist."

But he didn't say any of that, as it could clearly land him in jail or worse.

Instead, he returned the sheriff's unblinking, hard gaze and said, "My wife was understandably shocked when I called to tell her I'd found Peter's body and was being brought in for questioning. Her first instinct was to call our lawyer. I suppose Rod called you just to check in on me."

"I do understand that influential people have their law-yers," Sheriff Bruce replied. "Sheriff Owens tells me you are a person of some influence up in San Miguel. I'm sure you won't make the mistake of assuming you have the same degree of influence *here*, in *my* county."

Another pause, and Sheriff Bruce turned to the door.

"Now, you all drive home safely," he said.

The lookout opened the door and followed Bruce out, but then planted himself in the corridor across from the open door.

The four people left in the room, Tom, Maria, Weston, and Yost, exchanged glances, affirming they had all witnessed the same performance: the "constitutional sheriff" relishing the exercise of his absolute authority.

The sheriff had delivered a warning and Tom and Maria were free to go, but not without edging past the intimidating lookout, who did not budge when Tom said, "excuse me."

The two interrogators escorted them out of the building into the late afternoon light, where both of their cars were waiting in the parking lot—Tom's having been retrieved from Lionel's neighborhood by sheriff's deputies, not as a courtesy but as a way for them to corroborate the story he and Maria told them about how they had arrived at the crime scene on Hay Camp Mesa: that they had, indeed, followed Lionel there.

"What's with that guy in the corridor?" Tom asked Weston.

"Duke?" Weston asked. "He's the undersheriff, just doing his job."

Right, Tom thought. Intimidating witnesses.

Then Tom and Maria stood alone in the parking lot.

"Good thing you had that lawyer call," she said.

"No shit."

"What do we do now?"

She couldn't have meant it as an existential question, but that's how it sounded to Tom.

"I guess we go home," Tom said, opening the door to his car.

Tom had Sarah. He didn't know Maria well enough to know who, if anyone, she had to go home to. He watched her walk to her car. She looked deflated, or probably she was just wrung out. He certainly was.

"Stay in touch," he shouted.

She looked back at him, and nodded unconvincingly.

He watched her climb behind the wheel of her car and drive away. Would they see each other again? Maybe, he thought. Probably.

When Tom instinctively tossed the knapsack that he was carrying—Peter's knapsack—into the back seat of his car, he couldn't help but notice that it landed on top of another, similar knapsack. He winced, as if he was about to be struck. It was his knapsack, containing his computer, his water bottle, and his fresh socks and underwear.

But Tom had not been busted.

Apparently, none of the deputies had observed that there was a knapsack in the back of Tom's car and another one slung on his shoulder. No deputy had asked him why he was in possession of two knapsacks, two laptops, two water bottles, and two changes of underwear.

Sometimes, Tom thought as he pulled out of the parking lot, breathing easier, you get away with one.

But this was a brief reprieve fueled by adrenalin. Tom did not yet know the depths of his devastation because he had not yet had begun to grapple with the harsh fact that he bore some responsibility for Peter's death.

Chapter 22

THE LATEST BUG GOING AROUND

S orrows drift down like snow, forming layers. Winds reshape it into drifts. The layers of snow pile up and sometimes coalesce into an avalanche. People shovel and plow the snow, and pack it down with their boots and tires until it turns to ice. Sadness becomes the default emotion from which all other feelings devolve.

Tom might indulge indignation at the injustice of the universe and fury that Peter's promise was snuffed out. But there was something far worse than that, something bottled up: inexpressible guilt. He had failed to protect Peter, had allowed Peter to mislead him about why he wanted to "poke around" in Cortez, had allowed his relationship with Peter to go astray right when it was most important for it to be functional. He had failed as a mentor, as an employer, as an editor. It was hard to see how he would carry on.

Tom limped back the 70 miles to Telluride and embraced Sarah, sobbing an apology for having misled her about the purpose of his trip to Cortez. He met with Sheriff Owens, who questioned him closely and gave back not a sliver of information about the status of the investigations into the murders of Jay Cluff and Peter. Giving as good as he got, Tom said nothing to Owens about Sheriff Bruce's involvement with the Cluff family in Hay Camp Mesa Ranch.

He spent a painful hour with Hailey, expressing his deep remorse for failing to protect her partner, her lover, hearing back that Peter credited him with providing the opportunity for Peter to discover his life's purpose. Peter told her what he told Tom, that he was onto "something big," but without telling her what it was.

"He was just so excited, and that was enough for me," she said.

She revealed that she and Peter knew that investigating the Cluff murder in Cortez could be dangerous, and had discussed it, but looking back, she realized now, that they understood it only as an abstraction to be discounted.

"We were naive," she allowed.

"We all are, sometimes," he replied.

He had a similar hour-long phone conversation with Peter's parents, finding this second exchange of his apology to Peter's loved ones in exchange for forgiveness as gut wrenching as the first.

He also gave Samantha Peter's laptop, hoping she might know the password or be able to hack into it.

Then, he somehow cobbled together The Examiner's coverage of Peter's murder without revealing everything he knew or suspected, coaching Samantha to coach a young reporter through conducting interviews to produce a draft that Tom could not resist editing—which he never should have done, being so deeply and personally implicated in the story.

Having dispensed with obligations, Tom somehow managed to feel even worse. In the few days remaining before the funeral, he went through the motions of sleeping—uneasily—eating, brushing his teeth, getting dressed for the day, he accepted condolences; there were long periods of stillness; and he sank into ineffable grief that was congealing into something like cynicism, a loss of all faith — in himself, humanity, individual agency, journalism, or justice.

What was this unnamable, inexpressible exhaustion that felt far beyond any conceivable reversal?

Peter's memorial service was in Town Park just six days after his body was found. His mother Sheila, a psychiatrist, and his father, Phillip, an English professor, described Peter as an inquisitive child, whose innate curiosity found a perfect outlet in journalism. Friends recalled that Peter was often awkward; and he was funny, sometimes unintentionally. In Peter, these were attractive foibles. He liked to cook and host intimate dinner parties. He had become passionate about skate skiing. He and Hailey were on the Nordic trails at Lizard Head all winter long. In the summer, they went on day-long hikes high in the upper basins around Telluride. Hailey recalled how he was fascinated by the ghost remnants from the mining era: foundations of structures long since rotted away, steel cable that once hoisted ore buckets left to rust on the ground beneath where the buckets once hung. She revealed that she and Peter were planning to get married but hadn't told anyone because they were in no rush. They were young and thought there would be time.

Tom was called upon to deliver a eulogy.

"Peter Barnard had all the qualities of a great reporter," he said. "He would grab on to a thread and follow it wherever it led. When it went nowhere, he wasn't discouraged. He just started over. He was likable, so people told him things when he interviewed them that they hadn't planned to divulge. He had the patience to sift through details and sit through endless government meetings without losing his focus on why he was there. My job as a publisher and editor of a small-town paper became more interesting when Peter joined our staff as a reporter, because he always asked another good question, always had another idea for a good story, always delivered. I won't talk much about our personal relationship because mostly we were editor and reporter…."

And he started to break up.

"…. but he was a great kid. A great kid. He will be missed. His loss is inexplicable and unbearable. I am so sorry, Peter."

Peter was buried at Lone Tree Cemetery, in a smaller, silent ceremony right after the service, because, his parents said, Telluride was where he had begun to thrive, to find his passions, a good job with a good boss, a loving partner. They were Buddhists for whom meditation, counting breaths, served as their final eulogy.

Tom stood back from the grave, holding Sarah's hand, watching. It was a warm early autumn afternoon. The aspen on the southern hillside would soon blaze yellow with bright red highlights, a shot of glory before winter, oblivious to human lives, deaths or business cycles. But even the aspen was suffering, Tom knew, because The Examiner had published a story about Sudden Aspen Decline—the acronym, aptly, was SAD—a newly identified syndrome killing aspen groves at large scale due to abnormally hot and dry conditions in recent decades. The visible sign of climate change was yet another harbinger of doom that was deeply disturbing if you stopped to think about it. Instinctively, people chose instead to enjoy the fall color while it lasted, carrying on with daily routines for as long as they possibly could.

The mourners slowly started to peel away and leave. Tyler was struggling to get out of his stroller, so Tom leaned over to Sarah and whispered: "You go ahead and take him home. I'd like to stay here and think a while longer. Then I have to go back to work."

They left and Tom sat on a nearby bench. He was alone with his thoughts no longer than five minutes when someone sat beside him: the inevitable Chuck Small.

After a few moments, he spoke.

"For most of the folks buried here, dying young of a gunshot wound, or in a mining accident or snowslide; or from an infected wound; or during an epidemic of cholera, scarlet fever, or diphtheria, or from tuberculosis or especially pneumonia—none of it was unusual. The air was full of coal and wood smoke that contributed to lung diseases, mules and horses crapped all over the streets and the San Miguel River was an open sewer. It wasn't easy to find clean water. People used to assume that the odds were pretty good they would die before they were thirty or forty, and certainly people they loved would die young. They'd have children and a lot of them would die before they were five, so, shee-it, they'd just have another and hope for better luck. A long life was uncommon. Not like it is now. Now it's the other way. People assume they won't be shot and if they get sick, they're pretty sure they'll be cured. They expect their three score and ten, at least."

Tom didn't respond, so Chuck asked, "Am I bothering you?"

"No, you are pretty much on my wavelength right now."

"You ever walk around this cemetery? Notice how young people were when they died."

"Is that supposed to make me feel better about Peter?"

"Not better. But a different perspective on it, maybe. Back in the mining era, which was not that long ago, my grandparents' generation, they grieved as deeply as we do today. But they had to go through it a helluva lot more often throughout the course of their lives."

"I read that Arthur L. Collins was not buried here."

"Collins was too fancy for Lone Tree, had to be buried in Denver, but a lot of other interesting characters are moldering into the earth here. Mortal enemies in life, lying side-by-side for eternity."

"I'd like to see that."

"Let's go."

They walked a short distance.

"Look here," Chuck said. "One of many mass graves for avalanche victims. This one is marked."

The etching in the concrete marker read, "All Killed by Snowslide, Jan. 26, 1886," and there were four names: Joseph Preest, D. Overstreet, M.J. Mitchell, and Wm. Harford.

"We believe there are many other mass graves of avalanche victims that are not marked at all. The best ore was mined at the highest elevations, where the avalanche danger was greatest. In February 1902, 19 men died in a series of three slides near the Liberty Bell Mine, some of them while they were trying to rescue men buried in the first slide and others trying to rescue the rescuers who were buried in the second slide. All over the cemetery you'll see epitaphs noting that the person buried there died in a slide.

"Then there was the great Bullion Tunnel fire of November 1901 that killed 24 miners," Small continued, pointing to a gravestone set into the ground. The epitaph for Thorvald Torkelson, 33 years old, read: "Here rests the body of a dear husband who lost his life in the Smuggler Union Mine Nov. 20, 1901 in trying to save the lives of others. Missed by a loving wife."

Nearby were the graves of two brothers named Zadra, Francesco, who died at the age of 22 and Marco, who died at 33, both in the same fire, their epitaphs in Italian: "Rimasti soffacati nela Smuggler mine, Nov. 20, 1901."

"Vincent St. John cemented his renown as a union organizer by working 48 hours straight rescuing trapped minders in that incident," Small said. "It earned him the enduring love and respect of the miners, but it also damaged his lungs, which probably contributed to his death when he was just in his early sixties. Died in a boarding house in Oakland in 1929. By then he was alone, broke, and forgotten."

They stopped in front of the most prominent monument in the cemetery.

Tom read words etched on the monument out loud: "Erected by 13 to 1 Miners' Union in memory of John Barthell, died at Smuggler, Colorado, July 3, 1901," followed by a Longfellow inscription: *"In the world's broad field of battle, In the bivouac of life, Be not the dumb driven cattle, Be a hero in the strife."*

"Barthell was a Finnish immigrant," Small said. "He was with a group of strikers who approached scabs completing the night shift at the Sheridan dump, urging them to walk off the job and join the union. Company guards stepped between the strikers and the scabs and ordered the strikers to leave company property. Barthell shouted at the guards, 'You are under arrest,' probably because he'd heard it more than a few times and it was one of the few English phrases he knew, even if he didn't know exactly what it meant. They fired, killing him instantly.

"St. John had the vision to turn Barthell into a martyr, spending union dues to build him this monument, which was intended to rival anything that even the richest local banker's family might be able to afford. It symbolizes the union credo, that strength in numbers is grander than private wealth."

"Why did they call themselves the 13 to 1 Miners Union?"

"Thirteen major mines in the district versus one union. Of course, the mining companies didn't see it quite that way. They saw themselves as independent companies under attack by a global conspiracy.

Socialism. Anarchists. Taking orders from abroad. The union believed in strength in numbers to combat the wealth and power of the mine owners. The companies believed in individual enterprise and the creation of wealth as the bulwark for freedom and prosperity and thought they were defending themselves against an alien philosophy."

"The monument does what St. John and the union intended," Tom said. "Here we are a hundred years later, talking about them and what they endured.

"Gives you an appreciation of gravestones and monuments, doesn't it? The stones symbolize eternity, even though we can see all around us that they do decay, especially the concrete markers. The inscriptions erode and become difficult to read and the lives they memorialize become impossible to imagine. We don't know if there was anyone, besides his union brothers, to mourn Barthell. We can't know how many people were buried here with no marker, or with a wooden marker that has decayed away. There are certainly a lot more of them in this cemetery than there are people with stone or concrete monuments."

They strolled past more stones, infants dead at the age of three or ten days, memorialized by images of lambs or angels, a staggering number of people born in the late nineteenth or early twentieth century and dead by their teenage years, or in their twenties or thirties, cause of death often not noted. Many stones bore a symbol denoting the deceased's affiliation with a fraternal society: the Benevolent and Protective Order of Elks, the Independent Order of Odd Fellows, the Knights of Pythias, or the Freemasons.

"People's lives revolved around fraternal societies," Chuck said. "If you think about it, you can imagine why that was. There was no TV, no radio, only a handful of the first movies made it here. There were live performances at the Sheridan Opera House, for the well-to-do. But there was no public library or public park. Most people lived in shacks that were small and dark and cold even in the summer and they could go to the Odd Fellows Hall or the Masons Hall just to warm up and be around other people. Even the wealthy, concentrated in the Elks, liked getting out of the house. Plus, the societies were a way for people to provide for each other, kind of an insurance policy. If a husband died in an accident or a wife died in childbirth, the members of the fraternal society would be there for the survivor.

"Here lies James Clark, who was town marshal from about 1887 to about 1895. He kept law and order in town and supplemented his income by engaging in holdups outside of town, in disguise. Turned out his real name was James Cummings, and he had a price on his head for an earlier career, after the Civil War, of robbing trains and stagecoaches and banks. Not long after the town council fired him, someone shot him on main street."

Chuck pointed to initials under Clark's name: "C.S.A., Confederate States of America. He fought for the confederacy and was proud of it."

"Where are Francis Curry and Charles Sumner?" Tom asked.

"Don't know about Curry. He's not buried here, so far as I know. He kept on editing the Daily Journal for some years, and then he just faded away. He lost his relevance or sense of purpose, I suppose, once the union had been destroyed. Sumner was deported from Telluride during the martial law period in 1903, arrested with a group of union men. They were marched out of jail in the middle of the night, forcibly put on a train, and ordered never to return. But Sumner did all right, I think. He went on to edit newspapers in Idaho. But here's Charles Painter."

Painter died at 87 in 1943, according to the inscription on the gravestone.

"He built the Painter Building, across the street from the courthouse east of Elks Park. Where the Sunshine Pharmacy is now. It's where he published the Daily Journal and ran his property title and insurance business."

Painter was a major figure in historic Telluride, Chuck went on to explain, the first exalted ruler of the Brotherhood of Elks, the first mayor of the town of Telluride, the first San Miguel County Clerk, and the vice president of the San Miguel Valley Bank at the time it was robbed by soon-to-be-legendary outlaw Butch Cassidy on June 24, 1889. As founder of The Daily Journal and publisher of that paper during the reign of editor Francis Curry, he lent all his influence and prestige to the effort to bust the Miners Union.

"He didn't work in the mines or handle explosives, he didn't travel to high mining camps during avalanche season, might not have ever gone up there in the summer. He was rich so he didn't live in a drafty shack, and with all that he managed a long life. Lucky bastard."

"Is Eva Shoen here?"

Chuck pointed to the upper northwest corner of the cemetery.

"That's where there are a lot of recent graves," he said, his dismissive tone indicating they were therefore of little interest.

"Why are you so immersed in the mining era?"

"It started when I was a boy and would talk to my grandfather about his early days in Telluride. The wild west wasn't so remote to hear him tell stories. Then I moved here when I was in my early twenties, and it was still pretty much the wild west. Idarado, which used to be the Smuggler-Union, was still operating. We were hippies and the miners who were here then hated us, with our long hair and tie-dyed clothes and free love and drug-taking and amplified music. I was one of the few hippies who could talk to the miners. They were just like my grandparents. Some of them even remembered my folks. Well, after a couple of years, in 1974, we outvoted the miners and took over town government, which we pretty much had to do because they'd hired a town marshal who loved his job harassing hippies. His name was Everett Morrow, he wore this big Stetson and talked in an Oklahoma drawl and was like a character right out of 1900. Best thing you could say about him is he never actually shot any of us, but he did send more than a few to prison for smoking pot, which pretty much ruined their lives, and busted most of us at one time or another for some small infraction. When new hippies pulled into town, he'd do his best to scare them away before they got the idea of sticking around. First thing the new town council did was fire him. He tossed his marshals badge at them and said, 'The badge is yours.' Then he patted his holster and said, 'But the gun is mine.'

"Then the ski area got cranking and the mine shut down and almost all the miners left, and a lot of the original of hippies did too, because they outgrew living as freaks in an old ghost town, and then property values went nuts. And I started to see all of these connections between Telluride now and Telluride then. The more I looked into the past, the more I understood that everything has changed and nothing has changed. I just went deeper and deeper into it. Sheeit, life was hard then, but in some ways, I think I might prefer it to modern times. Telluride's had two golden ages: when the union was at its peak of influence, with seventy percent of the men in the district enrolled as members, even though it only lasted two or three years; and then between the time the hippies took over the town in the early 1970s and the big money started to move in by the mid-1980s. I guess I'm lucky I got to live through one of them."

Small paused, and then said, as if, despite all the thought he had given to the subject, this was a new insight: "I doubt that it's a coincidence that during both of those 'golden ages,' the town was run by people in their twenties."

"Youthful idealism."

"My generation certainly thought we were building a better world. The Age of Aquarius and free love. Vincent St. John was also devoted to building a better world. But so were the young businessmen who opposed him. Just in a different way. While St. John was fighting for an eight-hour workday and decent wages L.L. Nunn dreamed of electrifying the world with AC power. They were both visionaries."

Despite Chuck's lack of interest, they had been walking toward Eva Shoen's grave. Her memorial was a large, modern marble sculpture of a woman with long, flowing hair, in a reclining pose. The epitaph read, simply, "Mother."

"Do you remember her murder? The last murder in Telluride before Jay Cluff?"

"Oh yeah. It felt like we were living in a TV show. Like now, with Cluff and Barnard. I didn't know her, but people say she was a nice lady. It was sad."

Nearby there was a similarly newer marble monument with a bas relief of a boy skiing through powder carved into it.

"Buzz Johnson," Tom read. "1976-1991. He died the year after Eva Shoen."

"Some kids still die too young," Chuck said. "He was a great skier, son of a longtime local family. He died of meningitis after he spent time in a dormitory at a ski camp back east. He was really sick when he got back, and his dad took him to the clinic. The doctors treated him for flu and sent him home. He was dead the next morning. Meningitis can be treated, but it's often misdiagnosed if there's not a nearby or recent outbreak that has put doctors on alert.

"When something like Buzz Johnson's death happens in a small town you learn odd things, like how dangerous meningitis can be. For a few years after that, parents were very careful to ask the docs at the clinic if it could be meningitis when they brought their kids in for what was probably just the latest bug going around."

Chapter 23

REPORTERS COVERING THEIR BEATS

Time does not stop when a young man dies, certainly not for a minute longer than it takes to bury him.

If life somehow continues, a newspaper doesn't instantly fail either, not even when its biggest advertiser abruptly cancels her ads. Sitting at his desk an hour after Peter's funeral, behind a closed door, Tom gazed in a kind of stupor at the garish headline: "Examiner Reporter Peter Barnard Found Murdered" on the front page of the paper that hit the stands the previous day.

Was it the last edition of The Examiner that would be published after 123 years, briefly interrupted only for a few years during the Great Depression?

Tom still didn't know.

How long had it been since Peter texted to tell him that Jay Cluff had been killed? Just ten days. How long since Erica Ortiz pulled her ads? Eight days. How long since he had found Peter's body, and was a party to Lionel Cluff's death? Six days.

Two murders in ten days that felt like an eternity. His newspaper hanging by a thread. The mind plays tricks. Tom found himself thinking about what Peter would have been working on if Jay Cluff had not been murdered and he had not gone to Cortez to poke around.

Those were Peter's words: "I'd like to go to Cortez to poke around?"

"See what you can find," Tom had said.

"It's dangerous to poke a stick at a coiled rattler," Deputy Weston later warned.

If Cluff hadn't been shot, Peter would have been poking around a controversial question headed for the Telluride ballot to use a portion of a large parcel of land previously dedicated to open space for a new medical center. Was a new medical center really needed? Was it worth the sacrifice of open space? The snakes lurking under those rocks weren't rattlers, just local residents with axes to grind. Who would report that story now? He would not try to replace the irreplaceable Peter, would downsize his staff, would keep the paper alive if he had to do it all by himself, as he had done in Naturita.

He would keep hope alive.

Or was that just the Obama campaign's ubiquitous slogan slipping uninvited into Tom's stream-of-consciousness?

Writing the story of Peter's death had been nearly impossible because Tom and Samantha were sources with no capacity for journalistic detachment. They knew too much and not enough. Their informed speculation about the case might be particularly insightful or it might be self-serving. It seemed obvious that Jay Cluff's grandson, Lionel Cluff, had killed Peter, almost certainly in collusion with his aunt, Connie Cluff. But they could only theorize about what the Cluffs were trying to hide; could only suspect that the Montezuma County sheriff was implicated and would therefore not conduct a legitimate investigation. Nor could Tom assume that because Connie and Lionel killed Peter, they were also behind the death of Jay

Cluff. Neither Sheriff Bruce in Montezuma nor Sheriff Owens in San Miguel offered up any indication as to how their respective investigations were proceeding. Only the routine assurance that they were "pursuing all leads."

Should they include their discovery—what was possibly Peter's "something big"—that Cluff was in business with the Montezuma County Sheriff, selling remote real estate to white supremacists?

"It's too big," Tom explained to Samantha. "It needs a lot more reporting, and more context that doesn't fit in this story. Let's give it a few days so that we get it right."

Was there self-interest involved in Tom's editorial decision? A desire to avoid provoking Sheriff Bruce by having a reporter call him to ask about his secret tie to the Cluffs? The story couldn't be published without contacting Bruce for comment, even if his response was "no comment." What if Peter had contacted Bruce to ask about his involvement in Hay Camp Mesa Ranch, and that's why he was killed?

So, what did the young reporter Eric Hansen--coached by Samantha and closely edited by Tom--report, first posting the story online early on Sunday, September 14, and in print the following Tuesday?

EXAMINER REPORTER
PETER BARNARD FOUND MURDERED

By Eric Hansen

Telluride, September 16, 2008—San Miguel Examiner senior reporter Peter Barnard was killed while on assignment outside of Cortez. His body was discovered September 13 by Examiner publisher, Tom Austin, who had gone to Cortez to search for Barnard, with whom he had lost contact.

Barnard was in Cortez to report additional details surrounding the murder of Jay Cluff in Bear Creek on September 8. Cluff was a Cortez resident.

Barnard traveled to Cortez on September 11. Austin went to Cortez the following afternoon, after he was unable to reach Barnard by phone. Late the previous day, in a phone conversation, Barnard told Austin he had uncovered "something big," but he did not elaborate.

In tracing Barnard's steps, Austin stumbled on a scene on remote Hay Camp Mesa, about ten miles northeast of Cortez, where a man, later identified as Jay Cluff's grandson, Lionel Cluff, appeared to be engaged in disposing of Barnard's body. In an altercation, Cluff was shot and killed by Maria Sanchez of Cortez, a Cortez private investigator Austin had retained to help him find Barnard.

Montezuma County Sheriff Dan Bruce has stated for the record that he does not anticipate charges against either Austin or Sanchez.

"We are investigating the killing of Peter Barnard," he said in a written statement. Lionel Cluff is an obvious suspect. At this time, we believe the killing of Cluff was in self-defense."

Also this week, San Miguel County Sheriff William Owens said there is no new information to report in the investigation into Jay Cluff's murder.

That was it. A not-entirely-honest scrap of a story, only somewhat mitigated by a short Up Bear Creek column.

UP BEAR CREEK

What Should a Newspaper Report When a Reporter Is Murdered on the Job?

By Tom Austin

The headline above this column poses a question I can't honestly answer.

The fact is, I don't know what a newspaper should do faced with the extraordinary circumstances that faces The Examiner this week. I only know what I'm doing.

My friend, my employee, died while on an assignment I gave him. Then I found the body. I'm a witness to any police investigation into the circumstances of Peter's death, and I'm also a source for any journalist who writes about it, including, oddly, myself. I can't report all that I know because I can't draw the line between what I truly know and what I only suspect, what I can corroborate in a journalistic sense, and what leads, however unlikely, that police should pursue as a matter of solving the crime.

They don't teach this in journalism school.

In fact, I probably shouldn't be writing even this much for The Examiner. But there is no readership more interested in what happened to Peter than The Examiner's readership.

So, we have published as much as we can, with as much transparency as we can muster, as we grieve and prepare for Peter's memorial service at Town Park on Tuesday.

We will publish more in coming days as we work through
a tangle of legal, journalistic, and personal complications.

Wish us luck.

. . .

A knock and Samantha stuck her head in the door.

"Are you OK?"

"I'm still trying to make sense of everything."

"Let me know when you've got it figured out."

Tom nodded, indicating that she should take a seat.

"All by yourself, of course."

"I'm sorry, I…"

But she cut him off: "No apology!"

Then she hit him again with her uncanny insight.

"You're not the only one in pain," she said. "Because if you're to blame for what happened to Peter, I am too. He didn't tell me either."

"Tell you what?"

"That Cluff was in business with the white supremacist sheriff, if he knew that. Or why he went to Cortez, if he didn't. What he was doing there. He didn't tell me anything."

"That makes two of us."

"Exactly."

Their shared experience since the murder of Jay Cluff brought them closer than Tom had realized. He studied her as if he was seeing her for the first time. She was a small woman, with shoulder-length curly brown hair and a gap between her teeth. She'd been at the paper for a year, but Tom had not allowed their relationship to deepen because he inherently mistrusted her purpose for being there, to take The Examiner online. In any case, Peter was his second-in-command, leaving little room for her or anyone else to gain his full confidence. Now, sitting across from him, she looked both angry and vulnerable, and was demanding honesty from him.

"You weren't his boss," Tom said.

"I was his colleague, his digital editor, his friend. He should have told you. And he should have told me."

"He cut me out because he was afraid that I wouldn't let him go. I don't know why. I might have helped him do it safely. But why you?"

"Because he was afraid that I'd tell you and you wouldn't let him go?" She shrugged. "It doesn't matter now. I'm just so pissed at him."

She shook her head, working to dampen her emotions.

"I feel like I'm wallpaper," she said. "Something that's just there all the time in the background."

"You're not. I get it. What happened with Peter in Cortez, it happened to both of us."

"I'm sorry."

"No apology!"

That drew a smile.

"So that's how it's going to be," she said. "Neither one of us is sorry."

"I think we both are."

They sat quietly for a few minutes, grieving together, which was better than grieving separately.

"Maybe Peter found out about the Nazi subdivision after he got there," Tom said, breaking the silence.

"He could have called."

"Or he underestimated the danger."

"Not plausible. I think probably he was just being a jerk. It doesn't matter now. We'll never know. But we can't blame ourselves."

Tom felt his own emotions start to well up again. There had been more than enough of that. So he changed the subject. Back to the business at hand.

"Did you get into Peter's laptop?"

"I've tried a bunch of possible passwords. No luck yet."

She let a moment pass, as if she was calculating whether either one of them needed any more expiation, and whether Tom would submit to it if he did, and then she said: "What now?"

"We go back to covering school board meetings and Town League recreational sports. New medical center or open space? Does it matter?"

"Peter is gone. But people will still want to see a doctor when they're sick. And enjoy open space."

"We all want it all."

This was Tom's moment to reveal that there would be no paper to publish, because the town's realtors were following the lead of his biggest advertiser and had started to cancel their ads; the collapsing local economy, tied to the global financial crisis, had caught up with him and The Examiner. Even if they learned who killed Jay Cluff and why Connie and Lionel Cluff killed Peter, and were ready to publish it all, their voice would be silenced.

Instead, his conversation with Samantha had recharged his will to carry on, as if Peter's death could not have been in vain. Peter had to have died for something, for newspapering and for following leads to the bitter end.

And Samantha was a worthy successor.

"Have we got enough stories assigned?" he asked. "There's got to be more going on than the murders."

"Reporters are covering their beats."

She hesitated, then said: "I've got something kind of interesting, maybe, that I was hoping to discuss with you. I don't know if now is the right time."

"Now is as good a time as any. Is it big?"

"Well, it's weird. Maybe just a distraction."

"I'll take a weird distraction over covering the school board."

"It's about that restaurant you assigned me to write up, Elsa's Melting Pot. You know, my perk."

Chapter 24

ETHICAL GYMNASTICS

Samantha was glad—in an earlier era, before Peter disappeared—when Tom assigned her the restaurant "review." Stories about a business that advertised with the paper, or could potentially advertise with the paper, were handled mostly by Tom himself, and occasionally by Peter. Such stories required ethical gymnastics that not just any staff reporter could manage, an ability to walk the fine line between advertising and reporting, community service and self-interest. A story about a new restaurant was a particularly tasty perk because wining and dining made the transaction between restaurateur and reporter both impossible to ignore and impossible to openly acknowledge, certainly not in print.

From the restaurateur's perspective it was obvious: "You get a nice night out and I get a nice story in the paper. Even Steven."

For his part, the publisher will hope for weekly ads on the theory that the bump in business gained from a "review" demonstrates that people read the newspaper and will therefore see the restaurant's ads and will be periodically reminded to eat there. But do dollars spent on newspaper ads really come back in the form of increased customers?

Not so easy to track, says the restaurateur: "I ask people what brought them in, and they always say it was 'word of mouth'."

Any publisher or half-competent newspaper ad salesperson will suggest that the typical customer will often say "word of mouth" when it was actually an ad that moved them to eat out or make a purchase. What you hear from a friend—that kind of word of mouth—and the visibility provided by a newspaper ad are the same thing: customer awareness of your brand, and they reinforce each other. Restaurant owners too shrewd by half still try to create evidence that ads work, like a coupon in the ad, or a "mention this ad for a 10 percent discount," which the respectable salesperson will strongly discourage, because "coupons are cheesy, not worthy of your classy establishment, don't discount your product!" and the "value of advertising is not always so immediate."

"It's about broadening your visibility," the salesperson will argue. To which the restaurateur will reply: "I pay plenty in main street rent for visibility. What more do I need?"

Tom had explained this ritual sales dance to Samantha, part of her education in the wily economics of small-town newspaper publishing. For Tom to assign her the write-up about Elsa's Melting Pot represented an invitation into the top tier of Examiner management, along with Tom and Peter, because like Tom and Peter, Samantha had enlisted in the hand-to-hand combat of figuring out how to make money from news in a world shifting away from print. As the paper's great hope for a viable future, Samantha, mentored by Tom, just might discover the alchemy of turning digital written words into a stream of cash that might flow to the owner of Elsa's Melting Pot, Graham Hall, and from Graham back to The Examiner.

Tom had hired Samantha a few months earlier, at Peter's urging.

"Can you really save newspapers from the internet?" Tom had asked her during her interview, conducted by phone.

"I want to try," she replied. "I think in some ways a weekly community paper like yours might be better positioned than a metro daily, in the long run."

"Why is that?"

"There's less competition in reporting community news, plus the costs are more manageable. I'm not saying it will be easy. It will be a challenge, but one worth tackling. I got my degree in journalism, not computer science, because I believe in the content, what newspapers do, not in how they do it. The new technology is a threat, but also an opportunity if we can figure out how to seize it."

"I respect the fact that you aren't promising me that you know you can pull it off."

"All I can promise is that I'll give it my best."

Samantha was inclined after the interview to look elsewhere for employment, at one of those metro dailies where there were teams of digital reporters and editors trying to figure it all out, but Peter had called to encourage her to take the Examiner gig, and not to be put off by Tom's curmudgeonly demeanor.

"He pretends to be crusty," Peter told her. "He's really a teddy bear and will do whatever it takes to save The Examiner. Plus, if you take the job, you'll get to live in Telluride. Do you have any idea how rare it is to be able to live here and have a job in your field?"

"No."

"Run don't walk. Telluride is a great place to live and The Examiner is a great place to work."

Samantha took the job, but Tom did not let up on his deep misgivings about online publishing. She could understand why. Not only was he a creature of print, but he was realistic in calculating the odds against the paper's survival. Tom was no different from thousands of other newspaper publishers across the country. For several generations after the Second World War, to publish a small local newspaper was a great business. The papers' customers were virtually every business in their market. Small town businesses had no better way to reach their customers than with ads in the community newspaper. The papers had a monopoly on community news, which commanded community-wide readership. Small-town newspapers were not only profitable; their publishers were respected pillars of the community, power brokers in a unique position to shape public sentiment on virtually any subject.

Seemingly overnight, with the arrival of the internet—and at the same time that both population and locally owned enterprise was abandoning many small communities—these comfortable publishers could sense that obsolescence was stalking them.

Paradoxically in Telluride, thanks to the real estate boom that preceded the arrival of the internet, The Examiner was enjoying its period of greatest prosperity just as the threat of digitized news loomed. Which meant that Tom could better afford to hire Samantha and invest in online publishing than most other small-town papers. He had more to gain and more to lose.

Samantha saw the assignment to write a story about Elsa's Melting Pot as an opportunity to flesh out a possible source of digital revenue. She envisioned stories about every dining option in Telluride and an online restaurant directory, with curated customer feedback in a comments section and options for restaurants to pay for "featured" status, or even a direct link to their own webpage. Print publications—particularly alternative weeklies in college towns and big cities, city magazines, and visitor guides in resorts—had long published dining guides, charging restaurants to be listed and charging a premium for special prominence. This basic concept might adapt beautifully to an online dining guide published by the local newspaper in a small resort town.

For her night out courtesy of Graham Hall, and to enhance the social vibe, Samantha invited John, a ski patroller who worked as a landscaper in the summer, to join her. Her plan was to outsell the rug merchant-turned-restaurateur. While he sold her on Elsa's Melting Pot, she'd sell him on her new online dining guide.

He was waiting for her, like a cat crouched behind the sofa waiting for a mouse to scurry past.

"Welcome, welcome," he said warmly the night of her reservation. "Have you met my wife, Elsa?"

Dressed in couture—a tight skirt, patent leather heels and a ruffled blouse with a plunging neckline, looking nothing like a mountain girl—Elsa offered Samantha a limp hand. They shook hands and Graham escorted them to a table for four.

"We would like to join you for dinner, if you don't mind," Graham said. "So that we can make an evening of it, and you can experience all of the conviviality of fondue, which by its nature—the sharing of the fondue pot—is an especially social form of dining out."

He had scripted the evening in advance, just as she had, and was telling her exactly what he expected her to write.

At least, she thought, they were well-matched.

Chapter 25

ELSA'S MELTING POT

The restaurant occupied a cellar beneath the Hall rug gallery. "We had this space, which was underutilized," Graham explained, after the first glasses of wine were poured. It was roughly finished as an apartment but was not comfortable. Elsa and I would put up guests here. You see…." and he pointed to a large cabinet on a nearby wall… "the Murphy bed is still here. When we remodeled the space into a restaurant, I thought, 'Why remove it?' It might still come in handy."

"Who knows what for?" he offered with a salacious wink that did the opposite of mitigating the insinuation.

Samantha looked around the cellar. The walls were exposed rock, the foundation of a historic structure from the mining era, reinforced in more recent times by steel I-beams. It would have made a better dungeon than an apartment, she thought, but worked as a rustic restaurant.

"It reminds me of a fondue restaurant I ate at in Chamonix," she said.

"Exactly!" Graham said. "Telluride is the Chamonix of North America, and our historic buildings are similar, built of native rock. In the Alps, you often descend into a cozy basement to be served fine wine and cheese. The setting and cuisine suit the cold mountain climate and active mountain lifestyle. And our tourists will love it!

"To be honest, to survive in Telluride these days, we need to monetize every square foot of real estate. It struck me that a fondue restaurant would work beautifully here. Plus, fondue doesn't require a full restaurant kitchen. Just crock pots to melt cheese and chocolate, a bar for wine and spirits, some refrigeration, and a sink to wash dishes. We were able to build it all of that here quite affordably.

"That last part is off the record, of course."

"Of course."

Elsa appeared bored, and more interested in Samantha's date than in her husband's boasts about his business acumen.

"I have seen you around town," she said to John. "Maybe we have met? At a party, I think."

"I guess I've been to a few good Telluride parties!" he replied. "I've lived here for eight years."

The waitress, thematically Alpine-blonde and dressed in a dirndl, stepped up, smiling broadly.

"Welcome to Elsa's Melting Pot! My name is Tammy and I'll be serving you tonight."

"I'd like for Samantha and John to sample a little bit of everything," Graham said. "So just bring out small sample portions of our specialties. You know my favorites. Pace it so that we aren't overwhelmed."

"Sounds good," Tammy said.

"Tammy and her partner Ryan built this place and now they're running it," Graham offered behind Tammy's back as she left, loud enough to be sure she heard it. "I'm so lucky that I found them."

Tammy flounced away and Graham nodded to the bar, where a young man costumed in kitschy lederhosen and suspenders over a coarsely woven frock was positioned. Ryan nodded back and waved.

The evening was long, lubricated by too much wine, and felt to

Samantha more like work than pleasure as she and Graham bore into each other, each seeking advantage. He could barely force himself to pretend that he was listening to her pitch for the online restaurant guide. Maybe, she thought, she should have held her fire until a subsequent meeting, until after the story she wrote was published. But then she'd have less leverage.

Samantha found herself vaguely aware that Elsa and John had discovered that they'd been in Val d'Isere at the same time. She and Graham skied there the same year John lived there for a season on an international ski patrol exchange.

"Did you eat at a fondue restaurant there?" Elsa asked him.

"A couple of times"

"Maybe we were at the same one on the same night?"

He grinned: "I'm sure I would have noticed you!"

She envied their easy flirtation. They were enjoying the evening out, nothing to worry about.

The next morning, hungover, Samantha was at her desk, working on the story. She reread the lede.

"A visitor to Elsa's Melting Pot, the new fondue restaurant on Main Street in Telluride, might be forgiven for thinking, if just for a moment, that she had been magically transported to Chamonix.

"Which is precisely what owner Graham Hall intended.

"'There is something about fondue that suits mountain towns,' he explained. 'The coziness of the cellar setting, the warmth, the fine wine, the melted cheese.'

"And everything at Elsa's Melting Pot is delivered as promised, from imported European cheese, both served up on charcuterie platters and melted down to be served with crusty cubes of bread, to lovely side dishes, including a stellar lemony Caesar salad…."

She was interrupted by an unexpected visitor. The very waitress who served the wine, cheese, and charcuterie.

"Have you got a moment?" Tammy asked.

"Sure."

"Did you enjoy your meal last night?

"A little too much wine, to be honest. But otherwise, it was fun."

"Is that what you do? Write about restaurants?"

"This is my first one. Usually, I work on the newspaper's website."

"Oh."

Dressed in jeans and a sweater and wearing no makeup, Tammy seemed like a different person than the performer of the night before. Older, perhaps, in her early thirties, tired, and something weighing on her.

"Graham is quite a character," Samantha said, hoping it might break the ice. "It must be a trip working for him."

"That's what I wanted to talk to you about."

Samantha nodded to indicate she was listening.

"Have a seat."

"The restaurant isn't real," Tammy said as she sat. "It's a scam."

"The costumes you wear. I mean, we're not in the Alps, are we?"

Hearing herself, Samantha realized that she was off on the wrong foot, sounding superior, as if she was carrying her embarrassment over the "review" she was in the process of writing into the conversation. She changed her tone. "It's a theme restaurant," she shrugged. "But what can you do? Even in Chamonix, the fondue places are tourist traps and the waiters wear costumes."

"I wouldn't know," Tammy said, and then abruptly changed the subject.

"Ryan and I were camping in Town Park when we met Graham about a month ago," she said. "Graham walked through the campground like he was looking for someone. He picked us out, like we were exactly who he was looking for."

"How so?"

"We were in pretty bad shape, to be honest. Down and out. We'd been on the road for a couple of months, had headed to the mountains looking for a new life close to nature. We're from Florida. I was in a bad marriage and met Ryan. We had an affair. My husband found out and kicked me out, so Ryan and I just took off in his beater. Didn't know where we were headed or why. I left my daughter."

Tammy shook her head to shake the memory or to remind herself to stick to her story. Her abandonment of her child was a wrong turn. Irrelevant. Too much information.

"Ryan had some money saved up, but we ran through it. He's got diabetes. He needs insulin to stay alive and it costs $40 a day. Our car broke down and needs $1,000 in repairs, plus we'd been in the Town Park campground for eleven days already, and there's a two-week limit on how long you can stay there. We were planning on moving into the woods, you know, becoming woodsies, when Graham says 'hey.'

"'Are you looking for work by any chance?' he asks.

"He tells us he has a great gig for a good-looking young couple like us. Like we were something to look at! He's building this new restaurant and is looking for someone to manage it. Asks if we've done restaurant work and if we're handy. We tell him we're willing to do anything.

"'You can even stay at the restaurant while you're building it out'," he says. "'There's a bed in there, and a bathroom with a shower.'

"He says it's just room and board until the restaurant opens up, but then we can run it and he'll pay us, plus we can make bank in tips. I tell him we can't afford that because we need to pay for Ryan's insulin, so he thinks about it, like he's wondering if Ryan's life is worth it, but really he's doing the math in his head, $40 x 7 is $280, so he offers us $150 each per week, which barely covers the slin, but what can we do?"

"That's just completely shocking. I'm horrified!"

"I know, right?"

Tammy dabbed her eyes with a tissue.

"But we're trapped. We've been working 14-hour days, seven days a week, for a month, for basically nothing, fixing up that shitty basement. And we can't leave because we don't have a car and we need the cash for Ryan's insulin."

Tammy was done. Wasted.

"You're slave labor," Samantha said grimly.

Tammy nodded.

"Are you telling me this so I'll write about it?"

"Oh, God, no!"

"Why then?"

"You seemed like you'd understand."

"Have you thought about going to the police?"

Tammy shook her head.

"Ryan would kill me if he knew that I was telling you. That I was telling anyone. He says we just need to save up tips until we can afford to get the car fixed and drive out of here. And I keep thinking, when will that be? And then what?"

"I don't know how I can help you," Samantha said.

"I know."

Chapter 26

'YOU MIGHT WANT TO LAWYER UP'

Jesus," Tom said, after Samantha finished telling him the story. "She just needed a friend. Someone she could talk to."

"Which tells you how desperate she is," Samantha said. "To tell a story like that to a complete stranger. And as I'm listening to her, I'm writing the headline of my restaurant review." She raised her hands to put it in air quotes. "Enjoy Traditional Swiss Fondue Served by Wage Slaves at Elsa's."

Tom laughed, for the first time, he realized, since Peter's disappearance.

"I shouldn't joke, but…."

"You have to joke. We have to laugh, sometimes."

This is a distraction, Tom almost said, but he caught himself. Yes, it was a distraction but a welcome one—the laugh she elicited had come as a relief—and he allowed his mind to wander. Could Samantha possibly be thinking what Tom had instantly concluded as she talked, drawing on his own knowledge of Graham and Elsa? That the Florida couple were likely something more than wage slaves, that sexual services were part of the arrangement between Graham and Elsa and their good-looking "employees," a modern take on the brothels of Telluride's mining era, the Murphy bed put to good use, as Graham had implied.

But this was a crucial detail that, if it were true, Samantha didn't share with him, most likely because Tammy didn't reveal it to the stranger to whom she spilled her guts. It would be one trouble too many to share. Or maybe Tammy herself considered the sex more of a perk than a problem.

Tom's mind had wandered too far.

"It's a great story," he said. "No doubt about it. But if she won't go on the record, you've got nothing. Even then it would be tricky because we'd need corroboration to publish her accusations against Graham. Otherwise, how do we know it's true? And if it's not true, it's libel. And even if it is true, it's nothing illegal, right? They're all consenting adults."

Tom was thinking about sexual exploitation and had made the right call not to mention it. Because Samantha was focused on the labor issues.

"It's not legal to exploit workers like that!" she said.

"But tough to prove if they don't want to complain."

"They're too embarrassed."

"No doubt."

"I could interview Graham."

"Not without her blessing or you'd be violating her confidence. Plus, he'd never admit to any of it. You'd end up with her word against his. Which wouldn't be publishable."

"How do I just file this away and ignore it? It says so much about Telluride today, and America for that matter. The struggle to pay for insulin on one hand, unimaginable wealth on the other, and a hustler like Graham in the middle working both sides."

"Often, when a story isn't coming together, the answer is to do more reporting," Tom said. "Maybe broaden it into a piece about how retail and restaurants are struggling to pay their workers and how workers are struggling to survive. Talk to several business owners, including Graham, and get his explanation for how he found Tammy and Ryan, without challenging him directly. Maybe it evolves into something."

Then, Tom realized that sorrow is never far away, and might never be far away again.

Brought to mind by the rhyme of Graham's indentured servants and mining era brothels, his thoughts had turned to the Collins murder, the ultimate cold case, and from there back to Peter's murder and the Cluff murder, which seemed to be going cold already, as evidenced by the fact that he and Samantha were deep into discussion of an unrelated story.

"Today's service workers are not very different from the miners of a century ago," he said.

"You think that's the angle?"

"It's too abstract. Just an idle thought. It won't add up to anything for next week's paper, which is what you need to focus on now. But you may be onto a good story and should pursue it when you've got the time to dig into it."

Tom's phone rang. It was Sarah calling.

"I've got to grab this," he said.

Samantha stood to leave, and Tom answered.

Sarah was in distress.

"What's wrong?"

"Angie took Tyler to the playground. And I don't know where they are."

"How long has it been?"

"I was mixing a big batch of soap," Sarah said. "Since Tyler was OK with Angie, I started another one. You know, there are points in the process when you've got to watch it closely. So, a couple of hours. She promised she'd be back with him at 2 and it's already 3. When they didn't come home, I checked to see if she left her car keys on the shelf, and they're gone. So I went to the park and they're not there and neither is the car. I'm just leaving there. I'm on my way to you now.

"She had a day off work and accused me of not trusting her alone with her own son, so I said she could take him to the park. I should have taken the car keys, but I didn't think of it."

Sarah was breathing hard, obviously walking quickly, maybe jogging.

"She's probably been planning this. It's why she came back. I've been a total idiot."

He could hear her voice emanating from the phone and, at the same time, just out of sync, outside his office.

He stood to greet her at the door, and she collapsed into his arms, sobbing.

"It's not your fault," he said, pulling his office door shut behind her. "I've been no help."

"You couldn't help, not with everything that's going on. I'm so worried."

"I'll call the sheriff. Every minute that passes could take them another mile further away."

Tom got Sheriff Owens on the phone quickly, a perk of his position as the newspaper publisher, not to mention the two murder investigations each was investigating in his own way, and quickly explained the situation.

"We'll put out at an all-points bulletin," Owens said. "We'll find her. Have you got any idea of which direction she's headed?"

"Probably west, to Los Angeles or the West End. Or maybe Junction. Those are the only places she knows anyone. That we know of, at least."

By the time they got to Owens's office, there was news.

"Sheriff Bruce has got her," Owens said. "Down in Montezuma County. They're both OK. They're in his custody. In Cortez."

Sheriff Bruce? Montezuma County?

"Thank God," Sarah said, taking a chair facing the Sheriff's desk.

"Just to clarify," Owens said. "You are the child's legal guardians, even though your daughter is his natural mother."

"We're his parents," Tom said. "We adopted him when she abandoned him."

"But you gave her permission to take the child?"

Tom and Sarah answered simultaneously.

"No," she said.

"Yes," he said.

"It's not exactly yes or no," Sarah explained. "Yes, to the playground, with my permission, but not out of town."

"She showed up a couple of weeks ago," Tom said. "We thought it was the start of a reconciliation. But obviously not."

Owens nodded.

"A lot of families are complicated these days. Most police contacts are related to family conflict. Domestic disturbances of one sort or another. The question for you, is, do you want to press charges?"

Again, they answered at the same time, again disharmoniously.

"No," she said.

"Yes," he said. "A night in jail, or better yet, a month or two, would do her some good."

"But then what?"

"Well, we have to do something. Because if we don't, how can we keep Tyler safe? Do you think she's back using drugs?"

"No!" Sarah said, too quickly. "At least I hope not."

"Hope is not a good enough answer to that question," Owens said grimly. "Not when you're talking about a child's safety."

The three of them sat silent for a moment.

"Tell me about the drugs," Owens said.

"Angie was in your jail before," Tom said. "Almost five years ago. She was busted for ripping off her employer, a hotel in Mountain Village, and we came up from Naturita to bail her out. We didn't see you when we were here. You and I, we, hadn't met each other back then."

"I don't get directly involved in very many cases," Owens said. "Murders. Not that we have many of those. Except now, of course."

He was tapping at his computer keyboard. "Sounds like it was a Mountain Village Police Department matter, anyway, and we were just holding her for them.

"Her file is flagged," Owens said, staring at his computer screen. "She violated bail release after that Mountain Village arrest."

"She did," Sarah admitted. "She skipped town. Which is how we ended up with Tyler."

"There's an arrest warrant out on her," Owens said. "Sheriff Bruce's office didn't mention that when they called in response to the APB. He'll likely be calling to transfer her here, once he's seen the warrant, if he hasn't already."

He tapped a button on his phone and said: "Any more word from Montezuma County on the kidnapping? OK, let me know."

He hung up and reported to Tom and Sarah: "Not yet."

Owens was thinking ahead: "She could be sentenced on the Mountain Village charge, plus violating bail, and for kidnapping if we end up charging her for that. She could be put away for a few years. Maybe more, depending on how the D.A. and Judge Shuteran feel about the whole mess."

"Oh my God," Sarah said, burying her face in her hands.

"What do we do now, Bill?" Tom asked. With his personal life splayed open in front of the Sheriff, Tom was grateful they were on a first-name basis.

"I don't see that you have much choice," Owens said. "You are responsible for Tyler. Make sure you've got the paperwork proving you're his legal guardians with you and drive down to Cortez to pick up your son."

"I've got it," Sarah said, patting her purse.

"Good."

Owens stood, indicating the meeting was over.

"You might want to lawyer up, with all that you've got going on," Owens said, almost an afterthought, as Tom and Sarah headed to the door.

"Why?" Tom asked, as if Tyler's kidnapping had blotted out all the other events of recent days.

"Oh, I don't know. By my count, we've got three open homicide investigations. And one way or the other, you're involved in all three of 'em."

Three investigations?

Tom's reserve of composure was depleted. Beneath it lay paranoia.

But paranoia might have been extraneous. Was Tom imagining it or was Owens going out of his way—in this wholly inappropriate moment, in the midst of Tom's deeply personal family crisis—to confirm that the Lionel Cluff case remained open? And at the same time, owing to the coincidence of Angie being apprehended in Montezuma County, Owens was dispatching Tom back into the belly of the beast, the place where Peter was murdered and Lionel Cluff was shot in front of Tom's eyes, and where Sheriff Bruce reigned supreme and might well arrest him?

"And I am curious about something else," the sheriff said, adding insult to injury. "Are you going to report the attempted kidnapping of your son in the paper?"

Chapter 27

MIMING FIGHT MOVES

What was the point of that last jab? Was it as gratuitous as it seemed? Or was it every bit as intentional as the sheriff's suggestion that Tom lawyer up? It was as if Owens saw that Tom was on the ropes, staggering from repeated blows to the jaw, so why not take him down with a final gut punch? But to what end?

Tom's thoughts were racing, even as he took Sarah's arm to move her and himself quickly to their car for the urgent drive to Cortez to rescue Tyler.

Of course, he had not asked himself if Angie's attempted kidnapping of Tyler might be newsworthy. Nor did he welcome the opportunity, at this fraught moment, for introspection about his journalistic practices, and how his editorial decision making could relate to a story in which he himself was personally implicated—as, in fact, he was deeply implicated in the story about the death of his reporter, published just the day before. Which seemed to be exactly what Owens couldn't resist pointing out: that Tom was no mere chronicler of the news but was up to his eyeballs in making it.

On the surface, Owens might have sincerely wondered if the

attempted kidnapping was newsworthy. Outside the present context, it would have been a fair question. How did Angie's attempted kidnapping of Tyler compare with the numberless other "domestic disturbances" that Sheriff Owens referenced, which rarely appeared in the paper, apart from the occasional blind item in the police blotter? Where the local law enforcement agencies sometimes failed to redact names in the public police blotters that Tom and his reporters drew upon, the newspaper did the redactions for them. The paper's policy was to report names only in cases of felonies. But even in serious criminal matters, what found its way into print was entirely arbitrary, a matter of what caught a reporter's or an editor's eye or was specifically brought to their attention by an interested party; what they had space for; and what else was competing for their attention. Sometimes, when the news was slow and Tom had a lot of pages to fill because ad sales were heavy, he would scan the police blotter looking for a potentially bigger story he could assign to a reporter.

As if to celebrate Telluride's small-town virtue of having little crime to report, and thus to flatter the readership, it had become something of a tradition at The Examiner, under Tom's editorship, for the young reporters who transcribed the police blotter to render an unremarkable police engagement into something lyrical and faux literary. One of Peter Barnard's final bits of writing was a masterful example of the ironic sensibility that The Examiner had come to represent.

> IMPERVIOUS TO PAIN — On the evening of August 14, police received a report of a fight in progress at a local bar. Upon arrival at the scene, officers spotted two men walking away from the bar, one with blood on his hands and miming fight moves, apparently reenacting the fight.

When officers called out to the man, he began to shout incoherently and then proceeded to approach officers while bumping his chest and making other threatening gestures. He appeared to be drunk and delirious, so one of the officers, fearing for his personal safety, acted quickly to force the man to the ground. When the man tried to get up, the officer performed an arm-bar on the man to restrain him, but he was "impervious to pain," and continued to resist violently. During the ensuing struggle, the man bit the officer's finger, resulting in a significant laceration. Another officer joined in the struggle, but the man appeared to have "super-human strength." The officers, running out of options, threatened to use increased force if the man did not stop resisting. After one officer was struck in the arm, causing a loss of feeling, the officers were forced to use "hand control techniques" to counteract the offender's seemingly limitless source of energy. One of the officers punched the man twice in the face, subduing him long enough so that he could be handcuffed and placed under arrest.

Tom had read this bit of Peter's last-published prose when he returned from Cortez. It was printed in the same edition as the story of Peter's death. Was it purely sentimental that Tom found it artful? That he wondered if the writer would have gone on, had he not been cut down at a young age, to produce writing that was more substantial, and which might appear on a bestseller list, or even stand the test of time by finding its way into a literary canon? Yet, it wasn't only Tom who was impressed by the breezy qualities of The Examiner's Police and Thieves column.

The deputies who recorded their activities in the blotters from the three local law enforcement departments also stepped up their game, adding more detail than they used to, knowing there was an appreciative readership for the newspaper's recounting of their exploits. And that was also why it wasn't necessarily a jab that Owens asked Tom if his son's attempted kidnapping would be reported in the paper. The incidents rendered as small-town color in Police and Thieves were not really joking matters, from Owens's point of view, as Tom himself could now attest, given the deep emotional trauma of fearing for Tyler's safety and being dependent on a police response to rescue him.

Or Owens was not objecting to the glib tone of the police blotter but was instead making the simple observation that not everything belongs in print. In that case, it would be nothing more than a caution to Tom to be judicious in what he printed about Owens's investigations into the Cluff and Barnard murders.

More likely, Owens was just running his mouth, as he was wont to do.

But at that moment, it felt to Tom more personal than that. Tom was vulnerable four times over due to his domestic dirty laundry having just been aired in front of the Sheriff, his moral culpability in Peter's death, his potential legal liability in the death of Lionel Cluff; and his handling of his professional responsibility to make ethical editorial judgments. Not to mention the fifth blow that Owens presumably knew nothing about: the imminent failure of his newspaper. The exercise of cataloging the gaping holes in his armor made Tom feel light-headed, although it could have just been that he jumped to his feet too quickly to get the hell out of Owens's office.

Nobody is pure, Tom thought. Everyone has secrets they would prefer not to see published in the local paper's police blotter. Or do they? Maybe other people lead straighter and narrower lives than Tom could imagine.

Tom would sometimes lie awake in bed at night and revisit, in sequence, all his own crimes and misdemeanors, starting with skipping school one day when he was in eighth grade so he could smoke weed with a friend, and proceeding to his being fired from his big city journalism job, and on to even worse offenses that were painful to recollect, like cutting off communication with his mother for five years, not because she did a single thing wrong, but due to his own shame for having squandered all of the advantages of a loving childhood and great education. He would balance the litany of failings against his good deeds, mostly later in life, which included his love for Sarah, adopting Ray Walker, Jr. and Tyler, reconciling with his mother; and now, running a community newspaper with as much integrity as he could muster. He was proud to mentor aspiring young journalists, like Peter and Samantha. But he had failed Peter, adding a fatal act of poor judgment to the list of major misdeeds, further unbalancing the ledger. He could only conclude that there was more bad than good in his checkered life, pushing his odds for achieving any form of ultimate grace, if such a thing was possible at all, to a future that was likely further out than his probable lifespan.

Tom's time, like everyone's time, was running out, more quickly than most people realize. "Enjoy yourself," went a current popular song, originally written in 1949, covered by The Specials, set to a jaunty melody, "it's later than you think."

One thing seemed certain about Owens calling into question Tom's right to judge others or to publish stories about what he might know: it was aimed at blunting Tom's impulse to keep looking into the murders. There are many forces that may suppress truth, not only guilty secrets, but also, possibly in this case, the Sheriff's determination to conduct his investigations without interference and his distaste for how police business was reported in the press.

In any case, Owens's warning Tom to stay in his own lane backfired. Why should Tom assume that the sheriff, who managed to simultaneously come off as blunt and canny, was uncompromised? Was Owens the good cop he always assumed him to be? Or yet another rattler lurking beneath a rock?

Tom walked out of Owens's office and headed back to Cortez with Sarah to rescue their son, determined to learn who had killed Cluff and Peter, and why, without waiting passively and indefinitely for either Sheriff Owens or Sheriff Bruce to solve the case.

Because there is something locked deep in the human psyche that insists on understanding how and why violence erupts, as if understanding might be the magic potion to ward it off.

Chapter 28

PROBABLE CAUSE

D o we need a lawyer?" Sarah asked as Tom steered south to Cortez.

"Probably."

"Should we call Rod?"

"Not now."

How much of his mounting paranoia should Tom share?

Should he tell Sarah that he was now wondering if Angie and Sheriff Owens were both in league with Sheriff Bruce and the Aryan Patriots? That they were using Tyler as bait to draw him back to Cortez, where they could trap him? They were doing this because like Peter before him, Tom was heedlessly threatening to blow up their conspiracy, whose outlines were anything but clear but were potentially broad enough to have brought Angie back home *the very same day Jay Cluff was found murdered in Bear Creek?* Was there any other plausible explanation for why he was now back on Lizard Head Pass, heading south, right where they wanted him? Could all this be mere coincidence?

Yes, it could be. There were only three directions Angie could have gone upon leaving Telluride. The odds were one in three that she'd head for Cortez, back toward Los Angeles, as she had.

Tom willed himself onto a different train of thought. No conspiracy was necessary to account for the urgent mission of rescuing Tyler. Angie was more than a sufficient explanation. She had come back not to reconcile with her mother, but to take her son. She was more devious than they had given her credit for and had grabbed Tyler at the first opportunity: when Sarah let her guard down to make an extra batch of soap, thinking that she might ease her family's financial stress by bringing a hundred dollars more to the table. Angie couldn't know that she'd be stopped in Cortez, forcing Tom into a new engagement with the sovereign sheriff.

What did it matter? Regardless of how it had come about, Tom might be arrested in Cortez or share the same fate as Peter. Worse, he was exposing Sarah to the same risks. They had no choice but to rescue Tyler, so what was the point of indulging fear? Of expressing his fears out loud where they might not dissipate but would spread, infecting Sarah, who had more than enough fears of her own: How was Tyler? What would happen to Angie?

He almost blurted it out, almost said, I think I might be losing it, but thankfully Sarah broke the silence first.

"Tyler must be so confused."

Tom nodded grimly as he reached over to take her hand.

Then Tom was back at the place he was so relieved to escape just a few days earlier, the Montezuma County Sheriff's office, identifying himself to the front desk officer. And he was back under the steely gaze of the goon, Duke the undersheriff, who stood conspicuously in a corner.

When it was Deputy Ross Weston, the "good cop" who had questioned him about the double homicide, who came to meet them, Tom felt an odd sense of relief, introducing Weston to his wife as if he were an old friend. The feeling morphed into something less comfortable when Weston escorted them to the same small conference room where their first meeting had taken place.

"Maybe we could use a different room?" Tom said.

Weston shot him a sharp look, seeing no humor in Tom's quip. Or maybe he intended to question Tom's implication that it was coincidence that brought him back so soon.

"I can't believe I'm back here," Tom said. "On a totally unrelated matter, of course."

"Can we see Tyler?" Sarah asked.

"He's with a social worker," Weston said. "He's fine. I'd just like to ask you a few questions, and then, of course you can see him."

"OK," Tom said.

"Can you tell me what happened?"

Where to begin?

"We were distracted," Tom said. "We buried Peter just two days ago. We were exhausted, so we let Angie watch Tyler…."

The context seemed important, but Tom was violating the dictum to say as little as possible to a cop who might have reason to suspect you of a crime. Starting with the funeral of none other than one of the homicide victims whose death Weston was, presumably, investigating, Tom was reminded that there are no coincidences in life, much less in policework, if only because seemingly unrelated coincidences must illuminate each other somehow. In this case, to Weston, it was incontrovertible evidence that Tom's life was in a state of unholy collapse.

And then Sarah confessed: "I should never have let Angie watch Tyler. Not even for five minutes."

To which Weston replied: "Did you bring the adoption papers?"

Sarah handed them to him.

After glancing at the document, Weston looked up, pointedly less friendly than he had been after Tom's previous interrogation, and said, "We have some concerns regarding the child's safety."

"What?" Tom said, incredulous.

"Why should that be surprising?" Weston asked. "The Montezuma County Department of Social Services has begun an investigation. And until that's complete, your son will be placed in foster care."

"Oh, my God!" Sarah cried. "You can't do that to him!"

"No, ma'am," Weston said. "What we can't do is just hand him back to you. Not after what's happened."

Sarah turned to Tom beseechingly, as if he could somehow and instantly reverse this grave injustice.

"You can understand that we are in a state of shock," Tom said to Weston. "Can my wife and I have a few moments of privacy?"

Weston thought about it for a moment, then nodded, stood, and walked out of the room.

* * *

For Tom, the calculus was instantaneous. He didn't see it coming, blinded by the emergency of Tyler's kidnapping, but now it was obvious. Even if he were not corrupt, the Montezuma County sheriff could not help but think twice when the toddler who turned up with his alleged kidnapper at his jail just happened to be the son of a man implicated in a couple of active homicide investigations — or three active investigations, if Sheriff Bruce considered the Jay Cluff murder to be related to the other two, and he was therefore investigating it — and why wouldn't he be?

But Bruce was corrupt, given his secret political and business entanglements with the first murder victim, Jay Cluff. And there was no overlooking that both Montezuma County homicide victims, Peter and Lionel Cluff, were killed at Hay Camp Mesa Ranch—the very property that was secretly marketed by the Cluffs to members of a white supremacist militia group, with Bruce's endorsement.

From Bruce's perspective, add in the curious case of alleged kidnapper Angie Walker, the daughter of Tom's wife, wanted for previous crimes up in Telluride, now sitting in Bruce's jail, and there was plenty to investigate. Especially, one might suppose, for a man who was "sovereign" in his county.

Bruce had cause to be suspicious if not paranoid. Then again, so did Tom.

Was Angie colluding with Bruce?

Tom pushed the unhelpful thought aside once again, and moved his chair so that he was facing Sarah, their knees touching. He embraced her and nuzzled her ear, burying his lips in her hair where, he hoped, they couldn't be observed moving. He whispered: "They're listening."

Sarah nodded slightly, imperceptibly, Tom hoped; and he pulled out of the embrace and looked her in the eye.

"Of course, this is upsetting and wrong," Tom said in a stronger voice, meant to be heard, to convey a normal father's normal reaction to being told his son was being put in foster care.

Sarah nodded.

"But if we cooperate, we'll get Tyler back soon. Because there is not one shred of evidence that we are not fit parents."

She nodded again.

"We'll ask Deputy Weston if we can spend some time with Tyler, and then we will go and get legal help."

"OK," Sarah said, gulping.

"Are you ready?"

Sarah nodded.

Tom stood and walked to the door. He opened it to see that Duke was still impassively on duty in the corridor.

"Can you send Deputy Weston back in?"

Duke nodded.

While Duke was a too familiar and unnerving presence, Tom still had not heard his voice. It was probably high-pitched, Tom thought, and not the low growl that should emanate from such a barrel chest. Of course! That was the completely innocent explanation for why he never spoke.

A few minutes later, after Weston had returned to hear their request, the social worker brought Tyler into the conference room. The boy practically jumped out of the stranger's arms into the embrace of his parents. Though it was likely wishful thinking, the social worker, judging by the set of her eyes, seemed to Tom to be touched by the powerful emotions of child and parents upon being reunited.

"Is there anything you can do to release Tyler to us?" Tom asked. "We're his parents. We'll stay here in Cortez and won't take him out of the county until your investigation is complete."

"I'm sorry. It's not up to me."

Her nametag read "Annie Johnson."

"The Sheriff has found probable cause for an investigation," she explained. "That means we have no choice. We'll do it quickly. We always want to reunite children with their parents as quickly as possible."

"How quickly is that?" Sarah asked bitterly.

"A few days," Annie said. "A week at most. And you can spend some time with him every day until it's complete. *Supervised* time, I should say."

Chapter 29

COLLATERAL DAMAGE

Sarah told Tyler that the social worker, Annie, was a new babysitter.

"I'll see you tomorrow, OK?" she said bravely.

But Tyler struggled in the social worker's arms and screamed.

The moment the door closed, Sarah collapsed in a chair, sobbing. And Tom stood there like a dope, feeling helpless.

"This is something I surely hate to see," a man drawled. "A family ripped apart."

It was Sheriff Bruce, who had entered the conference room.

"Then why are you doing it?" Sarah said.

"I don't see where I'm the one doing it," Bruce said, taking a seat. He studied them for a moment and said, "You've got a helluva lot going on. And I'd say that is an understatement."

"It's a perfect storm," Tom said. "The Cluff murder, then Peter killed by Lionel Cluff. Lionel Cluff shot. In self-defense, of course. And now, these family difficulties."

Bruce studied him for a moment, then turned to Sarah and said, "I wonder, Mrs. Austin, if you might like to visit with your daughter.

I would imagine that you have subjects of some importance to talk over with her."

Sarah seemed hesitant, so Bruce continued.

"She's got a heap of legal difficulties," he said. "Might oughta be her own mother gives her the bad news."

Bruce summoned deputy Weston and instructed him to allow Sarah some time with her daughter. Tom nodded to signal that Sarah should do what the sheriff asked.

"I appreciate your consideration, Sheriff," Tom said after Sarah left.

"Let's just cut the bullcrap," Bruce said sharply.

"What bullcrap is that?"

"It's just you and me now, son. Just the two of us and we can settle things right quick if we both want to."

"I don't know what you mean."

"I said no bullcrap!" And the sheriff slammed his fist on the table. "You didn't just show up in *my county* by accident, did you? Sticking your damn nose where it's not wanted?"

"I came looking for Peter."

Having established that he had a temper, Bruce's demeanor shifted abruptly back to good-ole-boy.

"I've almost got half a mind to believe you. Maybe you are just dumb enough to think that you could send a punk reporter to solve a big murder, and not get himself killed. I reckon you learned your lesson there."

"I shouldn't have let Peter go. But he was just doing his job."

"You figure he found out the identity of Cluff's killer?"

"Lionel Cluff has to be a suspect."

"Lionel and his granddad were very close. I'd say it's more 'n likely that Lionel figured your damn reporter killed his grandad and so he administered some frontier-type justice."

"Not a chance. Peter wouldn't hurt a fly."

"I read that boy's stories in your newspaper. He didn't like Jay Cluff much, did he?"

"There are a lot of people in Telluride who didn't like Jay Cluff."

"Exactly! There are hundreds of potential suspects. Your reporter could have kept himself busy for months looking at all of 'em. So, what did he think he'd get outta coming down here?"

"To learn more about the victim. It's logical."

"Now, why do I find that so hard to believe? Am I just as dumb as a box of rocks?"

Bruce appeared to try another tack: "You know I could charge you in Lionel's death, don't you? I've got half a mind to do it."

"It was self-defense."

"Maybe. But I could charge you with involuntary manslaughter, or some such thing, and you could try and defend yourself. You might even get acquitted, though I'm not sure I'd be wanting to take my chances with a Montezuma County judge and jury if I was you. Not up against the evidence we would put in front of 'em. And now…. *now I've got your son in protective custody.*"

"What exactly do you want from me, Sheriff?"

"It's very simple, Mr. Austin. I want you to get the fuck out of my county and never come back or send any more punk reporters down here. Because if you do, I'll charge you in Lionel Cluff's death and I'll make damn sure you and your beautiful wife won't ever see that little boy of yours again. But if you are reasonable, why, I might let you take Tyler home with you right now, back in his mama's arms in five minutes, before any harm has come to him."

The sheriff's gaze bore down on Tom, who met his look with a with an equally hard stare.

"Well," Bruce said. "What do you say, boy?"

"We have a deal," Tom said.

"And to keep things real clean, I'm even gonna send Miss Angela Walker back up to San Miguel County and let Sheriff Owens deal with her. So, you won't have any cause at all to come back to my county. Not ever. Do we understand each other?"

"Yes, sheriff. I believe we do."

. . .

"We're being followed," Tom said.

Sarah looked back and gasped to see that a Montezuma County sheriff's deputy was tailing them.

"Bruce just let us go so that he could trap us," she cried. "To kill us. To run us off the road and make it look like an accident."

She turned to face him, panicked: "Why are you driving so fucking slowly?"

"If it's a scheme to hurt us and we speed off, it will only help them get away with it. We'd be evading arrest."

"What, then? What are they doing!?"

"He's been following us for a while. And he hasn't made a move. I think it's just the sheriff's way of intimidating us, making sure we know he means business. Escorting us out of his county."

They were nearing the county line.

"Look. He's dropping back."

Sarah fell back against the seat, scarcely relieved.

"I can't take this. For all we know there's a posse of Aryan Patriots up ahead, waiting for us."

"I know."

"If we get home safely, you are going to drop this entire thing. Promise me right now."

Tom didn't answer.

"For my sake, and Tyler's, and Ray's. No matter what Sheriff Bruce is guilty of, no matter what he's done."

"What if he murdered Peter?"

"I don't care. You have to let it go. Sometimes there is no justice. No hope for revenge. You accept that you may never get even, so you take your losses and move on, to survive. So that your family can survive."

"Look. Tyler is awake. We woke him up."

When Sarah turned to look at him, strapped into his car seat in the back seat, the boy started to wail.

"Pull over."

Tom stopped the car so that Sarah could jump out and get in the back seat to comfort Tyler. Then he pulled back onto the highway.

There was nothing more to be said. Not with Tyler awake. Tom listened as Sarah tried to distract him.

"Do you see the big moon?" she asked.

"Where?"

"There."

"Uh huh."

"Everything is OK. We are going home now."

Tom watched the road closely, lightly traveled this late at night, scrutinizing the few vehicles coming toward him or pulling up behind him — their headlights blinding — careful to stay below the speed limit, but anticipating that he might need to speed up and make a dash for his life, and for Sarah's and Tyler's lives. It was hardly unthinkable that the Aryan Patriots had targeted him for elimination. If they got him, the deaths of his family would be collateral damage.

He felt Sarah's tension and her reticence to express it for fear of upsetting Tyler any further.

"It will be OK," Tom said, as they drove through the tiny town of Rico. "We'll be home, safe and sound, in half an hour. Is Tyler sleeping?"

"Yes," she whispered. "Let's not argue and wake him up again. Do you really think we're safe?"

"Yes," he lied, knowing that she knew it was a lie, but glad to hear him say it anyway. And at least they were nearly in San Miguel County, where they would be relatively safe.

"What about Angie?" Tom asked, as they descended Lizard Head.

"We can talk about it tomorrow."

Finally, they pulled into Telluride.

But even their hometown felt forbidding. After all, Jay Cluff was murdered here not two weeks earlier, setting off the chain of events that led after many twists and turns to their long drive home from Cortez.

It was not even three days since Peter had been laid to rest. Since then, Angie had absconded with Tyler. Tom and Sarah had rushed to Cortez to rescue him, they had been threatened with losing him a second time, and Tom had been threatened with prosecution. They had been escorted, menacingly, out of Montezuma County and had driven home in terror.

It was nearly midnight when they got home, where sleep was inescapable and welcome.

Chapter 30

JUNK MAIL

Tom woke up the next morning to the smell of fresh coffee.

"Looks like a storm's coming in," Sarah said when he stepped into the kitchen.

"Too early for snow. It'll be rain."

He could hear the wind outside.

"They say snow," Sarah said.

"Peter was buried just Saturday. It feels like a very long time ago. Everything that's happening makes time go faster, or maybe it's slowed to a crawl. I don't know which it is. Whatever. I can't keep track. How come you always know what day it is?"

"It's so I won't get totally lost, I guess. But I'm numb. I'm in shock. Do you think Sheriff Bruce will leave you alone now?"

"If I don't mess with him. Because if he thought his best move was to hurt me, or to hurt us, he had the perfect opportunity to do it yesterday. He's gambling that the threat to arrest me or take Tyler or do God-knows-what will keep me from digging into Peter's murder. It's a smart move because if he acted on the threats, he would just lose leverage. He wouldn't be able to control what could happen next, what I might do, what I might know, who I might tell, or, if he knocked me off, who would investigate."

"He knows more than he's saying about Peter's murder."

"Definitely. But we still don't know why Lionel killed Peter and how it ties back to the Jay Cluff murder. It could be something between Bruce and Cluff or something within the Cluff family, tied to their conspiracy to do whatever they're trying to do. Take over Montezuma County and get rich off it, I guess. Whatever it was, Peter was getting close to it. But by killing Peter, whoever wanted to shut him up just dug themselves a deeper hole."

"Not if you back off. Who else, besides you, would investigate it?"

"Nobody, unless there are other crimes that the feds or the state are aware of."

"They're not. Nobody but the local sheriff pays any attention to what happens on the range. I've never met an honest cop."

"Well, you were born and raised on the West End."

"Most years there wasn't even a deputy from the Montrose County Sheriff's Office stationed in the West End. And when there was one, he was in somebody's pocket."

"What about Angie?"

"She was real bad yesterday. Nasty. There's nothing I can do to help her."

"Sounds like she was crashing. She must be back on drugs. I'm sorry."

"It's OK. I was willing to give her every chance. But I'm done. Now I want her to stay in jail. Maybe it will straighten her out, and at least I'll know where she's at."

"What are you going to do when she calls?"

"She wouldn't dare!"

"Of course she will. She'll call you from jail to ask for help because she's got nobody else."

"Well, if she does, then I'll think about what to do. Which will probably be nothing. Maybe after she's sentenced, I'll go visit her in prison. Probably not. But who knows? We've got too much other stuff to deal with right now."

"Samantha has got to be worried, the way I left yesterday. Is it OK if I call her?"

"Of course. I've got a batch of soap, ready to cut and wrap, so I can ship it out tomorrow. I'd like to get it done before Tyler wakes up."

"I'll take care of him if does."

How quickly normal life resumes: Sarah was making soap. Tom was listening for Tyler.

He put the call in to Samantha.

"Is everything OK?" she asked, clearly relieved to hear from him.

"I had a family emergency."

There was no point, right then, to tell her that the emergency had sent him back into the bowels of Montezuma County and a second encounter with Sheriff Dan Bruce.

"That has to come first."

"How about the staff meeting?

"I assigned a bunch of stories, some to freelancers, since we're short-staffed. Is that all right?"

"Yeah, sure. Had to be done. Still got a paper to publish."

Or did he?

"I'm sorry to put it all on you."

"No problem. All you've got is the government beats, but if that's too much, I can try to do them myself."

"I can do them in my sleep."

Tyler cried, from the next room.

"That's my son, waking up. I'll try to get in by nine or ten."

An hour later, with Sarah still occupied in her studio, and after Tyler was comforted, fed and distracted by his toy cars, Tom was scanning his email when he saw one that he almost deleted because it was likely junk mail. It had arrived an hour earlier, and was from the Cozy Inn in Cortez, a place he had never stayed.

He opened and read it.

"Dear Mr. Austin," it read. "This email is to confirm your reservation with us for Monday, September 22. If you need to cancel or change your reservation, please respond to this email."

It was signed: Mark Strong, Front Desk Manager.

A motel clerk with the initials M.S.? Mark Strong was clearly a pseudonym for Maria Suarez, but why would Maria bother with such a transparent ploy? Perhaps only to emphasize the need for great care and to indicate that she, Maria, was not really affiliated with the Cozy Inn.

"Dear Mr. Strong," Tom replied to the email. "You have the date of my stay incorrect. I plan to be there this afternoon, Saturday, September 20, checking in at around 2:30 in the afternoon. Can you accommodate that? Best, Tom Austin."

The reply was almost instantaneous.

"Dear Mr. Austin," it read. "Fortunately, we have a room available tonight. I look forward to seeing you mid-afternoon. Sincerely, Mark Strong."

Turning his back on Cortez and Montezuma County, and all that had happened there, was not going to be possible. Tom had vaguely intended to contact Maria as the dust settled, or as needed, but as intense as their brief time together had been, she had exited his life as quickly as she'd entered it. Now she was contacting him, and with a conspicuous degree of caution, which suggested she might be facing danger that was similar to or worse than the threat he had received from the sovereign sheriff. If Bruce didn't want Tom looking into Peter's murder, he sure didn't want Maria doing it either and he might not exercise nearly the same restraint in dealing with her as he had in dealing with Tom.

In any case, Maria obviously wanted to avoid using her cell phone or a personal email account and found a safer way to communicate with Tom, but not so safe that she was willing to put whatever it is she wanted Tom to know into the email. Maria must believe that she was being surveilled and had reason to fear that whatever it is she wanted to discuss with Tom would be of interest to an unfriendly party with hacking skills or police powers.

Chapter 31

WHO KILLED CLUFF?

I have to go back to Cortez."

"Have you lost your fucking mind?!"

And then, after Tom explained that he had to go back because whatever Maria needed from him could not safely be ignored, and it was in Tom's interest and Sarah's interest to know what it was—and because, as they had just discussed, it was entirely possible that nobody else was investigating—Sarah proclaimed that if he was determined to go, then she would travel there with him.

"You can't. We can't leave Tyler with anyone else. Not after what he's been through. And it's far too risky to take him with us. If we got stopped, they could take him away from us again. And we might not get him back this time."

They sat silent for a moment.

"What are you thinking?"

"I'm terrified. Something could happen to you if you go back down there. And then what would I do?"

"I know," he said, taking her hand. "But if I borrow a car that the Montezuma sheriff won't identify with me, and if I don't speed or run any red lights, and if I'm very discreet, and I slip down there to meet with Maria and then turn right around and come home, probably nothing will happen."

"Probably?"

"But if I don't do it, there could be a bigger risk."

"What?"

"Maybe she's learned that we're in danger here in Telluride."

"Oh, my God!"

"She wouldn't have emailed the way she did if it wasn't important."

"How do you know you can trust *her*? Maybe it's a trap. Maybe it's not even her. Maybe it's Sheriff Bruce pretending to be her."

"He just kicked us out of his county. Why would he want me back?

"Who knows?" she said, her voice full of despair. "He changed his mind!"

"We are struggling to understand what's a real threat and what's paranoia," Tom said. "And what's the safest way out."

Sarah's eyes brimmed with tears.

"I don't understand what's happening," she said. "Everything is falling apart. Nothing makes any sense. What did we do to cause all of this?"

"Nothing. There was a murder in Bear Creek. We had nothing to do with that. Angie showed up. We had nothing to do with that. The economy tanked. We definitely had nothing to do with that. Well, not much anyway. Then Peter went to Cortez. I guess I can't shirk responsibility for that one."

"You couldn't have known what would happen to him."

"I should have known it might be dangerous."

"You are the only thing in this world that I trust," Sarah said. "If you leave me here with Tyler, then you have to promise me that you will come back safely. Because if you don't, then I don't have any idea what I'll do."

"I promise. I will go down there, meet with Maria, and turn right around and be back home before dark."

⁘ ⁘ ⁘

Never mind that it was September, it was snowing hard on Lizard Head Pass, slowing Tom's progress. By the time he crossed the Montezuma County line at around three, the snow had let up. But Tom slowed down even more, mindful that a Montezuma County sheriff's deputy could be far more treacherous than any icy mountain road.

Arriving at the Cozy Inn, Tom encountered a young man, at the check-in, where he half-expected Maria to be sitting. When Tom identified himself, the man, who appeared to be Native American, handed him an envelope without uttering a word.

Tom opened the envelope when he was back in his car.

"Ute Mountain Casino," he read. "Go inside and I'll find you."

Presumably the desk clerk would let Maria know that Tom was on his way.

⁘ ⁘ ⁘

The Ute Mountain Casino was small, but it boasted a hotel and several restaurants in addition to the gaming floor itself. Tom didn't have time to orient himself because a uniformed casino security guard approached him before he was more than ten feet inside and said, "Mr. Austin? This way."

The guard led him to a small private dining room in Kuchu's restaurant. Maria was waiting there.

"This is my cousin, Clay," she said, introducing the guard. "He's helping me out."

"Pleasure to meet you," Clay said, extending a hand. "Maria's told me everything that's going on."

"Good to know," Tom said. "We need all the help we can get."

"It's good to see you," Tom said to Maria.

But she had no time for small talk.

"I told you I'd keep trying to put all the pieces together," she said. "To try to figure shit out. We still don't know who killed Jay Cluff, or why. If it was Lionel or Sheriff Bruce, why did they do it? Something is not adding up. And they definitely killed Peter, so maybe they did kill Cluff and Peter figured out why. But that first piece is still missing. Who killed Cluff? If we knew that, we'd know everything.

"It seems like Bruce is at the center of it. And if Bruce was working for Jay Cluff, and Cluff was at the center of some big conspiracy, well, somebody offed Cluff, right? So, there must have been someone or something bigger than him or someone who wanted to take his place."

"Connie Cluff?" Tom offered.

"Maybe, plus Peter met with her and maybe he said the wrong thing, but…."

"But?"

"First off, didn't we already figure that she didn't really want Peter dead? But maybe we were wrong and if it was Connie, did she kill her father? And if she did, why? You figured Peter's big story was that the Montezuma sheriff is a white supremacist. But it's not like Bruce ever made a secret out of that. He fuckin' ran for office on it. Hell, he'd be proud if you put a story like that in your paper. And it's no surprise that he was helping Jay Cluff sell cheap land on Hay

Camp Mesa to armed rednecks, cause that sure as shit ain't a scandal, not around here."

"Not around here maybe. But it would be a huge scandal way beyond southwestern Colorado. Selling real estate 'exclusively to White Christian patriots' is a federal crime. If Peter reported it, the U.S. Department of Justice would be breathing down their necks."

"Guess that shows how much I know. But maybe it explains what happened next."

"What?"

"I'm getting there."

Chapter 32

DENNY LAKE PARK

Maria had killed a man. Now she knew what it felt like. She didn't feel guilty or sorry. She was proud that she had reacted instinctively when Lionel lunged for a weapon. She was proud that she got him with one shot. She didn't feel bad for Lionel, either. He was scum and had it coming. Only now he couldn't be questioned about who ordered him to make the hit on the Telluride reporter, and that was a bummer. Maria would have demonstrated superior skills as a detective if she'd managed to keep Lionel Cluff alive long enough for him to spill his guts. Because he was weak and tied to a chair with her gun pointed at his temple he would have broken fast.

But where would that have led? Even if Lionel confessed, what would she have done then? She couldn't let him go or execute him on the spot so she still would have had to turn him over to Sheriff Bruce. And how would that have worked out? Not well, because Bruce and the Cluff family were probably all in on murdering Peter. If Lionel had been turned over to the sheriff, what could Bruce have done then? Even if Lionel agreed to take the fall on a murder charge—which was doubtful—they would have had to come up with a fucking amazing story about why he killed Peter on his own.

Maybe Bruce was thankful to Maria for wasting Lionel. Maybe the sheriff would recognize Maria's police skills and hire her back, bringing her inside the conspiracy to help with the coverup. She might even consider taking the job, because that felt like a much better place to be than where she found herself, lying in bed two days after she'd shot Lionel, depressed, out of work and about to fall further behind on her rent. Even if Tom remembered to pay her the $150 a day plus expenses he'd promised, she had only worked for him for 24 hours.

In that single day Maria had been fired, and then hired for her first private eye gig; she shot Lionel, was interrogated by the police, and had been released. Now she was working all the crazy angles, which had her head spinning like she was trapped in the Fun House at the Montezuma County Fair.

Then, as if she finally arrived in front of a mirror whose special effect was to place the viewer's enlarged torso at the bullseye of a target, she saw the unavoidable truth.

They're going to kill me, she thought. "It's all they've got. They only let me go so they could pick me off later when things quieted down.

Then she talked herself back down.

It's too late for that," she reasoned. Too many people know something's up. Any more corpses and they'll be writing their own ticket to a life sentence.

But they could disappear me," she thought. Except I'm not invisible anymore. I'm famous.

Her name and picture had been on the front page of the Cortez newspaper.

CLUFF GRANDSON SHOT

Missing Telluride Reporter Also Found Dead

By Philip Dray
Cortez Sun Staff Reporter

Cortez, September 12, 2008—Montezuma County resident Lionel Cluff was fatally shot on Saturday afternoon at the Hay Camp Mesa Ranch subdivision northeast of Cortez.

Cluff was shot by licensed private investigator Maria Sanchez of Cortez, according to Montezuma County Sheriff Dan Bruce. Sanchez had been retained by Tom Austin, publisher-editor of the San Miguel Examiner, to help him find a missing reporter, Peter Barnard.

According to the sheriff, Sanchez and Austin interrupted Cluff while he was apparently attempting to dispose of Barnard's body. Barnard was in Cortez to report the circumstances surrounding the August 13th murder of Cluff's grandfather, Jay Cluff, who was shot by a sniper in the mountains just outside of Telluride in San Miguel County. There have been no arrests in that case.

"Of course, these three deaths must be tied together somehow," Sheriff Bruce told the Cortez Sun. "We don't understand exactly how yet, but we're working with the San Miguel County Sheriff to figure it all out."

No charges against Sanchez are planned "at this time," Bruce said, since it appeared she had shot Cluff in self-defense, possibly saving not only her own life, but Austin's life as well.

"It was self-defense," Sanchez said in an interview. "We found him trying to dispose of a body, the missing person I was hired to find. He was going for a gun, so I shot him."

The young Cortez reporter, Dray, had asked Maria if she knew why Lionel Cluff shot Peter.

"I've got theories," Maria said.

"Barnard must have found something out."

"Yeah, but what?"

"I dunno. That Lionel Cluff killed his granddad."

"Maybe."

"Are you saying there are other suspects?"

"Well, sure there are."

"Are you planning to investigate?"

"Are you?"

"No way," the reporter said. "After what happened to Barnard? I'm happy to leave that to the sheriff."

Dray had no awareness that the sheriff might be one of those other suspects, and Maria wasn't about to tell him. She was happy to see when she read Dray's story, that he used only the one quote, about how she shot Lionel in self-defense. Maybe she'd be rewarded for saving a client's life with interest from other people who needed protection.

Her phone rang, but it was her mother.

"What are you doing in the newspaper?" she clucked. "When the prairie dog sticks her head up out of the hole, that's when she gets shot."

In the first few days after she shot Lionel, Maria had tried to reach Nizhoni Yazzie, a high school classmate who she worked with at the Montezuma County Sheriff's Office, and who still worked there.

But Nizhoni didn't answer or return her calls.

She thought someone might be following her, was kicking herself for talking to the newspaper, and was afraid to go back to her apartment, so she drove to a cheap motel and parked behind it.

"I'll clean rooms for a bed and an allowance to cover gas and food."

The owner looked up at her and then down at the newspaper sitting next to him, her mug plastered on it. She was on the lam and would be cheap and he could use a break from doing the housekeeping himself.

"Five bucks a room."

"Can you make it seven?

"Six."

"OK."

He handed her a master key.

"Housekeeping closet is down that hallway on the left. You'll find a uniform in there you can put on. You can spend the night in any empty room. Unless we're sold out. Then you got the floor of the closet. But we ain't never sold out."

A few hours later, with cash in her pocket, she walked to a convenience store, bought a can of Vienna sausages and beans, and then back to the motel.

There was a text on her phone from an unknown number: "Denny. 10 p.m."

It could be someone fishing, the text a fishing fly expertly cast into a riffle just upstream from the deep pool where Maria was hiding. The fly would be carried down to where the trout would be unable to resist rising to the bait and would be hooked.

Or it could be Nizhoni.

A couple of hours later, Maria drove to the City Market gas station, put $5 in her tank, and promptly burned some of that precious fuel by driving in circles, her eye on the rear-view mirror to try to spot anyone who might be tailing her. She made her way to the far end of town, parking on a quiet residential street a few blocks from Denny Lake Park.

She slipped down back alleys and across undeveloped scrub to enter the park at the opposite corner from the park entrance off the highway. Denny was known as a spot for late-night hookups, where high school kids escaped the prying eyes of strict Bible-thumping parents and cheating husbands met up with their girlfriends or got their rocks off with a cheap hooker. Cortez cops had to know about the illicit activity but looked the other way, probably so it would be there when they wanted to take advantage of it themselves.

Denny Lake Park, in other words, was a safe place to commit a crime. Or, Maria hoped, it was a place where Nizhoni could meet secretly with her.

It was just after ten.

Maria stayed beneath the trees at the edge of the parking lot, across from the lake, scanning the lake shore. She saw a light flash, in an apparent pattern, two long flashes followed by a short one. She flashed her own phone back, in the same pattern.

Like fireflies searching for a mate, the two sources of synchronous flashes moved closer to each other, then both went dark as Maria and Nizhoni moved to an embrace. An observer would have assumed they were just another pair of secret lovers and would leave them alone.

Nizhoni gestured to indicate they should move to deeper shadows in a nearby grove of cottonwoods.

They were alone but whispered, nonetheless.

"Girl, you are making all kinds of trouble," Nizhoni said.

"It found me."

"Nah."

"You're right," Maria said. "I walked into it."

"This shit is way worse than you know."

"Why did Lionel kill Peter?

"Bruce told him to."

"Do you know why?"

She slipped something into Maria's hand. An old iPod.

"You keep me outta this sister. I'm in too deep already."

And then she slipped away into the chilly dark night, as if lingering a moment longer than necessary could be the fatal mistake.

Chapter 33

SOMEONE BIGGER

But that was not the fatal mistake. It was something else.

Maria had taken care to make sure she wasn't tailed on her way to meet Nizhoni, but she was tailed returning home, which meant that a sheriff's deputy had found her parked car. She should have hidden it more carefully, or she should have made her way to Denny Lake Park on foot. Or it could be that a GPS device had been put on the car and Maria was tracked to where she parked, and possibly from there was followed on foot to the lake. She had likely been observed meeting with Nizhoni.

Whoever was tailing her now made no effort to lay low. He wanted her to know she was caught. He watched her get out of the car and unlock the door to her motel room. He parked so that his headlights shone brightly in her window. This might have been for intimidation. To scare her into leaving town. Or to trap her inside while he determined what to do with her, called for backup, or whatever.

"Or he was just a dumbass," Maria told Tom. "He should have just killed me right then and there. Because I am out the back window faster than a jack rabbit. Go to a friend's house and get a ride here, to the rez to hide out at my mother's house. But I'm not even sure that's safe, so I walk to an old shepherd's shack a mile or so away, off-road."

"You didn't listen to the iPod?" Tom said.

"It doesn't work. Maybe it's outta juice and I can't charge it cause I'm off the grid."

"You're fucking burying the lede!"

"Huh?"

"Newspaper talk. You must have listened to it by now, right?"

Maria ignored him in favor of sticking to the story as it played out.

"Next morning, I find Clay and tell him everything. Tell him I'm worried about Nizhoni."

"I make a few phone calls and find out she's dead," Clay said.

"Holy shit!"

"They say an overdose. Opioids."

"But we know they killed her," Maria said. "They would have done the same thing to me if they got me."

Clay retrieved an iPod from his pocket, put it at the center of the table where they were sitting, attached it to a portable speaker, and touched the play button.

"Hello, Dan, I've got a problem I need you to take care of for me."

The voice was unmistakable, and deeply familiar.

"What's that?" Sheriff Dan Bruce replied.

"There's a punk newspaper reporter headed your way, sticking his nose where it doesn't belong."

"Is that right?"

"Works for the paper up here in Telluride. His name is Peter Barnard. He needs to get lost, permanently, and fast. He'll be in your county this afternoon. He'll be obvious about it. He'll be asking questions about Jay. Let Connie know."

"I'll take care of it."

The call ended abruptly.

Observing Tom's stricken expression, Maria asked: "Who is she?"

"Her name is Erica Ortiz."

Tom's silent business partner had ordered the hit on his star reporter. And within hours of doing that, Erica had canceled her advertising with the newspaper she effectively controlled.

The Examiner, not just its reporter, was the conspirator's target.

Erica hadn't canceled the advertising because of the financial crisis. That was a convenient pretext for doing it. Erica's abruptness when she told Tom she was pulling her ads had been out of character. Knowing Erica, Tom would have expected her, even given the dire economic circumstances, to discuss alternatives to closing the paper immediately. She had been harsh with Tom not because she was stressed out about the economy. She was stressed out because The Examiner was closing in on a story that was dangerous to her, something that threatened her far more than the tanking real estate market: she was a partner with Jay Cluff in developing a white supremacist compound in Montezuma County. Upon publication, Peter's story would make her the target of a federal lawsuit and a "person of interest" in Cluff's murder. The notoriety would be devastating to her Telluride cred, both in her business and her social life.

Peter almost certainly asked her about ties to Cluff. Just as Tom couldn't know what specific questions Peter put to Erica, Erica couldn't know how fully Peter had informed Tom about whatever it was he was asking about. Not knowing, she moved quickly to eliminate Peter—and the paper, for good measure—hoping that Tom knew nothing about it. If he did, she likely would have learned about it by now, one way or another, meaning that her gamble almost paid off.

"You think she could have killed Cluff, too?" Maria asked. "Or had someone do it for her? Like Bruce?"

"She was obviously capable of it."

"Why would she?"

"There could be a lot of reasons. And they're the sort of things Peter could have found out if he had the time to keep digging."

How far might the conspiracy go?

Tom's thoughts were racing. If Erica and Cluff were partners on Hay Camp Mesa--and who knew where else?--then why not in Bear Creek?

He struggled to contain a flash flood of emotion.

"What?" Maria asked.

"Peter couldn't tell me that he was investigating my biggest advertiser, that he'd found ties connecting Cluff and Erica. He might have had reason to suspect her of being involved in the Cluff murder. He knew I was compromised and wasn't sure I would act with integrity. He couldn't trust me. He was defending the paper by taking me off the story, because I had a clear conflict of interest. He might have even thought I was complicit."

And maybe, Tom thought, he *was* complicit, getting fat off real estate advertising. Because Erica owned him.

Chapter 34

LIVE AT THE SPEED OF LIGHT

Thank God, you're alive," Samantha said when Tom reached her using a burner phone Clay gave him—a necessary precaution in case Tom's phone was being traced. "I've been trying to reach you."

"I'm sorry."

"I called Sarah. She's frantic. You have to call her, right now, then call me back."

"OK."

But Samantha kept talking, quickly, to telegraph information and speed Tom on his way to the more pressing duty of letting his wife know he was alive.

"I got the password to Peter's computer," Samantha said. "His girlfriend's name spelled backwards. I should have guessed it sooner."

"And?"

"I'm just reading his notes now, but Jay Cluff had a secret business partner, here in Telluride."

"Erica Ortiz."

"How did you know?"

"I just learned it myself. From Maria. I'm in Cortez."

"Peter interviewed Erica just before he went down to Cortez."

"He did?"

"You have to call Sarah right now, and then call me back."

And then she hung up on him, before he could tell her that he had hard evidence that Erica had Peter killed.

"Who's this?" Sarah said, when she answered the phone on the first ring.

"It's me."

"Thank God," she said. "I was sure some stranger was about to tell me you were dead."

Of course, she thought that. The call was from an unknown Cortez phone number.

"I'm OK. I'm safe."

She was sobbing.

"Everything will be OK now. Erica killed Peter. Now that we've got her, we'll be safe."

But she was struggling both to breathe and to comprehend what Tom was saying.

"Erica killed Peter?" she asked.

"Yes."

"She'll come after us next!"

"No. She won't. We're safe."

He told her everything, taking the time to console her.

""I'm OK and you're OK now," he said after they had been talking for an hour.

"Now you have to let me go so I can finish this thing off and come back home sooner."

* * *

The path out was blindingly obvious. The Examiner wasn't dead yet. And Tom was still a reporter at heart. Reporters report. It's what they do, just as soon as they've got enough to go with. And between them, he and Samantha, with Peter's help from beyond the grave—three diligent reporters—had enough.

Tom worked from the safety of a hotel room at the Ute Mountain Casino and Samantha from The Examiner office.

It required Samantha to do some additional online research, but they had it done by late the next day.

LOCAL BROKER ERICA ORTIZ ORDERED HIT ON REPORTER PETER BARNARD

Barnard Was Investigating Ties to Jay Cluff

(Posted at 9 a.m., Wednesday, September 24, 2008)

By Tom Austin, Peter Barnard,
and Samantha Stolley

Local businessman Erica Ortiz, owner of Telluride Premiere Properties, asked Montezuma County Sheriff Dan Bruce in a phone call on September 11 to "take care of a problem" for him by making Examiner reporter Peter Barnard "get lost, permanently, and fast."

He's "sticking his nose where it doesn't belong," Ortiz added. "He'll be obvious about it. He'll be asking questions about Jay."

"I'll take care of it," Bruce assured Ortiz.

The phone call, which lasted less than 30 seconds, was recorded by Nizhoni Yazzie, an employee of the Montezuma County Sheriff's Department. (Click here to listen to the full recording.) Yazzie died on Tuesday of an opioid overdose, according to the Montezuma County Sheriff. Just two hours prior to her reported time of death, Yazzie secretly gave the incriminating recording to an Examiner source.

Notes and documents found on Barnard's computer reveal that Barnard had uncovered a business relationship between Ortiz and developer Jay Cluff, who was murdered in Bear Creek on September 8, and had asked Ortiz about it in an interview on September 10.

There has been no arrest in the Cluff murder.

Barnard's associates lost contact with him late on the afternoon of September 11, the day after he interviewed Ortiz. His body was found by Examiner publisher and editor Tom Austin two days later, on September 13, outside Cortez, at the Hay Camp Mesa Ranch subdivision in rural Montezuma County. Austin had gone to Cortez to find Barnard, where he retained a private investigator. He and the investigator, Maria Sanchez, interrupted Lionel Cluff, a grandson of Jay Cluff, while he was apparently in the act of disposing of Barnard's body. Sanchez shot and killed Lionel Cluff as Cluff lunged for a weapon to turn on her and Austin.

[The Examiner has notified the Colorado Bureau of Investigation that it is holding Barnard's computer and the iPod it received from Yazzie in a secure location and will hand the evidence over to state or federal authorities upon request.]

In addition to the notes documenting his interview with Ortiz, Barnard also downloaded public legal documents to his computer, including a 2003 Partnership Agreement between Ortiz and Cluff and a related Montana property deed.

"This is not news," Ortiz told Barnard, according to Barnard's notes. "It's a private business matter. I'd respectfully request that you refrain from publishing it. I don't know why you would even bother Tom with it. I hope you haven't. I'm sure you can understand why."

Tom Austin is the publisher of The Examiner. Ortiz has been a major advertiser at The Examiner. In addition, Ortiz holds a 51 percent controlling interest in the newspaper, while Austin holds the remaining 49 percent. While there are contractual prohibitions against revealing Ortiz's interest, the publisher has determined that the conflict of interest presented in reporting this story requires the disclosure and the risk of any legal exposure in making it. The Examiner's operating agreement stipulates that the publisher, while holding a minority share of the business, has management autonomy in all matters except a potential sale of the business.

Barnard does not quote himself in his notes, so it is impossible to know how he responded to Ortiz's request.

However, he made no mention of the interview to Austin or any other employee at The Examiner. Nor did he disclose what he had learned about the Ortiz-Cluff business association. Instead, he sought and got approval to look deeper into the murder of Jay Cluff by traveling to Cortez.

After losing contact with Barnard on September 11, the two reporters bylined on this story (along with Barnard), Tom Austin and Samantha Stolley, set out to find the missing reporter in Montezuma County, Austin by going to Cortez and Stolley by conducting internet research. In the course of their investigation, they learned that Cluff also had a business relationship with Montezuma County Sheriff Dan Bruce. While the exact nature of the relationship is unclear, the sheriff endorses sales of property at the Hay Camp Mesa Ranch subdivision on a hidden page on the Cluff Properties website.

There are no links to the page, which can be accessed only by someone who has been given the link. (Click here to view the page.) On that page, the subdivision is described as "a highly secure location that will be sold exclusively to White Christian American Patriots" and as being located in a county "overseen by sovereign Sheriff Dan Bruce."

Bruce made no secret of his extreme political and law enforcement philosophy when he ran for Montezuma County Sheriff last year. His priorities, he told voters, would be to defend Second Amendment gun rights, to refuse to recognize the authority of federal land management officials, and to arrest any illegal immigrant. He described himself as "a foot soldier in the Sagebrush Rebellion" and a proponent of the "sovereign county" doctrine; and explained that in his view county sheriffs are the highest authorities in the United States permitted by the Constitution.

Several members of the Cluff family, including Jay Cluff and Lionel Cluff, donated the maximum amounts allowable under state law to Bruce's campaign.

The Hay Camp Mesa Ranch subdivision, consisting of 42 lots ranging in size from one acre to five acres, was approved by Montezuma County in February 2007 and was developed by Cluff Properties. Public records reveal that at least nine parcels in the subdivision were sold by Jay Cluff in June and July. Of the nine buyers, seven reported principal addresses in Searcy County, Arkansas.

Two additional sales this summer were brokered by Ortiz. Although it is clear from the recording of her phone conversation with Bruce that she is on a first-name basis with both the sheriff and Cluff, it is unclear at this point whether Ortiz is more deeply involved with Hay Camp Mesa Ranch.

A federal investigation in 2006 resulted in the arrests of six Searcy County residents on charges ranging from arson and human trafficking to weapons violations and murder. All of the arrested persons were identified in indictments as members of a secretive organization called the Aryan Patriots.

Of the nine persons from Arkansas who purchased property from Cluff Properties on Hay Camp Mesa, at least three were subsequently hired as deputies by Montezuma County Sheriff Dan Bruce.

Bruce did not return phone calls requesting an interview. A deputy returned the call to state that "there is no information about the investigation into the killings of Peter Barnard or Lionel Cluff that can be reported publicly at this time."

Asked if there were any breaks in the investigation of the murder of Jay Cluff, San Miguel County Sheriff Bill Owens said, "you can count on me to notify you if there is a break that I can make public."

. . .

"Did you see your email?" Tom asked Erica, when he reached her by phone, shortly after he and Samantha had finished writing the story.

"Yes," she said, her voice as measured as if he was asking her if she'd like another glass of wine.

"And you read the story I attached?"

"Yes."

"Do you have any comment before I publish it?"

"Off the record?"

"Sure."

"Fuck you," she said mock-thoughtfully. "But I guess it's my own fault. You've got nothing to lose, you fucking loser."

After a pause, Ortiz continued, "On the record?"

"Sure."

"No comment."

She hung up.

"Add a sentence at the end," he told Samantha. "'Reached by telephone, Erica Ortiz had no comment when asked about her business dealings with Jay Cluff and Sheriff Dan Bruce.' Then publish it."

"Done," Samantha said, and the story went live at the speed of light.

Chapter 35

META

Telluride was stunned by the news.

The region's biggest real estate broker was a criminal mastermind and most likely a far right-wing conspiracist, to boot. Not that it came as a total surprise.

Nefarious machinations by capital were in the town's DNA.

Of course, readers assumed that Peter's alleged killer, Ortiz, would soon be proven to have been behind the killing of Jay Cluff, too. The motive would be more greed, the greedheads turning on each other.

This was the first Examiner story to go viral, just as Peter, only a few weeks before, had predicted it would be, first spread on social media, then picked up by the Denver newspapers and, quickly, the national media. A battalion of reporters descended on the town, each of them working to ingratiate themselves with the local paper, its editor, Tom, and the living bylined co-reporter on the story, Samantha, forcing Tom and Samantha to lock themselves in Tom's office, where they watched the hits to the paper's website pile up.

The story had been viewed over 600,000 times in the first 24 hours it was online.

"Remind me. How exactly does this turn into dollars?" Tom asked.

"If people click on the ads, in theory we can increase our price for online advertising," Samantha explained. "Because we're delivering more eyeballs."

"But why would they click on ads? Just because they want to read our coverage of the Cluff killing and all the rest of it, that doesn't mean they'll click on a restaurant ad, or a real estate ad. Or even if they do, the broker who placed the ad wouldn't think it did him any good so that they would suddenly agree to pay us more for future ads."

"True," Samantha allowed. "Plus, the ad they are most likely to click is one of Erica's. Out of curiosity. And her ads are online because they weren't set to expire yet, so we haven't pulled them down. And I suspect she won't be happy to advertise with us in the future just because we can show that her online ad with us got a zillion clicks this week. Even if she makes a sale off it."

"Should we pull her ads down?"

"No way! They make the story about Erica's alleged crime seem way more real and incredible, unbelievable, amazing, which keeps it going more and more viral. The ads are context for our story that no other website can duplicate. You're reading a story about Erica killing our reporter, with his byline on it, right next to an ad with Erica's picture in it. It's so *meta*."

Samantha's tone was wondrous, as if she was only just realizing that as an online editor she had seized the ultimate prize of meta, whatever that was.

"Meta?"

"It means everything wrapped up in one thing. Its own complete virtual reality. Or self-awareness. It's a kind of irony, I guess. Something that refers to itself. It's what everyone online wants."

Tom rolled his eyes.

"OK, so you can't bank it," Samantha said. "But we can juice our revenue by putting up some national ads. With these numbers, they'll get some clicks. It didn't occur to me until right now, with everything going on, but it would probably bring in a little cash."

"Hell yes, do it," Tom said. "We might as well get something besides glory for all we've been through."

"Sure, but we're still dead. I mean, how do we follow up this meta story? Our coverage of tonight's school board meeting won't suddenly get views because Jay Cluff and Peter were murdered here, and we were all meta about it. Or that people will read about our sensational murders and then read my story about Elsa's Melting Pot, and suddenly Graham will have lines out the door and he'll be able to pay his advertising bills."

"He's profiting some right now, with all the reporters in town. They're a hungry bunch. But they'll be gone in a day or two, on to the next kid stuck down a well somewhere."

"Yep."

"We are Wile E. Coyote."

"Who?"

"You play the meta card, I counter with Wile E. Coyote. He was a character in the old Roadrunner cartoons. You remember them?"

She shook her head.

"Of course not. Are you too young or am I too old?"

"Both."

"Wile E. Coyote is always chasing the Roadrunner, and the Road-runner is always leading him over a cliff. Because the Roadrunner can fly. The coyote's legs are pumping so hard that he hangs in mid-air until he realizes where he is and looks down and stops pumping his legs. Then he drops like a stone."

"Don't look down."

"Exactly."

Tom looked past her at the wall of shelved volumes of archived newspapers. These printed and bound artifacts were meta in their own way—fully complete, referring back to themselves, adding up to an entire world—but as deep and impenetrable to him as a planet orbiting a star in the distant Milky Way.

"But maybe Hollywood will buy the story," he said. "Because, you know, it's so"—he shrugged—"'meta,' or something."

Chapter 36

A TANGLED WEB

The CBI had come to take possession of both Peter's computer and Nizhoni's iPod the afternoon the story was published, yet two days later there were still no arrests, leaving Tom, Samantha, Sarah, the visiting press, and pretty much the entire town of Telluride suspended in mid-air, legs pumping.

Then Tom received a visitor in his office, a law officer who flashed his badge to get past the crowd of reporters and in the Examiner door. It was his old buddy, Montezuma County Sheriff's Deputy Ross Weston, but the badge he now carried was that of an FBI agent.

"We're making the arrests now," Weston said, after explaining that he had been working undercover in Sheriff Bruce's department, having previously infiltrated the Aryan Patriots in Arkansas. "Press conference later this afternoon over at the courthouse. But I got permission to give you the inside track. You forced our hand, of course. And my undercover days are over, thanks to you."

"Do you blame me?"

"Not at all. I'm grateful to you. I mean it. Thank you. I'm happy my cover has been blown and I got out of it alive. And it's ending with a bang. With a bunch of solid arrests."

"How many?"

"An even dozen, including Ortiz, Bruce, Connie Cluff, your old buddy Duke, and another eight deputies and sheriff's office employees."

"You're welcome, I guess. But I'd trade them all for Peter if I had the choice."

"You presented me with real challenges, but you moved things along. I was quietly doing my undercover work, then you sent the kid reporter down and he walked right into the trap your friend Ortiz set for him.

"You're thinking Ortiz encouraged him to hit Cortez?"

"Just a hunch."

"Did you let them kill Peter because he interfered with your investigation?"

"I can understand why you would say that."

But he didn't get defensive. He changed the subject.

"When your stepdaughter and son turned up, that's what really blew things up. Because Bruce was so paranoid by then, he was sure it was a plot. He couldn't say what the plot was, exactly, maybe an FBI plot, or a loyalty test coming from Aryan Patriot headquarters, but he was determined to turn it to his advantage."

"I was thinking the same thing. That it was a plot. How else could I have ended up back there? I was sure that Bruce had gotten to Angie somehow, and she was part of the conspiracy. She was running drugs for him, like Lionel. Or she was in the Patriots."

"I did what I could to protect you."

"Oh, yeah?"

"I convinced Bruce to let you take your son home. Told him if he didn't, and if he made any kind of move against you, he'd just invite more scrutiny. Because you're a person of prominence. Told him to bide his time. Let things quiet down."

"I owe you, then."

"No more than I owe you. We're even. We both found ourselves inside a nasty conspiracy and we both did what we had to do."

"We both failed Peter."

"Undercover work is inherently dangerous. Obviously, reporting can be, too. It's the Bureau's policy to intervene if a civilian's life, or an agent's life, is at risk. We're good, but we're not perfect, and I wasn't informed about the plan to kill Peter. Bruce kept all the soldiers, the underlings, assigned to different tasks, and he assumed his phones were bugged, and that there could be an undercover agent inside his office. Because that's what happened in Arkansas. Never suspected me, of course, at least no more than he suspected everyone else, not that I know of.

"Bruce's mistake was thinking that Nizhoni was totally under his thumb. He was fucking her. Or let's just call it rape. Maybe he got emotionally caught up and let down his guard with her. Who knows? Anyway, she recorded the conversation he had with Ortiz out of the office. He probably took the call on a burner phone when he was at her place, someplace we didn't have bugged."

"Then he had her killed?"

"Duke made him. After they caught her meeting with Maria Sanchez. You remember Duke?"

"The goon at the sheriff's office."

"Right. The Patriots put an 'enforcer' inside every cell. The enforcer's job is to be the national organization's eyes and ears, make sure there aren't any cucks on the inside. Bruce was the cell leader, but Duke didn't report to Bruce. He reported directly to national. The idea is that Bruce and Duke were supposed to keep each other honest.

"And it worked just the way it was supposed to work. Nizhoni betrayed them and even if Bruce might have wanted to spare her, Duke wouldn't let him. He made Bruce kill her himself, to prove his loyalty. It's all in Bruce's confession. Duke was standing there watching Bruce force feed his lover a half-dozen pills. And Bruce says to her *while he's killing her*, 'You know I love you, Nizhoni.'

"What they didn't know is that she'd taped him on the phone with Erica and slipped it to Maria. Neither did we. Not until you published it."

"Oh, what a tangled web we weave, when first we practice to deceive," Tom said.

"People think that's Shakespeare, but it was really Sir Walter Scott," Weston said. "I was an English Lit major at Yale."

"Is that a typical education for an FBI agent working undercover?"

"It doesn't hurt to have a feel for devious characters and complicated plots. This one's totally Shakespearean. White supremacist group takes over a rural county sheriff's office. The 'high' sheriff's power goes to his head. He and his fellow conspiracists, who recruited him and put him in office, start fighting over the spoils and somehow one of them is killed off. A newspaper reporter starts poking around and the conspiracists figure they can just kill him, make him disappear, because he made the mistake of setting foot in their county. But they get sloppy and hand the job to an incompetent who doesn't quite finish it by disposing of the body like he was supposed to. The body is found, by you, so they can't say the reporter just vanished, like they planned. So the whole shebang starts to unravel. Before we can make a move, the dead reporter's boss is handed an incriminating recording and blows the thing wide open. They kill Nizhoni. With corpses piling up, the FBI busts the operation."

"It's good, but there's a hole in your plot."

"What's that?"

"Who killed Jay Cluff, and why?"

"We'll figure it out. Once they are all indicted and have separate lawyers and are being questioned. They're a bag of ferrets. They'll turn on each other and start cooperating, ratting each other out, hoping to get lighter sentences."

"One more question?"

"Sure."

"Is Erica Ortiz an Aryan Patriot?"

"Hell, yes. They needed a banker, right?"

"How long have you known?'

"We've had an eye on her for months."

"Damn, she had a great cover."

"The best," Weston agreed. "Hanging with the rich Telluride libtards."

That was true as far as it went, but Tom was thinking of a different cover.

"Did you know she was my silent partner the first time you questioned me?"

"Nope," Weston said. "We only learned that reading your newspaper."

Chapter 37

'BIZARRE, MACABRE'

There were too many reporters to fit them all inside, so the arrests were announced at a press conference on the front steps of the historic San Miguel County Courthouse. The federal prosecutor for the District of Colorado was joined by CBI and FBI investigators, including Weston.

Telluride real estate broker Erica Ortiz and Montezuma County Sheriff Dan Bruce had both been arrested, the prosecutor announced, along with ten other Montezuma County residents, on various charges including public corruption, drug trafficking, and the murders of Peter Barnard and Nizhoni Yazzie. The indictment charged that Peter Barnard was killed by Lionel Cluff at the direction of Bruce, Ortiz, and his aunt Connie Cluff.

"We expect to make additional arrests, and to bring additional charges against those already in custody, in coming weeks and months," the prosecutor said. "We moved to arrest the individuals who were arrested today before our investigation was complete, because we had to put a stop to the illegal activity, which had escalated to include these two murders. And which, unfortunately, we were unable to prevent."

With the visiting press fixated on the podium, Tom approached Sheriff Owens at the edge of the crowd.

"It's their show now," Owens said, nodding toward courthouse steps.

"They're not saying anything about Jay Cluff."

"It's still under investigation."

"How is that even possible?"

Owens sighed.

"This is on background. You didn't hear it from me. OK?"

"OK."

"I'm told that Bruce confessed quickly after he was arrested. They had plenty of evidence to nail him on the Barnard and Yazzie murders, and on a bunch of other crimes. But he swore up and down that he had no idea at all who killed Jay Cluff. And I've got to say, there are things about the Cluff murder that are inconsistent. Bizarre, even. Macabre."

"Bizarre? Macabre? What's that?"

"I can't tell you.

"It's funny how things turn out," Owens added. "If nobody had killed Jay Cluff, then Barnard never would have gone down there to investigate and he'd still be alive, and Nizhoni Yazzie might be alive, too. And Sheriff Bruce would probably still be fortifying his sovereign county. He'd have been busted eventually. FBI was onto him. But not yet."

Yeah, Tom thought walking away. That is real funny.

Owens frequently misspoke. But he often revealed more than he intended in doing so.

Why had he just revealed that the Jay Cluff murder case was something substantively different, possibly not related to the Aryan Patriots? Because he didn't like being shoved offstage by the feds? And because he wanted Tom to know that he still had something up his sleeve?

Tom wondered if Owens had shared the bizarre, macabre evidence with the federal or state investigators.

He was eager to share his new intelligence with Samantha. He had seen her earlier across the crowd at the press conference, but now she was nowhere to be seen. She wasn't at the office either.

The prosecutor had completed reading his prepared statement and had begun to take questions when Samantha felt a tap on her shoulder.

She turned her head. It was Tammy, agitated.

"I need to talk to you," she whispered.

"Can it wait? I'm working right now. This is my job. I'm covering this press conference."

"It's a bunch of b.s."

Samantha was torn.

What could be more important than the arrest of the Montezuma County white supremacists who had murdered her friend Peter? And who had been busted thanks in part to her own reporting? She had already tried to follow up Tammy's initial tip about being "slave labor" to Graham Hall and had reached a dead end.

A few days earlier, Samantha was telling a friend about Elsa's Melting Pot and the slave laborers, Tammy and her boyfriend Ryan, whom Graham had picked up at the Town Park campground.

"I'm not at all surprised," Barb said. "Graham and Elsa are total pervs.'"

"How so?"

"I was at a party at this trophy mansion in Mountain Village and was looking for a bathroom when I opened a door to a bedroom, and Graham and Elsa were in there getting it on. I say, 'Excuse me,' and start to back out when Elsa says to me, 'Come join us, Barb. Graham wants to lick your pussy'."

"Ewwww," Samantha said. "That's just so cringe."

Samantha thought immediately of the Murphy bed in the restaurant that Graham was so proud of, the bed that might come in handy even after the apartment was converted into a restaurant. Maybe Tammy and Ryan weren't just wage slaves. Maybe they were sex slaves. Or willing sexual partners, at least. Maybe Elsa's Melting Pot served fondue until ten and kinky sex until dawn. Maybe that's what Tammy meant when she said the restaurant was a scam.

The next afternoon Samantha made her way to Elsa's before it was open, thinking Tammy might be free to talk.

"Oh, hi," Tammy said, as if they barely knew each other and maybe she wasn't even sure who Samantha was. Hadn't they spoken just a week earlier about how she came to work at Elsa's Melting Pot? If so, it was forgotten.

"I heard that Graham and Elsa are swingers," Samantha said.

"Oh, yeah? Maybe they are. I wouldn't know."

"Well, have you ever seen any kind of sexual activity at the restaurant? Maybe after hours?"

"What if I did? This whole fucking town is like a 24/7 sex club."

The brushoff seemed final to Samantha. There was nothing to Tammy's earlier story about working as an indentured servant at Elsa's Melting Pot that she could follow up. She put it out of her mind. Only now, here Tammy was back again, urgently demanding her attention.

The meat of the press conference was over, the questions posed by the out-of-town reporters of little interest.

"OK," Samantha said, turning away from the speakers and taking Tammy by the arm. "Let's go."

They walked away from the crowd to a nearby alley.

"So what's the b.s.?" Samantha asked.

"That guy who was shot in Bear Creek?"

"Jay Cluff."

"He was at the Melting Pot the night before he was shot."

"He was?"

"Yes. He had too much to drink and hung around after we closed. And we started to party."

"Party?"

"Yeah. We were fooling around. We were getting hot with each other."

"With Jay Cluff?"

"Graham hit on Cluff. You know, inviting him to join in. Graham's A.C.-D.C. Cluff freaked out. I mean, he wanted to party, but not with Graham. With Elsa. He went after her hard. He was too rough, so she tried to push him off, which made him lose it even more. He slapped her and then he started choking her. Graham and Ryan had to pull him off her and kick him out."

"Holy shit! This really happened?"

Tammy nodded.

"The next morning, Elsa wasn't herself."

"And?"

"She went up Bear Creek and shot him."

"You're sure?"

"There's proof."

"Elsa cut off Cluff's dick and brought it back to the restaurant and she showed it to us. She showed it to all of us."

"She showed you Cluff's dick?"

"Here," Tammy said, offering Samantha a brown paper bag. "It's in here."

Samantha couldn't help stepping back.

"Me and Ryan, we're blowing this sicko town."

Samantha was frozen as Tammy stepped forward.

"Take it."

Samantha took the bag and Tammy slipped away down the alley.

. . .

Tom opened the bag that Samantha brought back from her meeting with Tammy and emptied its contents onto his desk.

Cluff's dick was a black, shriveled, desiccated little thing, like a dried-up dog turd you might see on the River Trail.

But with the unmistakable form of a human penis.

Bizarre, Tom thought. *Macabre*.

Chapter 38

THE LAST WORD

The mystery was solved. This was the "peculiarity" that Owens had alluded to in Peter's interview with him after Cluff's body was found, the sordid clue that law enforcement withheld from the public because only the killer, or someone close to the killer, would know about it. And this was also why Owens had insisted during the same interview, somewhat cryptically, that the killer just might be female, as if he could not imagine that any man would be so cold blooded as to slice off a dying man's genitals and would then take those genitals for a trophy.

There was, Owens no doubt had considered, the possibility that the killer had tossed the missing member into the woods, where it would have been quickly devoured by ravens or mice, never to be found. Even so, the sheriff had correctly deduced that there was something deeply psychological in the killer's motive, and nothing overtly political, making Cluff's political notoriety an enormous red herring.

Once arrests were made, the evidence against Elsa would be overwhelming. The physical evidence of Cluff's preserved penis would be buttressed by testimony from three witnesses who could easily be charged as accessories if they refused to cooperate, and would have little choice but to corroborate each other's statements, not knowing what the other two witnesses would say.

It was a perfect example of the famous "prisoners' dilemma."

For Tom, the resolution of the crime meant, among other things, that The Examiner would end its long run with a second sensational story. Another reporter for the paper, Samantha, had solved the first mystery that had captivated the town by sticking with an unrelated story that might not lead anywhere, cultivating her relationship with a source who wanted to spill something, and by *poking around*. And it came fast on the heels of Peter's posthumous reporting, which had helped solve his own murder just a few days earlier.

What better last two acts could any 123-year-old newspaper have?

To preserve the scoop, and to keep the story as meta as possible, Tom and Samantha decided to run the same play they'd run with their previous scoop, writing the story and contacting Owens for comment only after it was ready to publish.

"Cluff Clocked" was the headline Tom wrote when Cluff's body was found. Now, sitting at Samantha's computer, giving the story about who killed him a final read before sending it into cyberspace with the tap of a key, he frowned.

"Elsa Hall Tied to Cluff Murder," he read. "We can do so much better than that."

"What have you got?" Samantha asked.

She watched as he typed and then laughed, startled.

"It lacks for dignity," Tom allowed.

"But more than makes up for it as clickbait."

"Do you know what the ski coaches tell the kids on the mountain?"

"I'm still pretty new here."

"Go big or go home. This is the last headline I'm ever going to write. Dignity be damned. I'm going big."

CLUFF DE-COCKED

Elsa Hall Arrested in Cluff Murder

(Posted at 6:03 p.m., September 27, 2008)

By Samantha Stolley

The Examiner forwarded compelling evidence this afternoon to San Miguel County Sheriff Bill Owens, linking Telluride businesswoman Elsa Hall to the September 8 murder of Jay Cluff in Bear Creek.

Asked his reaction to the evidence, Owens stated that he would be arresting Hall and asked The Examiner to hold publication until the arrest had been made.

Owens called at 5:57 today to announce that Hall was in custody.

The arrest of Hall, who operates the Hall Persian Rug Gallery and Elsa's Melting Pot restaurant with her husband Graham Hall, came after Melting Pot employee Tammy Anderson told Examiner reporter Samantha Stolley this morning that Hall committed the murder after Cluff had sexually assaulted her the previous evening, after hours at the restaurant. Hall then mutilated Cluff's body, removing his genitals, which she later showed to Anderson, as well as to her boyfriend, Ryan Roth, who also works at Elsa's Melting Pot, and to Graham Hall.

Anderson handed the reporter a brown paper bag containing what appeared to be desiccated male genitals. It was this evidence that The Examiner delivered to Owens.

Anderson stepped forward now, she said, because she was frustrated to observe today's press conference announcing arrests in the murder of Peter Barnard at the same time the Cluff murder case remained unsolved. It had been her plan to deliver the evidence she carried with her to officials at the press conference, but she was intimidated by the crowd and gave it to this reporter instead.

Hall was arrested only hours after federal prosecutors announced the arrest of Telluride real estate broker Erica Ortiz and Montezuma County Sheriff Dan Bruce for the September 26 murder of Examiner reporter Peter Barnard. Barnard was killed while reporting Cluff's death, when he inadvertently stumbled onto criminal activity in Montezuma County, which was not directly related to Cluff's murder….

There was, on the same front page of the last printed edition of The Examiner, dated September 30, 2008, but published late to allow for late breaking news to be printed, a separate story about the arrests of Ortiz and Bruce.

And, tucked at the bottom of the page:

UP BEAR CREEK

Examiner to Cease Publication
Sudden Drop in Advertising Forces Closure

By Tom Austin, Examiner Publisher and Editor

It's been a glorious run, not just the last four years that this publisher has had the honor of serving this historic newspaper, but the entire 123-year run.

The Examiner was acquired by Charles M. Sumner in 1900. In that job, my illustrious predecessor reported on the labor "troubles" of his era, including the notorious murder of Arthur L. Collins, General Manager of the Smuggler-Union Mine, which brought martial law to Telluride.

Sumner was literally run out of town for his troubles.

This week we are reporting the resolution of local murders that similarly rocked the community, and in some ways similarly reveal fault lines in our society. Telluride now as then is a place of monied interests in pursuit of ever-greater wealth, and political strains pitting workers against employers, which can erupt in violence. The turbulence can take out an editor and take down a newspaper, as, in fact, it took out Charles Sumner and as it has done yet again today.

Telluride has always loved its history, and The Examiner is not only historic but has often revisited the past.

So here for the last time is a bit of interesting — and perhaps relevant — history.

Sumner edited one of two newspapers in Telluride's historic period, The Examiner, which supported workers during Telluride's Labor Wars that raged between May 1901, when the miners in the district went on strike, and

December 1903, when martial law was declared. The other paper, The Daily Journal, supported the mine owners and operators and the town's business interests.

The Labor Wars took a sharp turn against the miners on Nov. 19, 1902, when Collins was shot by a sniper while playing bridge in his home office in Pandora, adjacent to the Smuggler Union Mill. Although nobody was arrested, and no one has ever been identified as the killer, there was a presumption that the Miner's Union was behind it, and that presumption led to investigations and indictments of union men, and the declaration of martial law in Telluride.

Sumner hung on as The Examiner's owner, publisher and editor in the tumultuous months after the Collins murder, but in July 1903, having gone deeply into debt, he was forced to sell the paper. On December 23, 1903, he and other union men and union sympathizers were marched onto a train in the middle of the night by soldiers and warned never to return.

Why tell this story, now?

It has been said that "history rhymes."

Telluride has not been embroiled in a bloody labor war the last three years, culminating in a declaration of martial law. And yet, is it not monied interests like those who railed against Charles Sumner and who boycotted Sumner's Examiner and forced him to sell that last week pulled their advertising from today's Examiner?

It is the sudden loss of advertising, led by the betrayal of the alleged murderer of an Examiner reporter, prominent local realtor, Erica Ortiz, that is the proximate cause of this paper's failure.

There are, in all fairness, two other "elephants in the room": a global financial crisis and the rise of digital publishing that has disrupted traditional media and particularly bleeds community newspapers. Even without the turmoil surrounding the events of recent weeks, this newspaper's days were likely numbered.

Although I would have appreciated a few more years to allow the financial crisis to ebb and to try to solve the puzzle of sustaining community journalism in the brave new age of Facebook and Google, it was not to be.

Who will uncover Telluride's next murderous swamp of corruption, even if it's a hundred years from now?

As I bid our readers farewell, let me state that it has been an honor to walk in Charles Sumner's footsteps.

The Cluff murder and the loss of our own precious Peter Barnard as he reported that murder, tested your hometown newspaper to the hilt.

I can only hope that, before expiring, we met the challenge.

Tom could take some measure of satisfaction that it was his small-town newspaper that solved the crimes. He had the last word.
It could as easily have been a fellow right-wing conspiracist turned

against him who killed Jay Cluff, someone like Duke. Or a business associate with a grudge, like Ortiz; or an eco-terrorist or a solitary actor like Chuck Small. But it was, instead, a woman triggered into taking revenge on a man who sexually assaulted her, turned in by an employee she and her husband had exploited. It was Peter, a beloved, funny, talented young reporter, who died at the hands of thugs who flattered themselves by appropriating high-minded but nonsensical political language. Meanwhile, it was systemic greed and the machinations of his benefactor, Erica Ortiz, that cost Tom his newspaper.

That and the relentless march of changing times, consigning everyone to their allotted place in the archives.

EPILOGUE

1. APPARENTLY UNKNOWABLE

Tom sat alone in his office, pondering how and when he would vacate it and bring 123 years of history to closure.

The archives were a particular problem. The shelves of bound newspapers that occupied the wall of his office across from his desk once again seemed to challenge him, asking, What about us? They contained uncountable hours of journalistic endeavor, generations of reporting stretching from Charley Sumner at the start of the last century to Tom's tenure in the previous few years. They had been preserved in the vain expectation that the intelligence they contained might be important to someone, someday.

Would anyone a hundred years in the future remember the murders of Jay Cluff up Bear Creek and of Peter Barnard, the Examiner reporter who was covering the story?

In light of that question, the murder of Arthur L. Collins seemed especially pregnant. Was there anyone other than Chuck Small and Tom himself who still cared about it? Tom had reread Sumner's coverage of the Collins assassination several times while investigating the Cluff murder, as if it the past might somehow illuminate the present.

What Tom didn't anticipate was that the present can also illuminate the past.

He retrieved the 1902 volume of The Examiner to read Sumner's story again, as if to bid it a final farewell before it and the rest of the paper's archives were consigned to the county dump.

Tom wasn't forcibly exiled from Telluride by soldiers like Sumner was, but the loss of the Examiner was something they shared. Tom understood viscerally the complexity Sumner grappled with in the aftermath of the Collins killing. Some of Sumner's words jumped out at him like they hadn't before. Sumner was trying to accomplish far too much with this one story: expressing trepidation about what this assassination would portend; arguing that it was therefore inconceivable that the Miners Union would have carried out the crime; and offering abundant clues that might help identify the murderer and exonerate the union. As a friend of the union, Sumner was also defending himself from the retribution that did, in fact, soon come his way. Like Tom in covering the Cluff and Barnard killings, Sumner was an inextricable part of the story he reported, making him both compromised and deeply knowledgeable.

THE CRIME OF AN UNHUNG CUR

No matter what may have been his grievance, his fancied wrong—no matter how strong may have been his provocation, there is no justification in the assassin act of Wednesday night. The desperado who committed the crime may have had all sorts of trouble with the management of the Smuggler Union; he may have been smothering a grudge for years to await a favorable opportunity to carry out his nefarious plan; on the other hand his grievance may have originated but the day before. But in either event it makes no difference. An unprincipled, disreputable, cowardly caricature of humanity who would wantonly take a life when the object of the attack was entirely unsuspicious and defenceless—who would deliberately shoot through a window of a room in which women were present, has no business in a civilized community. He has no business on this earth. The assassin, sneak and coward are abhorred by all men. You can often condone the actions of a man who will face an enemy to fight him—but a murderous dog, never.

Sumner's lede was a howl of indignation bordering on defensiveness, directly addressing an accusation he had certainly already heard, that the union had carried out the crime and that he, Sumner, was partially responsible. Sumner had inveighed against violence during the strike, whether it came at the hands of union strikers or scabs, frequently invoking union president Vincent St. John's similar exhortations to his own members to protest peacefully, regardless of the provocation. Now he felt the need to do so again, with even more urgency, because this latest act of violence was cataclysmic.

Sumner continued by reporting what was known about the night of the murder:

This community was thrown into excitement about 10 o'clock Wednesday night by the startling news coming down from Pandora that Arthur L. Collins, manager of the Smuggler-Union Mining Company, had been shot while sitting with a number of friends in the sitting room of the Smuggler offices. In the party were O. B. Kemp, chief clerk, A. B. Blainey, chief electrician, and Mrs. Blainey. They had been playing cards. Mr. Collins sat with his back to the window, and directly across the table from him sat Mrs. Blainey. Contrary to his usual custom Mr. Collins had not drawn the curtain. It is evident the assassin had waited for just such an opportunity, and a charge of buckshot was fired through the window at close range.

What conceivable assassin would be on the lookout for this utterly unforeseeable opportunity, contrary to "usual custom?" Was there a conspirator inside Smuggler Union, someone who abetted the plot by arranging the seating at the card table the night of the killing, leaving the curtain undrawn, and alerting the killer to the opportunity?

The next piece of Sumner's reporting seemed to confirm this thesis:

> About the time the shooting occurred, Theodore Becker, assayer, and H. P. Smith, assistant electrician, who had been in town, were on their way to Pandora when they heard the shot, and after commenting on its sound, gave the incident no further attention. A short time after they passed a man with a gun strung across his shoulder coming down the track.

> It is remarkable that the villain got away so quickly. He must indeed have been a desperate character, for in order to shoot through the window he was compelled to stand directly under an electric lamp, or at least in the broad light of it, and as it was early in the evening and a good many people about it is a peculiar circumstance that he escaped unnoticed.

Was Sumner suggesting that the killer had good reason to feel confident that he would not be apprehended because he had inside accomplices guarding his flank? They were, perhaps, the very witnesses Sumner named, two of Collins's employees, the Smuggler-Union's assayer and assistant electrician.

Sumner went on to raise another perplexing question:

> The causes leading up to the shooting of Manager Collins are hard to determine. During the strike of a year ago a good many bitter feelings were engendered, but as matters were amicably settled it can reasonably be said that those enmities gradually died out. Had not such been the case it can be seen where a climax would have come before this, and at a time when there was extreme tension in local affairs. It is generally believed that some dissolute character who entertained an intense hatred toward Mr. Collins took advantage of existing conditions and committed the terrible deed with an intent of throwing the responsibility on others. There is every reason to believe that such is the case. People are prone to jump at conclusions and the assassin realized it.

This was closer to an accusation than a speculation. Sumner clearly understood who benefitted from the crime, which hinted at a likely motive: Collins's murder afforded unidentified "people" an opportunity to blame unidentified "others." Contemporary readers would easily recognize that Sumner's "people" and "others" were the opposing sides in the Telluride's bitter labor war: mine owners and their hired union busters on one side, mine workers and the union on the other. Sumner foresaw that Collins's killing would reignite the conflict, with labor on the defensive.

Sumner then revealed that despite their deep differences, owing to their outspokenness on opposite sides of the labor war, he had something in common with the deceased mine manager:

> Going back to the time of the strike, it is recalled that anonymous letters were of frequent occurrence. In a conversation with Mr. Collins at that time he told the writer of receiving several letters, and we showed him two epistles that had been sent to this office, threatening the editor of this paper. Officers of the Union and others also received a number of the same sort of letters. There seemed to be a few persons in the community at that time who possessed a mania for writing unsigned letters, and but little attention was paid to them.

Just whose interests were served by stoking the enmities *on both sides* with these anonymous, menacing "epistles?" Were these "few persons" with a "mania for writing unsigned letters," readily identifiable to contemporary readers? If so, was Sumner pointing a finger at the likeliest suspects?

* * *

For a different perspective, Tom reread the account of the murder in the competing paper, the Telluride Daily Journal.

MANAGER ARTHUR COLLINS OF THE SMUGGLER-UNION MURDERED LAST NIGHT.

No Clue to the Inhuman, Cowardly Perpetrator of the Monstrous Crime.

When news of the cowardly tragedy circulated around town this morning, the community was shocked as it has never been before, though we have encountered many and grievous calamities. But these came in the form of accidents and catastrophes that apparently were unavoidable. But for a leading citizen, and one of the most prominent and highly respected citizens of the community to be murdered, shot in the back through a window while seated in his home, it simply paralyzed the whole community.

People are too shocked to talk or express an opinion. There are ominous observations that something must be done, but no one seems to have any suggestion as to what that something shall be.

It is evident that if vigorous action is not taken, Telluride may expect a Molly Maguire campaign such as terrorized the Coeur d'Alene region for years, resulting in the assassination of more than a score of the best citizens.

Here was an explicit call for revenge against the union, characterized as Molly Maguires, published by Sumner's rival, Francis Curry, a few days before Sumner published, suggesting that Sumner was responding to Curry.

Curry's attribution of the Collins murder to Molly Maguires was expedient but not persuasive. It was a subject of scholarly debate whether the Mollies were real, in Ireland, where the much-feared secret society purportedly originated, or in the United States, where they allegedly migrated. Real or not, it was child's play to level the slur "Mollies" at any union organizer, and particularly one of Irish descent like St. John. Curry's prescription was to blame the Mollies, urge state militia action to decisively to break the union, and be done with it. Labor peace and mining prosperity would be instantly restored.

Sumner had the more difficult problem: to suggest that the murder was the work of either an individual with a personal grudge or, more likely, a conspiracy whose motive was precisely to bring about the crackdown that Curry fervently advocated. This was why he argued that a plot to kill Collins would have been too dangerous to have been carried out by the union. But more to the point, the murder was not in the union's interest. Despite his obvious failings and narrow virtues, Collins had, after all, negotiated the three-year settlement with the union on behalf of the Telluride Mine Owners Association and was no longer a target of union enmity at the time of his killing.

Perhaps it was just the opposite. Maybe Collins's mortal enemies at the time of his murder were his former allies in the war on labor, whom he'd betrayed by settling with the union.

Both Sumner and Curry understood nuances Tom could only grasp at: Where lay the sympathies, for example, of the sundry witnesses to the crime? Left unexamined by both editors was the overarching reality of opposing ideologies. Curry defended an economic system that subjected masses of miners — virtually all immigrants — to short, brutal lives of unremittingly hard and extraordinarily dangerous labor to the benefit of a handful of mine owners and managers and their distant investors, with just enough of the benefit trickling down to local owners of ancillary businesses that supplied the mines to establish a defensible social order. Sumner sought justice for the workers. Perhaps both Sumner and Curry saw that Collins had worked himself into a dangerous middle ground, with enemies on both sides.

How well did Tom understand his own moment in time? What did he leave unsaid? What would a reader a hundred years in the future make of The Examiner's coverage of the Cluff and Barnard murders? Did these crimes reveal fault lines in the social structure of the time and place or foretell the future? Any person engaged in the act of journalism, in writing "the first draft of history," lacks the perspective of "what happened next." There is a sense of remorse in recognizing that today's consciousness is of no value to those who marched in a parade that has gone by. The corollary is an inverse of nostalgia, and equally nagging: To those marching in today's parade, tomorrow's consciousness is beyond comprehension, not only unknown, but unknowable.

Who killed Collins and why was also, apparently, unknowable.

2. NO SMALL INTEREST

Tom resolved not to send the archives to the dump. Knowing he was being sentimental and wasting precious money doing it, Tom decided to rent a small storage unit in Montrose and set about boxing the volumes for transport. In the process, he noticed a seam in the wall, which upon closer inspection was a door. It might have been difficult to see when it was freshly built, but the wood had warped, and the door opened easily.

Inside were papers, yellowing notepads, loosely bound sheafs of brittle paper and bundled correspondence, and a couple of journals, all of it covered with the neat penmanship of the last century. A quick inspection revealed that these were papers stashed by Charley Sumner, no doubt left behind when he was removed from the Telluride jail late one night in the winter of 1903, marched onto a train bound for Montrose, and ordered never to come back. Years later, after martial law ended, he might have been able to recover the papers, but obviously chose not to.

Nobody had seen these papers in 105 years.

Tom handled them gingerly and started reading.

There were flyers advertising musical performances of the Tomfooleries, a brass band for whom Sumner played the trumpet. There were written sketches of incidents Sumner had evidently witnessed, including notes titled "Vint wedding, Oct. 2, 1902."

"21 pers … Oscar & Cora, Frank, Luigi & … shades drawn…

The most intriguing writing that Tom found was a journal entry of a meeting between Sumner and the legendary Pinkerton Detective James P. McParland.

Sumner was evidently trying his hand at memoir, the prose far more polished than his hurriedly composed writing for the newspaper.

I recognized the famous detective the instant he walked in the door of The Examiner office in the spring of 1902. He was tall and heavy, wore a bushy mustache, and spoke in an Irish brogue.

"I was hoping I might have a word with Mr. Charles G. Sumner," he said.

"You are speaking to him," I said, rising to my feet and extending a hand. He was close to my height, but a hundred pounds heavier and 25 years older. Though I disdained him, I had to admire his taste for fine clothes.

"It is a pleasure," McParland said. He had a firm grip, which I matched. "I have heard a good deal about you."

"Nothing bad, I trust," I said.

"I am James P. McParland and wish to introduce myself. I am an investigator working on behalf of the Telluride Mine Owners Association."

"Ah, yes, Mr. McParland, your reputation precedes you."

"I wonder if there might be someplace more private where we might have a word."

The only other person in the office was my business partner Charles Fluke, who was working at his own desk.

"I keep no secrets from Mr. Fluke," I said. "Please have a seat."

Fluke nodded a greeting and McParland settled into an armchair across from my desk.

"I would like to be able to speak frankly, Mr. Sumner, and would ask your word not to identify me if you should choose to write anything we may discuss in the pages of your sheet."

"You have my word," I said.

"Very well," McParland said. "I take it as an important part of my work to ensure that newspaper editors are properly informed as to the full dimensions of the situation we are dealing with. You may know that my agency and I have deep expertise in matters related to the criminal activities of labor unions. Mr. Bulkeley Wells and Mr. Arthur Collins of the Smuggler-Union Company, along with other mine operators, are greatly concerned that labor relations in this mining district should be purged of corruption."

"We have heard a good deal about criminal activity in the district, Mr. McParland," I said. "But there has never been anything proven against the union. The local union president, Mr. Vincent St. John, speaks forcefully against violence at every opportunity."

"Ah, yes, but that is quite typical of how the Molly Maguires operate. It is a simple effort at deception for a man to decry violence at the same time he is perpetrating it."

"Do you believe that the Telluride Miners Union is under the influence of the Molly Maguires?"

"I don't believe it, Mr. Sumner. I know it. The Mollies maintain such tight secrecy in the conduct of their conspiracy that even many of their closest associates within a union, and those outside of it, are unaware of their involvement. The signs of this sort of a Molly conspiracy in Telluride are entirely plain to read and it is only a matter of time before it is proven."

"How is such a case proven?" I asked.

"Now that is a secret of my trade," McParland said. "A court of law will find the evidence compelling, as a court did in Pennsylvania."

"I see," I said.

I did not mistake McParland's meaning, knowing as I did, that he had sent twenty union men to the gallows in Pennsylvania by persuading a court that they were Mollies.

"It is crucial that a newspaper editor like yourself does not unwittingly act as an accomplice to the Mollies," McParland said. "Indeed, in some districts, there is evidence of a newspaper itself falling under the direct influence of the criminal conspiracy. I regret to say that we found that to be the case in some precincts in Pennsylvania and in Idaho as well."

"Do you suspect that Examiner may be under this dastardly influence?" I asked.

"It would be most unfortunate if it were."

"I appreciate the concern, Mr. McParland, and the warning. I can assure you that this newspaper is entirely independent and is under the influence of only its two owners, myself and Mr. Fluke. I am not a Mollie, and as best I can determine, Mr. Fluke is not one either. As far as I know, there are none within the Telluride Miners' Union, either."

"I will take you at your word with regard to your newspaper, Mr. Sumner." McParland said, standing. "But I caution you not to be deceived by the union. And I would urge you to weigh my words carefully."

He turned to leave then turned back and nodded at Fluke.

"Good evening, Mr. Fluke. And to you, too, Mr. Sumner."

Then he was gone.

"Well, Fluke," I said. "I believe that we have just been threatened with the gallows."

A man of few words, Fluke did not react visibly.

"You're not a Mollie, are you Fluke?" I asked.

"I am one now," he growled.

* * *

Was this the final clue to the identity of Collins's assassin? Might it have been the legendary union buster? Might this have been the start of an expose wherein Sumner planned to reveal what he knew?

If so, it wasn't to be found in the collection of papers Tom had discovered. If Sumner completed a book on the subject later in life, it had likely never been published. But this anecdote revealed that Sumner had been personally threatened, and by a man whose threats were not easily dismissed.

Tom learned from digitized newspaper archives that Sumner died at the age of 80 in a nursing home in Pocatello, Idaho. He was, according to his 1956 obituary, "one of the most colorful of early-day western editors and was editor of the Pocatello Tribune for some 15 to 20 years. He spent his young manhood in Colorado and participated in the early mining troubles there in Cripple Creek and other camps… In the early days Mr. Sumner was widely known in Idaho for his editorials and verse. He played a prominent role in Republican politics in Idaho and was active in the campaigns of the late Senators James H. Brady and Frank Gooding and Governors Davis and Moore."

The references to Sumner's having "participated in the early mining troubles" made it sound as if his exploits in Colorado amounted to mere youthful indiscretion. The mention of Cripple Creek and omission of any mention of Telluride was highly conspicuous considering that Sumner spent far more years in Telluride, the historic importance of Sumner's Telluride period, and Sumner's outsized role in Telluride's labor "troubles."

Just a few months after Sumner was exiled from Telluride, in June 1904, he married Lulu Belle Currier in Grand Junction.

From the online archives of the Grand Junction Sentinel:

> The bride is a striking and handsome young woman. She is cultivated and has enjoyed the best advantages of a modern education. For a short time, she worked as a stenographer in several of the city's law offices and later connected herself with the business office of this publication and continued in that position until severing her connection therewith about one week ago. Since her residence in this

city Miss Currier has met and charmed people and numbers a wide circle of friends and acquaintances.

The groom, Charles G. Sumner is well known in the city. He is the eldest son of Captain and Mrs. Sumner and is generally known, as his boyhood days were spent here. For several years he owned and published the Ophir Mail in San Miguel County and later was editor and publisher of The San Miguel Examiner in Telluride, and affiliated with other papers, in different sections of the state. Lately he has been connected with The Sentinel force….

Scrolling through digitized editions of the Sentinel, a familiar heading caught Tom's eye: It's the Altitude, the title of the column Sumner penned for all three papers he worked at in Telluride, and which he apparently brought with him to Grand Junction. The item was brief and, perhaps purposefully, easily overlooked, one small item in a long string of news snippets—familiar reports of out-of-town visitors, social gatherings, births, and deaths—many of them, no doubt, paid announcements.

IT'S THE ALTITUDE

It is of no SMALL interest that a party with knowledge of the momentous events that disrupted the Telluride mining camp is now living in Grand Junction. It is to be devoutly hoped that SMALL one day spills his guts, so that the facts of the matter might be delivered to posterity.

This "small" item had almost certainly escaped notice by anyone until it caught Tom's eye a century after it was published. It now reached Tom as a cryptic message from the past, slipped into print by Sumner when he was just 30 years old — working as a printer for someone else, not an editor at that moment — before he would go on to claim the professional and political respectability he later enjoyed: the word "small" capitalized and repeated for emphasis.

3. A PERFECT CRIME

Tom made his way to the Telluride Elks Club, where, he presumed, he would find Chuck Small. Though Tom was not an Elks Club member, Small did not register any surprise at seeing him. It was as if, for Small, the cast of Telluride characters, past, present, and future, came to him in a constant stream of motley drinking companions, some of them in the flesh, others in his intemperate imagination.

The club was barely populated at three in the afternoon.

"Hell of a paper," Small said, nodding toward the last copy of The Examiner on the bar in front of him. "I mean, shee-it, you figured a way to go out with a bang! Cluff de-cocked! Might as well engrave that on your tombstone now."

"I thought it might have been you who killed Cluff."

"Me?"

Startled, Small burst out laughing.

"To make some history of your own," Tom explained. "Like whoever killed Arthur L. Collins did."

"I should have done it! It didn't occur to me, or I sure as shee-it would have!"

"You pointed me to Arthur L. Collins, and Vincent St. John, and Charles Sumner," Tom said. "Now I've done my bit by writing another chapter of Telluride history, not quite as historic as the labor troubles."

"I don't know about that. Nobody but me, and maybe you, gives a rat's ass about history. It's just old news to most people." He nodded toward a row of dusty portraits of former Elks, hanging on the opposite wall. "They are as real to me as you are. Most of 'em are buried over in Lone Tree Cemetery, we still occupy their buildings, and they're watching over us right now. It just doesn't seem all that far back in time to me."

"There's Charles Painter," Tom said.

"Yep. Published the rival paper to yours."

"But on the other side."

"Aww, you'll join him in Hell before you know it."

Tom laughed.

"I'm more like Charles G. Sumner. I won't make it to the Elks Club wall. I'll end up obscure and forgotten, like he did."

"You could avoid that fate by joining the Elks. You could become an officer and end up on the wall where you might hang out another hundred years. It's not that hard. All you've got to do is be sponsored. Hell, come to think of it, I'll sponsor you!"

"That's it?"

"You have to swear that you believe in God, you have to pledge allegiance to the flag, and you have to have friends who are Elks and will testify to your upstanding moral character."

"I could lie about God and the flag, but who's going to testify to my character?"

"Ha! Bribe 'em. It'd pay for itself. If you die an Elk, you get a free cemetery plot over in Lone Tree. And before that you get a lifetime of cheap shitty food and cheaper strong libations right here with me for company, except for those rare nights we decide to go to the New Sheridan for a change of scenery."

"You have any idea what happened to Sumner?"

"He moved back to Grand Junction after the troubles. Ended up running papers in Idaho."

"A Telluride man relocated to Grand Junction after the troubles? Just like your grandparents. They probably knew him."

"They did. I met him. When I was a kid. I was maybe five, six years old, so it would have been in the early 1950s. My grandfather Frank Small used to take me to the park. And one time he had a visitor from Idaho. It was Mr. Sumner."

"You remember from when you were that young?"

"One of those odd things that get lodged in memory."

"What do you remember?"

"A couple of old men sitting on a bench reminiscing," Small shrugged. "I didn't think much of it."

"I think it was more than that."

"Why?"

"Because you remember it. And because of this."

Tom pulled a sheet of paper from his pocket and handed it to him.

"It's the Altitude!" Small read. "It is of no SMALL interest that a party with secret knowledge of the momentous events ....'

"Well, I'll be Goddamned! Sumner wrote that!"

"Is he referring to your grandfather."

"I'm sure he is."

"Do you know what he's talking about?"

"It's not something to talk about. That's what my mother told me. Never, ever talk about it."

"Even now? All these years later? You're pushing eighty and still listening to your mother?"

Tom said nothing, letting Small come to his own decision to "spill his guts to posterity."

"Well, if I don't tell you now, then nobody will ever know, will they? And at least you're interested. Nobody else is. My parents have been dead for a couple of decades; granddad's been gone for almost fifty years, so why the hell am I keeping their secret now?"

"Why are you?"

"For the same reason I got so damned interested in Telluride history in the first place. It's why I've spent my life here. Because there was this secret at the heart of it. It was personal and part of history, a mystery that I wanted to inhabit. Who killed Arthur L. Collins? What I heard on that park bench is that granddad killed someone in Telluride. I told my mother what I heard that night when she put me to bed. And she said I must forget that I heard such nonsense and must never repeat it. It was deeply shameful.

"When I finally got to Telluride as a young man in the late 1960s, a lot of old timers were still here, and I started to piece it together. Those who were still here were not friends of the union, almost by definition, because the union sympathizers had been driven out. To them, the troubles at the turn of the century were a time when anarchists and rabble-rousers, mostly foreigners, had to be defeated for the good of the town, for the good of the country. They didn't like hippies for the same reason. Because we were communists! It was Linda Smith who ran the historic society back then who told me granddad disappeared, left town, slipped away, right when Arthur Collins was killed. People who knew him figured he probably shot Collins."

"Why would he?"

"Well, shee-it, someone did it," Small shrugged, "so why not him? People who came to Telluride at that time were looking to strike it rich, or at least to survive. When granddad died a couple of years later, I went home for the funeral. My mother was packing his stuff up to take to the dump, there wasn't much, but I found one thing he'd held onto. It was a letter from the Pinkerton Detective Agency commending Frank Small as a man of upstanding character and discretion, and it was signed by none other than James McParland, director of the agency's Denver office."

"Do you still have the letter?"

"Would you like see it?"

"I would."

The two of them left the Elks Club and ambled across town to Small's house, one of the last remaining miner's shacks in town—along with Tom's rental—that had not been restored into a vacation home. Tom waited on the porch while Small rummaged about inside, returning with the letter in an envelope yellowed with age.

Tom removed the letter from the envelope and read it:

PINKERTON NATIONAL DETECTIVE AGENCY
Denver Office
1410 Larimer Street
Denver, Colorado

January 23, 1903

To Whom It May Concern:

Mr. Frank Small is a man of upstanding character and discretion who will complete any task with which he is entrusted. This Agency has issued this letter to assure any employer that Mr. Small is worthy of your deepest consideration.

Sincerely,
James P. McParland
Director

. . .

There it was.

Arthur L. Collins was assassinated by none other than the Great Detective he and other mine company executives had hired to bust the union. Charles Sumner had figured it out, and had started to write about it, but had never reported it except in a blind item in a gossip column. Sumner probably lost his nerve and wanted to move on with his life, past the pain. Or maybe he calculated that McParland was too dangerous an adversary to cross. For an articulate and gregarious man, Sumner's lifelong silence when it came to Telluride was further evidence that the mining companies and McParland had utterly vanquished Vincent St. John and his Western Federation of Miners, in Telluride and far beyond.

Not until the end of his life did Sumner circle back to meet with Frank Small in Grand Junction. Maybe he imagined he would right the historic wrong by finally revealing McParland's plot to frame St. John for an assassination he himself commissioned. Possibly Sumner had run out of time by then to get the job done.

For McParland, carrying out a heinous crime against Collins and pinning it on his enemies was consistent with his modus operandi. He had started his illustrious career by framing twenty Pennsylvania coal miners as Molly Maguires, sending them to the gallows in 1887-88. He did it without remorse; indeed, he feasted on it for the rest of his career.

The labor peace that had broken out in Telluride was not in McParland's interests. He needed to recharge his crusade to crush the union. He likely took out Collins because Collins had negotiated the contract with Local 63 of the WFM on behalf of the Telluride Mining Association. If Collins had betrayed the cause and was of no further use to McParland alive, McParland found a way put him to excellent use dead.

McParland failed in his effort to pin the Collins murder on St. John. But a few years later, in 1906, he succeeded in bringing charges against Saint for the assassination of former Idaho governor Frank Steunenberg. McParland personally obtained the confession of one Albert Horsley, a/k/a Harry Orchard, in the bombing that killed Steunenberg, coercing Orchard into implicating St. John and other WFM officers in the plot. St. John was acquitted following a sensational trial in Grand Junction, after Orchard, despite a year of coaching by McParland, couldn't keep his story straight under cross-examination.

Before he had Harry Orchard, McParland had Frank Small.

Small, who was English, like Collins, was among the multitudes of immigrants who arrived in America in the 19th century to better themselves. He found himself as a young man in a rough mining camp, where a Pinkerton offered him the job of killing Arthur Collins, offered it to him precisely because he was an itinerant—unremarkable, indistinguishable, unknown, and hungry. The payout was just enough cash for him to purchase a toehold in Grand Junction, where he was able to put down roots, start a family, and live out his life in obscurity, living long enough to see his grandson become a hippie.

It was Chuck Small's granddad who pulled the trigger, but it could have been anyone. If McParland was the real villain, his murder of his own client, Collins, was just one of dozens, maybe hundreds of similar crimes he carried out in his long career, and not necessarily the worst of them. He was an archenemy of organized labor—immigrants!—despite being an immigrant himself. Just as Sheriff Dan Bruce, a century later, was willing to employ any violent means necessary to advance the proud cause of white supremacy, wrapping himself in the flag and profiting from it.

Still, Tom thought, there was a terrific book staring him in the face. Tom could chronicle the epic war between Vincent St. John and Arthur Collins from the perspective of Charles Sumner. Sumner learns that Collins was assassinated by McParland to frame St. John but finds himself silenced by the loss of his newspaper before he can report it, leaving the murder of Collins to stand as a perfect crime, an unsolved mystery that would endure as compelling testimony to the malice of union men for as long as it was remembered.

Only to be solved by Tom Austin a century later.

4. NEXT ACTS

The snows came down hard just after Christmas, a month after Barack Obama was elected president. There was a big dump, followed by a few days of sun, followed by another big dump and more sunshine.

In January, Denver newspapers and television news channels reported that Erica Ortiz, already charged in state court for murdering Peter Barnard, had been indicted by the feds for participating in the Montezuma County Sheriff conspiracy as its banker. She had secretly financed the Hay Camp Mesa Ranch subdivision with Jay Cluff as the front man. The indictment noted that Ortiz and Cluff ran other similar schemes, including the proposed development of Telluride's Bear Creek.

Tom and Cluff had more in common — both providing cover for a criminal mastermind — than either of them could have fathomed.

A couple of weeks later, still free on bail and with her murder trial set to begin, Erica and her beloved lifelong co-conspirator, Ramon, ducked the rope marking the Telluride Ski Area boundary. Together, they entered Temptation, the most notorious of the avalanche chutes in Bear Creek. They were buried under tons of snow, not far from the mining claim Jay Cluff had been defending when he was shot. Their corpses would not be recovered until spring.

The same week, Angie was sentenced for violating her probation to 18 months in a minimum-security state prison. Sarah, whose soap business was prospering, retained hope that the jailtime would finally straighten her daughter out.

Six months later, Graham Hall was sentenced to ten years for being an accomplice to his wife Elsa's murder of Jay Cluff. The court took pity on their wage slaves, Tammy Anderson and Ryan Roth, who had been apprehended in Grand Junction after fleeing Telluride, sentencing them each to a year's probation.

Elsa was handed down a thirty-year sentence. Montezuma County sheriff Dan Bruce and his accomplice Connie Cluff each got forty for their crimes, including the murder of Peter Barnard.

Thanks to a recommendation from Special Agent Ross Weston, Maria Sanchez gained admission to the FBI Training Academy in Quantico, Virginia, where she would finish at the top of her class.

Samantha Stolley was recruited by The New York Times, where she went on to a brilliant career, helping the Times successfully navigate the transition to digital media.

Chuck Small died quietly in his sleep at home in Telluride at the age of 81.

Tom Austin published his historical novel, *The Examiner*, purporting to solve the century-old assassination of Arthur L. Collins, in the spring of 2011. It won him respectable reviews, decent sales, and a new career as an author.

AUTHOR'S NOTE

The historical characters in this book—Charles Sumner, Vincent St. John, Arthur L. Collins, James P. McParland, and others identified by name—were real. Everything recounted in these pages related to Telluride's mining era is supported by the historic record, both primary sources (historic newspapers and other archived documents) and written histories, especially the generously footnoted *The Corpse on Boomerang Road: Telluride's War on Labor*, by Mary Joy Martin (2004, Western Reflections Pub.)

It is Martin who corrected previous anti-union Telluride histories, revealing the heroism of the Telluride Miners Union in the face of Pinkerton treachery, and this book owes her an enormous debt. *The Examiner* borrows only a small fraction of the devious machinations employed by union-busting interests that Martin uncovered and documented.

Both Chuck Small and his grandfather Frank Small are fictional inventions, and any resemblance to actual persons, living or dead, is coincidence, as is true for all the circa-2008 characters in this book.

The deductions offered by the fictional character Tom Austin about who killed Arthur L. Collins—an agent of Pinkerton James P. McParland—and why, are reasonable speculations gleaned largely from a careful reading of Charles Sumner's reporting in the San Miguel

Examiner. The passages in this book from historic newspapers are verbatim, with some passages abridged for purposes of narrative fluency.

The passage attributed to Sumner about his meeting with McParland is fiction, as is the letter from McParland commending the fictional Frank Small.

Barring the discovery of a hidden trove of documents, a fictional conceit, the murder of Arthur L. Collins will almost certainly never be solved.

About the Author

Seth Cagin and his wife Marta Tarbell founded The Telluride Watch newspaper in 1996, selling it in 2014. He is the co-author of three books of non-fiction, *Hollywood Films of the Seventies: Sex, Drugs, Violence, Rock 'n' Roll and Politics* (Harper & Row, 1984); *We Are Not Afraid: The Story of Goodman, Schwerner and Chaney and the Civil Rights Campaign for Mississippi* (Macmillan, 1988) and *Between Earth and Sky: How CFCs Threatened the Ozone Layer* (Pantheon, 1993).

The Examiner is Cagin's second Tom Austin novel. *The Uranium Drive-In* (2011) recounts Tom's investigation of the disappearance of his wife Sarah's first husband.

If you enjoyed *The Examiner*, you may want to follow Tom Austin back four years to Naturita, where he was editor of The West End Forum.

The Uranium Drive-In, the prequel to *The Examiner*, is also available at Amazon Books.

Here's a head start:

1. MISSING

Ray Walker missed his daughter's wedding last night."

Billy Pederson spoke without inflection, as if to give away as little as possible, but then, the Montrose County sheriff's deputy always talked that way.

"Missed it?" Tom asked. "You mean he just didn't show up?"

To learn of a missing man from Deputy Pederson was a professional responsibility for Tom, who was the editor as well as the publisher of the West End Forum, but he was also a member of the small community of Naturita and neighboring Nucla, and was friendly with Ray Walker, so it hit him on a personal level at the same time.

"Sarah says they didn't have a fight or something like that to explain it," Billy said, referring to Walker's wife. "Says he was really looking forward to it. Plus he still hasn't come home yet. Sarah says he got a service call on Wednesday afternoon and took off in his rig and never come back."

"He missed Angie's wedding?"

"Yep," Billy said.

"And they went ahead without him?"

"Had to. It was all planned and paid for."

"That must have been a real fun wedding."

"Real fun."

"Why didn't Sarah report it quicker that he was missing?" Tom asked. "That doesn't make sense."

"They'll be time to ask her that, I reckon."

"Damn."

Tom leaned back in his chair. His mind was flooded with more questions but he had an immediate concern: Would he have to rip up his front page and write a new lead story for the Forum? Press time was only an hour off.

"He probably run off the road somewhere," Billy said. "I need some help looking. If he run off the road and survived it, then he's hurt and we gotta find him fast."

"Well, if that's what happened, then he's already been out there four nights," Tom said. "It's been cold. He's probably dead…."

"Yep." The deputy was grim but matter-of-fact. "But maybe not. And even if he is dead, we've gotta look anyway."

"Got a picture?" Tom asked. "I'm sure I've got one somewhere, but…"

Billy was already sliding a snapshot across the desk. Tom picked it up. Ray Walker was in his early forties, his face weathered by a life lived mostly outdoors on the West End. He wore a full beard and a mesh cap emblazoned with the name of his business, Walker's Auto Repair. Ray worked on Tom's ancient Toyota, and half the other cars in the West End. He stared into the camera as if he were posing for a mug shot, no trace of friendliness or a smile in his expression. Ray was a good-natured guy, but there was no suggestion of that in the photograph. Sarah Walker, or whoever had given it to Billy, had not taken the time to look for the most flattering picture of the missing man but had grabbed one that came immediately to hand. Tom shuddered at the thought that Ray could be lying off the side of a highway, trapped in his mangled truck, maybe unconscious, slowly dying, wondering if he would be found in time, if he was conscious at all.

"Paper's out tomorrow, right? We'd appreciate a story if you can get it in," Billy said. "Maybe somebody's seen him or his truck. But we've got to start searching now. Cross the street in an hour."

"Right," Tom said. "Let me write it up and get the paper out; then I'll help."